midnight

a McKenna Chronicle

elizabeth miller

midnight

a McKenna chronicle

Midnight, a McKenna Chronicle

Cover Art by Najla Qamber Designs

Editing by Lauren McKellar and Hot Tree Editing

Synopsis: One destined meeting. It alters journalist Charlise "Charlie" Carter's course. When asked to work on a Republican candidate's campaign, she's unprepared for the intense reaction she has toward the young presidential hopeful, Colin McKenna.

Unable to resist Charlie's allure, McKenna succumbs to his desire and they find themselves exploring a passionate physical relationship that is soon tested by not only their own secrets, but his political advisors.

Traveling the country in pursuit of the presidential nomination, his career aspirations and complications from the past collide with their desire to be together, threatening to tear them apart forever. Midnight tells a compelling story of burgeoning trust, intense passion, and secrets that could cause it all to unravel in a heartbeat.

ACKNOWLEDGEMENTS

First and foremost, I have to thank Bryan, Jackson and Sean, who have sacrificed their wife and mother during evenings and weekends so that I may live my dream and see it to fruition—with love and thanks and hugs and kisses. Lauren McKellar, editor extraordinaire. I will be forever grateful for your support, direction and encouragement. No words can express my gratitude. Hot Tree Editing for working with me on the Midnight revisions. All the countless blogs and fans—thank you for your tireless dedication and for your love of reading. To everyone who has taken the journey with me, falling in love with Colin and Charlie – Thank you, thank you, thank you! Your enthusiasm and encouragement keep me going!!!

Xoxo -EM

PROLOUGE

I ALWAYS THOUGHT I was immune to want or need, that I would sleep through the rest of my life and never feel my heart thunder under the weight of a stare. Shivering from a touch or humming through a kiss was not for me. It just never happened. Days clicked into place one black-and-white slide at a time; college graduation, lunch with Mom, shopping with my sister. I'm happy, but not with the kind of dizzying joy that keeps me from concentrating on anything but a *Him* or an *Us*.

Last night I went to bed by myself, as I have every day before. But now, now a prickling knowledge shimmers over my skin and forces my eyes open.

I am not alone.

He's the perfect man: full lips, a chiseled jaw, and a smirk that wars between dirty and sweet. Tall and broad and in my bedroom, he's bathed in the early morning light. I swallow down a question as he leans in to press his hands on either side of my face, watching me watch him.

"There are few things in the world I'd call mine," he says in his perfect, deep voice. "You belong to me."

I whimper. I whimper and reach for him. My fingers dive into his hair and pull him down, crashing my mouth against his. He matches my hunger. We kiss, hard and deep, long strokes of his tongue against mine, and I demand more. I'm a ticking time bomb and he started the clock. My pulse, his lips, my breath, his heat, the calm possession, I'm tied into a knot of *yes, please* and *don't ever leave*.

He tastes like everything I've ever wanted or needed. And I won't let him go. Not now that we've found our way to each other. Our souls are on a first name basis. Forever has come and gone and we've just met again. *Mine*.

My world explodes into a bright light when he presses between my thighs and my lids snap open.

"Oh, God," I pant and swipe the damp hair from my forehead. The familiar glow of a streetlight tugs my mind into my room and my life, where a gorgeous man doesn't affect the state of my panties. "Sleep, Carter." My voice is angry, as is the punch I throw to my flattened pillow. An early morning starts in hours and leaves little time for wishful thinking. But it doesn't stop the flush burning up my chest, or hope, as I squeeze my eyes closed to find the dream that will never be reality.

ONE

POLITICS IS NOT MY strong suit; in fact, I hold a high level of disdain for it, and maybe more so for politicians. My simple philosophy categorizes the whole system just above the criminal clientele inhabiting the State penitentiary. Politicians are pompous asses in very expensive three-piece suits. They may hold the appearance of kindness and concern, yet behind the façade they plunder the pockets of Americans, spending taxpayer money as if it grows on the trees surrounding their million-dollar mansions.

The irony that I've been asked to meet Indiana Senator Colin McKenna about a much sought after social media position on his campaign team is not lost on me. I don't know anything about him. The late call from Sonja Bates, an editor I work with, didn't allow for any investigation, and given my beliefs about the American political system, I have little knowledge of the platforms on which he professes support. I'm more interested in reading the classics than about who's banging who in Washington.

The thought of following the progress of a stale campaign for months is rather depressing, but my dried-up life savings outweighs any concerns. I'm turning onto the University of Notre Dame campus because my freelance work dried up and I'm broke.

Sliding from my beat-up Chevy Blazer at just past two in the afternoon, I hurry through the parking lot with only a few minutes to spare. The January wind whips in lashing licks. It prompts my jog into the Morris Inn, where I jump in the line of reporters waiting to enter the auditorium. After a credential check, I'm motioned to the far end, where an elevated stage sits in front of a U-shaped configuration of tables. Behind this area are rows of seats for the general public, which are filled to capacity.

I stand aside to remove my coat, accepting the last open chair on the very edge of the assembly. A pretty brunette woman sits next to me, preparing a portable mini recorder on the table in front of her, along with a binder for written notes. I watch, fascinated, as she meticulously reapplies her lip gloss and ensures every strand of hair is in place.

I'm suddenly aware of my white button up. The cotton didn't fare well through the four-hour drive, so I run my hands down the fitted sides to smooth out any wrinkles and tuck the hem into my black pencil skirt. Afraid my auburn curls suffered the same wilting fate, I twist and pin them up into a loose bun and hope my presentation will pass inspection.

As I pull my iPad from my bag, a balding man appears on stage and the hum of the crowd calms.

"Ladies and gentleman, it's with great pleasure I introduce you to a man I had the good fortune to teach not long ago at this very university. His goals and ambitions were clear even then; his drive to succeed unwavering. Embodying honesty and sincere candor, he will lead this country into the next decade with a direct connection to the needs and desires of the people. Senator Colin McKenna."

The crowd erupts into a riotous ovation. Clapping out of politeness, I watch the candidate walk onto the platform, shrouded at first by the shadows at the edge of the stage. Hoots and whistles follow him as he makes his way to the forefront. This is the reception of a popular musician, not a politician.

My hands still midair, breathing forgotten. Colin McKenna is a mirror of the man from my implausible dream. I'm in a trance, a moth caught in a spider's web without the ability to escape. He's absolutely gorgeous. Elegant yet sculpted in sharp lines, he fills the seams of a three-piece suit with a radiating sexuality. He doesn't look like any politician I've ever seen before. He's young—really young—for a presidential candidate.

A screen hangs behind him, projecting his features large enough for those in the very back to see every brilliant nuance. His jaw is etched from stone, softened only by a slight indent in his chin. Full lips, perfect teeth, and dimples, and I fear I may need a fan to cool the heat on my cheeks when he smiles. Rows of dark lashes frame eyes like I've never seen before: a brilliant blue with a slice of brandy shooting through the left one. Thick brown hair is perfectly placed at the crown of his head, smoothed back into a short and neat cut. I want my hands in it. I want my fingers pulling on it as if they were meant to live there. *Holy hell.* Desperate to refocus, I stare at the podium and the university's symbol embellished on the front—staring anywhere but at Colin McKenna.

It's only a moment before my gaze is drawn back. The noise of the crowd has yet to die down. He gives a slight bow of his head, as if embarrassed by the attention, and gestures for the applause to quiet. A hush falls across the room.

"Today I stand before you with our future and the health of our nation lying ahead of us. I have heard the cry for change in Washington, heard the hope that this election will be different than all that came before it. Together, and with my leadership, your desire for a brighter future is within our grasp."

I find myself staring wide-eyed as he speaks. Surely this man, albeit a very attractive one, shouldn't have this effect on me. I look around. Many are as struck as I am, watching with silly grins or simply gaping. A camera flash sparks my sanity and I realize I've forgotten to hit record. Fumbling, I do so, knowing I must have missed the first few minutes of his speech. Straightening my back, I lift my gaze to the Senator as he confirms his bid on the White House.

"I've made it my life's mission to care for this country and those who call it their home," he says, squaring his shoulders. "As I continue on with the pursuit of this dream, it's time I seek the most absolute position in which I can lead with integrity, pride, and passion. I will not let you down; I will not let this country down. I will bring the United States of America into the next decade stronger than it has ever been." The crowd erupts and once again I feel as if I'm at a concert, suspecting an overly hormonal teenager will throw her bra on stage.

When the cheering calms, he continues sharing his key initiatives should he be elected. After a few more minutes it's over and the dialogue is opened to the members of the media. He's quizzed about his beliefs, his priorities during the first year in office, and so on. I'm once again thankful for the iPad, because I'm having trouble concentrating. It's only when I catch the tail end of a question that I sit taller in my seat.

"...abortion and women's rights?"

My breath catches but his response comes easily. "There must be a balance between personal rights and the right to live. Life is precious and we must think in that context when considering ending it."

Indignation pulses like a second heartbeat, bubbling to the surface. "Would you take away a woman's right to protect herself? For reasons you couldn't know, would you take away a woman's control over her body and possible health?" It's as if I was thinking out loud, yet it was stated with conviction for everyone to hear. All heads swivel toward me, looking for the dumb ass shouting out in argument with Mr. McPerfect. But I don't back down. I would like to know.

I need to know.

It's his turn to stare. His intense gaze holds mine for what feels like an eternity before he addresses me with consideration. "A child has a right to be born, a right to live." His eyes continue with their hypnotic spell as others invade the moment, hurling questions. He hesitates, studying my face and hair before he shifts his attention away.

Relief floods through me as I sink back into my seat. *What did I just do?*

The questions and answers flow until the conference comes to an end, and with a brief glance my way, he exits the platform. I let out the breath I didn't realize I was holding and stand so fast my chair tips back.

"Hey, now, there's no need to throw furniture. The speech wasn't so bad, was it?"

Oh, shit. Is he talking to me? The thump of my heart hits my throat and reluctantly, I turn.

He has an easy grin centered on a handsome face; handsome in a California surfer kind of way.

"Ms. Carter?" When I nod, he continues, "Evan Daugherty, the senator's campaign manager."

"Right, yeah." Flustered, I stumble through a greeting and his smile spreads.

"I have a private space set aside for us to talk. Come, he's anxious to speak with you."

I don't know if this is a good idea; after the reaction I had toward Senator McKenna, this assignment is looking more and more unfavorable. Yet I follow, even as nerves settle in my stomach. The only distraction as he leads me past the stage and through a large conference space bubbling with campaign staff is a stunning blonde, who plays voodoo with her eyes. They narrow and spit needles as she tracks my progress. I lose sight of her when accepting Mr. Daugherty's waved offer for one of four plush chairs in a private tiny room.

As I drop down to sit, the senator fills the doorway. By his mere presence, Colin McKenna commands attention, and he definitely has mine; every nerve in my body is highly attuned to his proximity, shimmering like a spark waiting to ignite. He's tall, so tall I crane my neck to look at him. I force my gaze to his face, but he's too—I don't know, he's too… him—so I let them trail to his chest. No longer fully suited, he wears only a dark gray vest with a white shirt, collar open. And then lower. I catch myself staring at his muscled thighs and the bulge that lies slightly higher, barely concealed by the slim line of his matching charcoal slacks.

He clears his throat and I blink my way up his rock-hard body. His smile broadens and I lose myself in its brilliance, before I call myself stupid and stand, fumbling with my bag.

"Thank you for agreeing to meet with me on such short notice," he says in a husky tone made to send shivers down my spine.

As my palm connects with his, a line of electricity shoots up my arm and the air feels full of an almost palpable energy. His brow furrows and his smirk dissolves into the straight line of his lips. I wonder for a second if he feels it too, and then the intensity of his stare causes a hot flush to spread up my chest like a wildfire. Those damn eyes; it's as if they're searching mine for answers to unasked questions. My lips part to respond to the mysterious inquiry, but no sound escapes my now parched throat. Shaking my head, I recover and slip free from his grip.

With our physical connection broken, his smile returns. "Please have a seat. May I offer you anything?"

I sink into the soft chair, crossing my legs, and his gaze follows to my leopard-print heels. But I don't feel ferocious as I did when I walked out of my apartment this morning. The confidence I held as I slipped into my favorite print has been stripped away, and all that's left is me. Charlie Carter, sister, daughter, a pseudo-journalist from a small town with limited experience. And in front of me is a god among men. Colin McKenna isn't the boy next door—he's the lion ready to slaughter the lamb.

I count to three to ensure I won't squeak out an answer. "No, thank you—I'm fine."

We're face-to-face as he sits on the couch, knees apart, one arm stretching to rest on the back cushion, relaxed. "I hope you had an uneventful drive. Where is it that you live?"

"Royal Oak, just north of Detroit—Michigan," I add after a beat, and then think stupid isn't a strong enough term.

"That must have taken you most of the morning. I'm sorry we didn't give you more notice to plan an accommodating travel schedule."

I wave away the concern in his tone. "It was fine, I didn't mind the drive."

He nods. "I understand Sonja has reviewed with you my thoughts on creating an extensive social media campaign, a chronicle if you will, relating to my candidacy and me personally. I want to connect with those who use social media as their primary means of communication."

"And you believe I may be the person best suited to do this?" I'm incredulous. I fail to understand how my limited resume qualifies me for this assignment.

"I do." He continues by changing the subject. "It seems you and I have differing opinions on topics that are very pertinent to the moral compass of our country. I'm intrigued to learn more about your position."

This is not a conversation I want to have. Not with him. I could kick myself for opening my mouth and wish I had shoved my glorious leopard-print heel into it instead. It takes a deep breath and boiling blood before I can offer the truth. "I don't believe a man wholly unconnected to the state of a woman's body should judge and prevent a possible life-saving procedure. How are you, or any other politician, qualified to determine what a woman may do with her own body?"

"And what about the baby, Ms. Carter? Who will protect the innocent life taken each time an abortion is performed?"

I flinch. "There are some instances in which neither one would survive if not for the option. It's in those circumstances I believe a woman has the right to choose her own life over the beginning of another." The intensity of my position shows as my voice reverberates my answer, forceful, even though the tone is low.

Nodding, as if to close the topic he says, "It's very rare that someone voluntarily and so spontaneously opposes my opinion at an event sponsored by my camp. I need to be connected to people, even those with beliefs that differ from my own. I like that you offer another side of the picture painted before me."

"Is it my opinion you seek, or my ability to write about yours?" I ask. *What is it he wants me to do?*

His eyes spark. "Both. Tell me, how do you approach a topic to present it in a fair light, approach it from a true, unpolluted perspective?"

"I withhold all personal judgment of the individual or subject. It's not my job to provide a conclusion for the reader; it's my responsibility to share the facts as I understand them." I've regained my footing and the fledgling confidence returns. "I learned very early on most people are not as easily read as one would believe. I let them tell me their truth, and listen carefully to the art of people. You would be surprised by what you hear."

Raising his fingers to his mouth, he begins to pull on his lower lip, and it does something to me. The same something it did last night, and I shift in my seat, hoping he doesn't notice my thighs squeezing together. "And what if the topic is of no interest to you?"

"Life is interesting, Senator. I don't need to have a passion for everything in it; I have to find what's remarkable for the readers. That's what will engage them in the blog and the topic itself."

I look at Evan, who has remained silent through the entire conversation, standing against the far wall, arms folded against his chest. He grins as if he's in on a joke I'm not aware of. "Was that your tactic when you created and maintained the highest rated personal blog for three years straight?"

My heart explodes in my chest. "Oh, that." I bite my bottom lip and wait for my pulse to settle. "I um, it was a lucky coincidence at a time when not many people were talking about plus size fashion. I wanted to chat about it and I didn't care much if anyone wanted to listen."

"Millions did. Why'd you stop?"

I shrug my indifference. "It was drawing me into the spotlight and I prefer to remain behind the scenes."

Evan's smirk turns into a smile at the same time McKenna leans forward, hands clasped. "Ms. Carter, I'm about to embark on a tour of the United States seeking the Republican presidential nomination. I would like for you to accompany me as I campaign. Use your expertise to understand my motivations and connect my beliefs and me to voters via the Internet. Will you come?"

It takes a moment to formulate a response, and the only thing I can think to say is "Charlie." His right brow lifts in question. "Call me Charlie. Ms. Carter or Charlise is too formal."

"Charlie," he says as if tasting my name, savoring it. When I don't answer he tries again. "Charlie, I want you to contemplate my offer. Would you meet me tomorrow for breakfast?" he asks, yet I think by the command in his tone he only expects an affirmative answer. "It will give you an opportunity to learn more about me and the campaign."

I'm drawn to this man, his masculine, chiseled jaw and cheekbones, straight nose, blue eyes, and the glorious waves in his hair. This is uncharted territory, and I'm not sure accepting his offer is the right thing to do—for him or for me.

"I haven't booked a room to stay through the night."

He glances over my shoulder. I turn to the window and the snow that has started tumbling from the sky. Big, wet flakes fall, the roof of the building next to ours already thick with buildup.

"I'll take care of the room for you this evening. Don't drive in this weather."

I agree with him, but not because of his demand. It'll take double the time to get home in this mess. "Okay."

"Good." He stands, staring down with an unreadable expression. "I would like for you to enter into our agreement knowing little about me or my campaign. Base your perspective on what you learn firsthand. Can you promise me you'll forgo any research from this moment forward?"

I'm surprised by his request. Most journalists engage in extensive preparation prior to embarking on such a journey. "Will you promise to be forthright and honest with information when I ask for it and have a need to know?" I search the sculpted lines of his face to determine the truthfulness of his answer.

"On my honor," he says, and for some reason I believe his sincerity.

"I promise."

"Until tomorrow then."

Standing, my hands fan over my skirt to ensure it's lying smoothly over my rounded hips. His eyes flick over the area I just caressed and then he turns and steps from the room.

"Until tomorrow, Senator," I whisper to his retreating backside.

TWO

Sitting at a small table in front of the restaurant's only fireplace, the senator's head is tipped to his cell. The few patrons left from the morning rush have a singular focus and I fall in line with them, relieved he misses my inspection. More relaxed than I saw yesterday, he's wearing a dark blue cable-knit sweater with a high collar. It hangs open, exposing a muscled neck and the white T-shirt hidden underneath. I can't look away, and it's not because his sleeves are pushed to his elbows, exposing thick forearms as if he's more professional athlete than presidential hopeful. It's a feeling, like we were separated years ago and our reunion took too long to occur. Now that we're together, I don't want to miss a breath or a word or smile.

He looks up and the feeling spreads below the belt. I might say my world stands still. If people remain in the near vicinity, I stop caring. In a simple moment it's me watching a cute boy with my heart somersaulting in my chest. But fairytales don't exist in real life, and the connection is broken by a shattering crash in the kitchen.

I glance to the hostess and her batting lashes when she deposits me next him. He stands in greeting. "Is there anything you need, Senator McKenna?" she asks in a voice much too breathy for a day job.

He shakes his head a fraction and says, "Charlie."

That one word lives within me as a shiver. This pull, the draw I feel toward him, is beyond surprising. It's never happened before. I can't figure out why now, why him? Then it hits me. I'm not alone, everyone has this reaction. Few people possess the type of magnetism that casts a spell, yet he has it in spades. With my inexperience I don't stand a chance to fight off his magic.

Keep it professional, Carter. I let the chant loose in my mind and hold out my hand, not expecting the sparks when he makes contact or the sudden lump I can't swallow when his thumb draws warm circles on my skin. We stand staring; his eyes seek out mine and I wonder what he sees: the injured child or the sheltered adult?

A diversion comes by way of the waiter offering coffee. "Yes, please." I beam with gratitude at him as he pours it, and then at the senator for pulling out my seat.

"Thank you," I say and sink down.

He's just as quick to relax next to me. "I hope you slept well?"

Okay, I can do this. He is, after all, a man; there are no lions at the table for breakfast. A smirk lifts the side of his mouth and I forget why we're here. Oh, right: conversation, campaign, social media. "I did, and you, did you sleep well?"

The smirk stretches to a smile. "Better than I have in months."

"Good." I wish I knew what he's thinking. Yesterday he was completely unreadable. Today it's as if he's lowered his shield and stepped away from battle, allowing me a glimpse of the man behind the mask. I glance to the fire snapping next to him, appreciating the heat on my bare legs.

"Are you cold?"

I shake my head. "It feels nice; I didn't have my thermals to keep me warm last night." I clench my jaw to hold a straight face.

He tips his head back and laughs. "Thermals?"

It's deep and genuine, warming me from the inside out, and it spurs me on. "It's very cold in Michigan, at nighttime especially. Thermals are warm; you should try them."

"I think you say that in jest, Charlie."

"You doubt thermals are warm?"

"No, I doubt you wear them."

I shrug. He's not subtle as he looks over my face and hair and then he catches sight of my shirt, his right brow lifting in question.

"A sudden fan of the Fighting Irish?"

"You like it?" I ask, opening the jean jacket I had stashed in the Blazer. Underneath is a kelly green T-shirt sporting the college's logo. "I wasn't prepared for the overnight stay, so I improvised with a gift shop find. Who knew they sell everything." And I do mean everything. My ass is peppered with the same logo because apparently there's a market for Notre Dame panties. Combine everything with my skirt from yesterday and I look more student than business professional.

"It's the same color as your eyes." There's heat in his voice, so much so my stomach flutters. *Okay....* It's time for coffee when all I can think about are his lips, and what his mouth tastes like, how it would feel on my neck.

I focus on my mug, and the cream and sugar. "I like kissing sweet and light. No...." I hold out my hand, horrified. "I mean coffee—coffee should be sweet and light. How do you take yours?"

He smiles behind his cup and now his eyes spark like the flames by his feet. "Dark and strong."

As in deep and wicked. Oh, for the love of God. I stop to think as the strangest thing sits on my shoulder and whispers in my ear, *you're not nervous or intimidated.* And this is not like me. I don't flirt or banter with boys, let alone a lion. The ease of it, though, is what's sending warning signals to my brain in bright blinking lights. A sign blaring careful-Charlie-this-is-life-changing is blinking in neon in the near distance, yet I can't help but follow its stated course.

"Was that your first question?" he asks with a dimple digging into his cheek.

"One of many, yes."

"You don't want to know my credentials?"

I contemplate him, the soft wave of hair that escaped from the rest to lie on his forehead and the day's growth of whiskers covering his jaw—smooth yet rough. In a flash of recognition I know his charm can win over the most difficult conversations, but underneath the perfection he has the potential to lose control. And that's what I need to discern—how dangerous is he?

"No. I'd expect Evan Daugherty and the rest of your team vetted you against the pack before you spent millions to get where you are today. You're asking me to leave my family for months, and to do that, I want to know the man under the suit. Tell me who Colin McKenna is."

He tilts his head and I get the same calculated assessment. His eyes trip on my lips and then he pulls at his bottom one with his teeth before it pops free. "We don't have anything between us but words, Charlie," he says, leaning in. "But I need one thing from you."

He rests his hand on mine. I hadn't noticed I'd clenched the edge of the table, but the underside of the wood is rough where I've dug into the grain. I stare at his long fingers; feel the warmth and the weight and the zing of possibility that travels up my arm.

I drag my eyes to his. Green to blue, and I willingly sacrifice myself to the slaughter. "Anything," I whisper

"Trust," he says. "I'll always give you my honesty and I expect the same from you."

Oh. I nod, but sense he's hungry for more. He wants my truth: the dark secrets of my soul.

My heart stumbles over the prospect and I get lost in a vat of overwhelmed. I don't do change. I lived with my parents until they cut the tie and urged me into adulthood. I like my people, my places, and the familiarity of my day-to-day. The safety all of it brings. And he's offering—what exactly? *Rein it in, Carter*. This is an interview, not a proposition. But I fixate on his left hand, still lingering over mine. There is no wedding ring and no indentation of one on his finger. He's beyond gorgeous, successful, and running for president; I'm surprised he isn't married.

"My wife died." He pulls away and rubs the spot as if in memory of the ring that once was.

My eyes cling to his. "I'm so sorry, I…."

"It was years ago. Are you hungry?" he asks, motioning for the waiter.

Starving. But not for food, for the something new he's offering. For the change that scares me as much as it excites. I swallow my heart as it pounds in my throat and pick up the menu. "Um… I'd like the blueberry pancakes with bacon, please."

"And I'll have the president's special. What?" he asks when my brows shoot up. "It's on the menu."

I wave away his grin and set aside the crazy notion this conversation is anything but straightforward. "So what did you do before politics?"

"McKenna Industries."

"And?"

"I rehabbed failing businesses. They still do. When I ran for office I transitioned the firm to my COO, but I remain the key stakeholder. My forte is determining why a company is deteriorating, get it moving in a new direction, and sell it for a profit." He looks directly into my eyes as he finishes, "I like to find broken things, discover their secrets, and make them whole; mend and repair until they're far better than before my interception."

I squirm under the weight of his stare, as if he's looking into me, searching again for my truth. "What's the secret to your success?"

"I learned very quickly that it wasn't about me; it's not about my title, or the skills I have, or what I can do. It's always about the people: their capabilities and motivation. People won't follow someone because they have a title; they'll support and do the right thing when influenced by someone they trust. Honesty and transparency are pivotal to a successful endeavor. With those principles and hard work, I push the companies and the employees beyond expectation, surpassing what they believed themselves capable of. Once it's successful, I sell it and start all over again."

"So why did you make the change to politics?"

He shrugs. "It's always been my dream. Fundamentally, the business concept is the same, yet it's on a bigger level. Very simply, it's about peeling back the layers one at a time, identifying the problems, fixing them, making it better than it ever was and moving on to the next layer. It's the ultimate challenge and I do it justice."

I nod. It makes sense. "But you're so young."

"Should I wait until I'm fifty?"

"Maybe. I thought you had to, actually."

"Thirty-five is the minimum age to run. I'm thirty-six; I'll be thirty-seven by inauguration, if I'm elected. You think I'm not qualified?" he challenges.

"No, I don't know you well enough to say that. I think there are a lot of people who will jump to that conclusion, though."

"It's one of the reasons why I need you." My heart free-falls. I know very well he's talking about business, but I feel his comment deeply.

Get a grip, Carter.

My reaction is bizarre. How is it that for years I've been immune to desire and at first sight of this gorgeous, completely out-of-my-league man, I'm salivating like a hormonal teenager? None of this makes any sense.

"I have so little experience. What if I fail you?" This is the truth; why would he look to me to assist him in this lifelong endeavor?

"Don't make yourself uneasy. I'm very familiar with your experience. I don't leave many things up to fate, Charlie, not in pursuit of the position I hope to have. I need you," he says again. "You're young with a fresh perspective."

"But how do you even know who I am?"

"Evan has read many of your articles and came across a website you devised for Jay Tyler; he's impressed, as was I when I did my research."

My head swims. It makes sense he would delve into my past and qualifications, just as I would have done with him if I'd had time. The senator would be very thorough and in depth. He'd uncover everything.

"Think about how good we could be together," he says as our food appears.

But all I can think about is the loaded meaning behind those words. We suspend conversation while we eat, and I'm amazed at how easy it is to be with him. The moment stutters into déjà vu, as if we've had a hundred mornings like this one.

"How are they?" he asks, pointing to my plate.

"Delicious. And your president's special?"

"Are you turning your nose up at my choice?"

I shake my head. "No, I'd never call scrambled egg whites boring."

He chuckles. "It's called healthy."

Boring, I mouth. "Here, try some of my pancakes; you can taste the difference between dull and insanely good." I push my plate toward him an inch, encouraging him to take a bite.

He cuts away a triangle from the stack and I watch as he raises it to his mouth. Our eyes connect and the heat is back, raging uncontrollably at our table for two. It was only a pancake, for the love of God. How can it turn into this unbearable tension?

I have to look away. My appetite is suddenly gone; I can't concentrate on anything but my heart and the thrumming energy under my skin.

"Charlie?" His voice is deep, with a rasping edge to it. I peek at his face where a small smile offers encouragement. "It's been a long time since I've had anything insanely good, so thank you—for the pancakes."

So he's sweet too. Damn man.

"Will you leave today?" I ask.

"As soon as breakfast is over."

"Oh." I wasn't expecting that. "And if I accept, when will I join you?"

"Will you accept?"

Now is the time to make a choice. To take a chance on living outside of my box. Albeit a comfortable and safe haven, it's time to stretch into a new me.

"Yes."

His response spreads into a heart-stopping grin. "Good. I'd like you to spend a week at my campaign headquarters here in Indiana, and then meet me and the others on the trail."

"Who are they?"

"My team, the people I trust the most. You're a part of them now."

"Oh." The weight of the endeavor is heavy on my shoulders. "I'd like a few days to get my things in order. Will you send me the itinerary? I'll also want an outline of your expectations for the blog and social media sites. With your input, I'll put together a proposal." It feels good to talk business.

"Yes, absolutely." He glances at his vibrating cell. "McKenna." His tone is different on the phone, different than his tone with me. Looking directly into my eyes, he responds, "Give me ten minutes… In addition, I'll need you to get Ms. Carter specifics on the campaign as soon as possible… Yes, Monday." After a pause he hangs up. His face, once relaxed and at ease, is fierce and he's back on the hunt.

A second later he removes his napkin from his lap and stands. I assume he has the bill routed to his room because we're done. Just like that. Breakfast is over and I have a new future. He steps behind my chair to pull it back.

"Thank you, Senator." I stand and turn. Lost in a to-do list the size of the Himalayas, I head to the door.

"Charlie!" His sharp tone snaps my gaze from the paisley carpet to the waiter: a huge platter full of dishes is barreling toward me. The senator grabs my waist and tugs my back to his chest to avoid an embarrassing collision. In an instant, an absurd, illogical force grips tight and I'm its marionette, a puppet controlled by an unseen figure, bound to its demands. Closing my eyes, I bask for an instant in his embrace; the heat radiating from him to me fractures my heart into scattered palpitations.

A low rumble vibrates between us as his fingers dig into my hips. *Oh, God.* I swear his lips brush against my ear. I know he whispers, "*Tell me you feel it too.*" His breath is rough, it is, I feel it, but then he pushes me away. None of it can be true when I turn to find he's raking his hand through his hair from root to tip, jaw tense.

"I'm so sorry, I didn't see him."

"Please," he says, motioning me to take the lead and past this crazy moment. He doesn't have to worry; I'd jog if it'd fast-forward through my awkward reaction. He pushes the door open from beside me and we exit the restaurant together. When we're alone in the lobby he takes hold of my arm and I swing around to face him.

He looks me over one more time, getting stuck on my lips and then my hair. His gaze lands on my eyes and I see a struggle rolling around in his blue storm. But he shakes his head, as if freeing himself from confusion.

"Evan will send you everything you need to be comfortable with a Monday start. I'll meet you the following week in North Carolina."

I reach for his outstretched hand and stare at our connection. He's warm, firm, and electric, very much like his eyes that draw me in and hold me captive. It would be very easy to get lost in them; lost in him.

"Good-bye, Charlie."

"Colin, have a safe trip." It's the first time I've said his name. I know it and I think he may too, from the parting of his lips. "Good-bye," I whisper. Pulling my hand from his, I turn and rush toward the exit. I don't dare look back; if I do I may say or do something I can't recover from.

The sting of the cold January air is a welcome slap against my face, breaking through the haze created by this crazy intensity. Imagined or real, it's profound and disturbing. Holy shit; we're going to work together for months. Now that I'm away from him, I'm rethinking my agreement; I need to stay away from Colin McKenna.

THREE

"THE BIGGEST RISK IS never taking one. How many times have we heard Gram say that?"

"Speaking of Gram, let's talk birthday bash," I say, trying to move us past the last ten minutes of our conversation.

"Oh, no you don't, sister," Ali admonishes. "You're not changing the subject. I want to finish talking about the hot senator and then we'll move on to parties. Now walk me through this crazy notion of yours to resign before you've even started."

"Ali." I sigh. Maybe it wasn't the smartest idea to call her from the car, leaving only one hand on the wheel. "I know my mental status is questionable and will be even more so if I decline this assignment, but please consider what I told you."

"I've heard everything and you know what it sounded like?"

"What?" I mumble, knowing she's going to tell me anyway.

"A lot of orgasms in the making. Most people don't feel half of that intensity in a lifetime, and you're contemplating ignoring it for a reason I can't figure out."

"I just told you: I could ruin him!" I lean my elbow against the driver-side window to prop up my addled brain.

"Oh, please. Little Charlie Carter cannot bring down a presidential candidate. You haven't done anything wrong."

"You know that's not true," I whisper. It still hurts to think about.

"Would you stop beating yourself up over something that happened fifteen years ago? You deserve to move past it. Besides, your secret's safe. Medical records are sealed; anyone searching that deep would have a privacy violation on their hands, which is breaking the law. Do I need to go on?"

"Thanks, Doctor Carter. I appreciate your reassurance."

"It's part of my sisterly duties. One day at a time, remember?" she says, repeating my lifelong mantra. "Just go, have some fun, enjoy meeting new people. Get laid—it's like an ice cream cone on a hot day: it makes everything better."

"Ali Carter!" I scream, but smile as I do.

"Come on, Charlie. If you would just let yourself relax, you'd love it; trust me."

"You're terrible, but I love you. Seriously, Al, you're the best."

"I know." She giggles and then gets serious. "I love you, Charlie girl. Promise to call and text all the time so I know you're okay?"

"I promise. E-mail me later about balloons and the guest list. Gram will love the surprise and I'll work the party into my schedule. I've got to run, I just pulled up."

"Give the senator a kiss for me. Bye."

I hang up and get nervous at the same time. I've thought of nothing but this offer for the last seventy-two hours. Minutes out from my first day, the panic takes hold. I'm excited, yet I'm out of my league. Insecurities threaten to break down my carefully constructed wall of confidence, but this will be good for me. It will. The sky acts as confirmation of that thought, bright and clear, as I slip from the Blazer, pulling my messenger bag with me. I swallow my angst as I drape it over my head and walk the parking lot. One day at a time.

Campaign headquarters is an old schoolhouse that's been renovated with big picture windows. It looks like any other structure in a business district except for the bell that remains on the roof. That and red, white, and blue has exploded into signs and banners. *McKenna for the People* is everywhere, on the lawn, hanging from the brick, and even etched on the glass door.

"No time like the present," I whisper to myself, and push through to my new future. A snappy brunette with straight bangs and a huge smile singsongs her greeting, "Hi, I'm Molly, and who are you?"

I can't help my answering grin. "Charlie—" Before I can finish she jumps up from her seat.

"We've been expecting you." She motions me to follow. "I'll take you back to Evan."

"I thought he was gone this week," I say, racing to keep up with her. At least I got something right, I think, while watching her rush ahead. Molly's oversized sweater, skintight pants, and mile-high booties mirror my own charcoal and black creation.

"There was a last-minute change to some plans." She glances over her shoulder to look at me as we rush down a curved hall. Pictures of the senator are hanging everywhere but no one is sitting around and staring. The bustle of fifty people hits us as we reach the body of the building. Tables are stacked with fliers, more signs, envelopes, mailers, and phones. Every surface is covered. Men and women, young and old, work side by side. It's loud, chaotic, and thrilling at the same time.

Evan's on the phone and hammering on his keyboard when we reach his office. Missing is the smirk he held when I saw him days ago. "I don't care what it takes—make it happen, Smith. We need to get him before Davidson. Next week—call me when it's confirmed." He sighs and tosses down his cell.

"Charlie." Standing, he reaches for my hand. "Welcome. I wish I had time to chat, but I'm…." He frees himself from my grip to pat his chest pocket and then his pants, while his eyes scan his desk.

He sighs when Molly pulls a pen from under a stack of binders and hands it over. "Thanks," he says, tipping it toward her and then me. "My good-luck charm. I never leave home without it."

I try to hide my smile behind my hand. He's so serious, and seriously cute, while verging on use of a pocket protector when he slips on glasses. Dark rims don't conceal his gray eyes sparking with mischief.

"Laugh now, but give it a few weeks and you'll have your own rabbit's foot. Don't look, but Tim." He stares over my shoulder. "Underwear, and don't ask me how I know this or how often he has them on. Now, Randy, it's his wife's—"

Molly cuts him off with a laughing cough. "I think she has the idea. And for the record, mine is a secret. No one will ever know."

"Where is the fun in that?"

"Trust me," she says as her cheeks take on a subtle flush. "The fun is all mine."

Evan's brow lifts and he nods his appreciation as she turns, walking away with an exaggerated hip swing.

"Hmm, well, I like the way she operates. Welcome home, Charlie."

I laugh. This might not be so bad after all. "Thanks, where should I start?"

Grabbing a stack of files, he hands them over. I pretend to crack under their weight, but my knee bend is not too far off. The documents almost meet my chin. "For your reading pleasure, you have access to the senator's personal and campaign finances. Learn how he uses the funds. Get to know his platform. As part of this team, you need to be able to speak to his vision responsibly. Start with these. There's an open desk in the back."

I twist to follow his nod and find the empty space through the deliberate chaos. "Thanks." Stepping out, I hesitate at the door to look at him. "I, uh, I thought you would already be on the trail. Colin, he mentioned traveling this week."

He taps his finger on the desk. It's peppered with papers and a large calendar is almost hidden underneath the piles. "Change of plans."

"Oh." I nod and try to hide the shiver racing up my spine to tickle my nape. *He's here*. Lord, if my heart won't calm down, I'll need to seek medical attention.

"We'll be back and forth from Indiana for a while before taking to the road," he says, and sits.

"Great, cool. Um . . . Okay, I'm going to go read." I roll my eyes. If he hadn't second-guessed his choice for social media journalist before, he is now.

But he just nods. "Good, and Charlie? I'm glad you're here."

"Thanks, Evan. Me too." I realize when I say it that it's the truth.

Leaving his office, I bob in and around people, tables, and piles of signs. McKenna is everywhere in print and in the air as calls are made to persuade votes. I find my new normal in a five-by-six space and sink into Colin's brain.

I review everything: donations, gifts, and individual wealth. He has a wide range of supporters and he's circumspect on how he spends their money. I swallow a *holy hell* when I get to his personal finances. The man has more money than the state of Michigan and that's not much of an exaggeration.

At quarter to one, a lanky guy I would place just shy of thirty pops his head into my cubicle.

He grins and holds out his hand. "Tim Hagger."

My smile is instantaneous because images of his well-worn briefs pop in my head. "Charlie Carter."

"First day?"

I laugh. He's channeling Evan's smooth sophistication but not quite getting there. His hair is too perfect and stiff with spray, and the day-old scruff on his chin is shaggy, as in Scooby Doo. "Is it that obvious?"

"It's the homework." He points to my desk and the open binders. "We've all been there; the quiz starts in the morning."

"Really?"

"No." He smiles with what looks like hope and takes his sweet time checking out the low dip in my sweater. I squirm under the inspection—not interested. "No testing allowed. Want to eat? We had food brought in from a deli."

I'm hopeful "we" is accurate and agree. Or, my rumbling stomach does.

Tim likes to talk. He fills each step we take with something. The lunch room is a cleared table with sandwiches and chips spread across it. Tim goes down the line until my head is dizzy with introductions. I'm so full of everything new I may not have room for the chicken salad.

"Hey." Molly tugs my sleeve.

"Thanks," I say, happy to sit in her proffered chair.

"So, you're heading out with John Montgomery next week?" she asks just as I take a bite from a surprisingly good sandwich.

"Hmm?" I wipe dribble from my chin and swallow. "Who?"

"The Montgomerys?" She looks around and then tips her head down as if she's sharing national secrets. "The senator's former father-in-law, John, is his communications director. He travels with him all the time."

I shake my head, surprised. "I didn't know."

She twists her lips into something close to disgust. "Have you met Ella yet?"

I laugh. "No, at least I don't think so. Who is she?"

"You would remember if you did; she has a permanent I-hate-the-world-and-I-will-make-you-know-it look. She's John's daughter, Colin's sister-in-law."

Voodoo crosses my mind. "Does she throw daggers with her eyes?"

"That's her," she exclaims. "Keep your distance. On her best days she aims to wound, and you, I think she might be out for the kill."

The hair on my arms doesn't like the sound of that, prickling up with goose bumps. "Why me? I've never done anything to her."

"This is all pure conjecture, but I'm solid with puzzles. Back in the day, the senator dumped Ella when he met her sister."

"Really?" Even I cringe at the piercing tone of my voice. "Why does she work for him, then? I mean, it would suck to be around an ex all the time."

"I think she believes in second chances and having another woman travel with him"—she elbows my side—"is enough to put a bull's-eye on your back. Ella wants him bad enough, I wouldn't put it past her evil highness to have thrown a ball instead of a wake when her sister and niece died. She's that rotten."

"Niece?" I ask, and toss down the last half of my sandwich.

"You didn't know?" Molly's face falls. "The senator lost his wife and three-month-old in the car accident."

I hold my thumping heart in my chest. "God, that's horrible."

"Horrible, and for the last five years Ella's been trying to sink her claws in him. John's not stupid either. He knew his son-in-law was destined for the White House so he stayed tight and helped him get voted into the Senate. I've heard he's ruthless in his tactics to ensure he's elected."

Just as I ask for details a bell trills, the kind to announce class is dismissed. Molly smiles and grabs our trash. "Back to work."

THE AFTERNOON MOVES AT the same pace as the morning: fast and full of all things McKenna. I'm amazed by the media workings of a massive campaign. The pressure is on. The last presidential election was decided by the winner's advanced Internet communications. My strategy will have to be better and easier to use to garner more participation than prior candidates.

At the end of the day, Tim arrives to correct a programming error on my computer. He's crowding me in, so close I can attest that his cologne is more gag-worthy than swoon. But as he's doing his best to align his thigh with mine a new awareness shivers over my skin. I'm compelled to look up. The pace of the office has slowed so it's not hard to find him. The lion found his den. Sans tie, his white shirt is open at the collar and tucked in to pants that hug his masculinity. Ali would say he's dangerous, hair verging on black in the waning evening light, eyes hooded and sinking to the same daring depths. The sight of him, so intent and staring right at me, pushes all the air from my lungs.

I knew he'd come, and I'd prepared myself for the racing heart and ragged breath. I was ready for fun and flirty and for flames burning up my cheeks. But I didn't know it would hurt. I couldn't plan ahead for the ache that lives in my chest when he doesn't acknowledge my wave. I hadn't thought to be thankful for an empty stomach, until it flips when his gaze flicks to Tim. His jaw clenches as tight as the fists by his sides.

I didn't know how empty I'd feel when he glares at my lips and my mouthed *hello*, but ignores it and retreats into Evan's office. Not a word, nothing but a tense slam of the door behind him.

Oh, okay. Tim's parting tutorial is lost in my ringing ears. I stare at the monitor, the blinking cursor—as that one minute with me here and Colin all the way over there—rolls on replay. I'm not sure what I did, or what has changed in the past seventy-two hours, other than everything. I hide my hurt behind the screen and berate myself for the absurdity of it. What did I think he would do? I'm clueless about men, and in my naiveté I thought we had some sort of connection.

"Charlie?"

"Ahh," I scream and nail my knee into the desk. "Holy shit, Evan."

He chuckles as I rub out the sting. "Sorry, I thought you saw me coming."

I shake my head. I must have been lost in la-la land longer than I thought. The office is silent and the windows dark.

"It's late, you should go."

"There's nothing to go home to; living out of a hotel this week, remember?"

"Right." He turns, stopping to rest a hand on the knob. "I have plans, otherwise I'd—"

"I'm fine." I cut him off before he can finish. "I brought my Kindle. You know, romance at your fingertips." God, I'm pathetic. I motion him away. "Go. Have fun."

Don't worry about me; I know how to do alone.

I SLEPT LIKE SHIT. I'm cranky and the dark water this place calls coffee is not helping my mood. My yawns are bigger than my hand and I can't hold them back. The third cup better work magic or my new team is going to get to know Charlie Carter better than anyone could imagine on my second day of work. Sleep is good, I like blankets and sinking into soft pillows, but last night the lumpy bed and thoughts of Colin McKenna did not make a perky princess. More like Snow White's grumpy sidekick.

Ugh, I got it wrong. What a monumental miscalculation on my part. Shivers be damned, my Notre Dame reaction was obviously from the frigid temperatures and not some magical moment.

The kitchenette is smaller than my office. From sink to hallway takes two steps. I know it'll take an espresso to bring me out of this stupor by the time I reach the door. As I pull the disappointing drink from my mouth, I'm bulldozed by Ella Montgomery when she rounds the corner. Inches shorter than I am, her hands are in perfect position to launch the disappointment from my grip. I feel an ounce of remorse for the borrowed Bugs Bunny mug when it shatters into a starburst against the polished concrete floor. She's not playing.

"What the…?" Her shrill pitch falls off as she focuses on my face, eyes catching on my lips and hair. She stiffens into a red-faced hellion, and it's not a good look. "You don't belong here," she says with venom falling from a fang.

"I'm sorry, I didn't see you."

She steps closer and for self-preservation I back up. "Let me put this in simple terms; terms you'll understand. Stay away from me, and stay away from Colin."

The rancor has reached her eyes and they bulge like the reptile she is.

"Are you dull?" She snaps her fingers as if I'm not paying attention to this spectacle. But it's really too good to miss. "I'll repeat it, so your simple mind can make sense of simple speech. Stay away from Colin." Her small frame rises until we're nose to nose. "You have no business being here and you certainly don't have any with him. If it were up to me, you'd be rolling papers for your route wherever it is people like you are born. So don't apologize. Clean up your damn mess and do something." She spins on her heels and leaves me with a brain full of *what just happened here*?

That little show found an audience, most of whom turn away when I look around. Everyone except Molly: she's already tugging my wide-eyed frozen-android self to the corner to save my suede boots from death by horrid coffee. "I told you she's a crazy bitch."

I laugh but it sounds like a broken record. "Does she treat everyone like that?"

"For the most part; but I think you got an extra dose because she's boiling with jealousy over your travel schedule."

My wobbly smile falls flat. "She doesn't have anything to worry about there," I say, bending to pick up pieces of the fractured mug.

"Leave it, I'll get the broom."

As Molly departs down the hall, Colin approaches. The seductive rhythm of his voice beats in time with my racing heart. I stand and drop my hand against my thigh. *Shit.* Squeezing my eyes closed does little to lessen the sting of separating flesh; warmth spreads far too quick to mean anything but too big for a Band-Aid.

One step has me at the sink with running water. I gasp through the bite as it hits the open wound.

"Charlie?"

Double shit. The shiver I so desperately wanted to blame on the weather is zipping across my shoulders as if he demanded it happen. A second later, Colin's breath is hot against my ear. He flips my hand over and his chest rumbles behind me.

"Can you walk?"

I snap my eyes open, immediately regretting it when his tense jaw blurs in and out of focus.

"I don't do blood well."

He grabs a clean towel from a drawer, knotting it around my palm. "I can see that. You look like you don't have any left in your body, you're so pale."

Wrapping his arm around my waist, he practically lifts me from the floor. I take advantage of his heat, pressing my nose into the pure male musk in the curve of his neck. Spice and everything nice has me smiling into his skin. Sandalwood, he smells like sandalwood, and my body tingles in all the right places. For just a second I imagine I'll have the chance to live in this beautiful place forever. He sighs and tightens his hold. It's only a moment, but it's a good one, with his fingers digging into my hip and the hard edges of his pectorals and abdomen pressed against me.

It's over before I can say his name, and we're moving side by side to his office.

"Sit. I'll get the first aid kit." The command comes as he guides me onto a couch. I've no room for argument when he uses that tone, so I relax with my head back and eyes closed.

A pulse has started in my hand. Just when my breath finds the same beat, a flutter of knowledge prompts my eyes open. Colin is staring from the doorway, watching me. I search for the easy banter we found at breakfast, anything to break the tension sweeping through the room, but he does it by walking to my side and sinking down.

He places the first aid kit on the coffee table and says, "Let me see."

I thrust it in front of him, but I don't watch the towel come off or peek as he pokes around. "Charlie." His tone forces my eyes to his. "You should go to the hospital for stitches."

I push myself up and try to pull away, but he holds on. "No, no hospitals." For many long-ago reasons, the clinical antiseptic halls of a hospital nauseate me. "Please, can't you help me?"

He sighs. "I'll need to clean the laceration. It will hurt."

"I trust you." I grab his arm; even through the expensive cotton his strength ripples beneath my fingers. My breath finds that ragged pace and my body comes to life, flushed and achy, under his appraisal. "Please."

Shaking his head—to get me out of it or to admonish my decision, I'll never know—he searches for the materials needed to clean me up. "Close your eyes."

Again he commands, and I tease with a "Yes, sir" and a mock salute. But a second later I'm hissing, "Holy shit."

His hand clenches around my wrist, pulling so I can't escape as the disinfectant burns. I groan and roll my eyes to catch his guarded gaze.

"I'm going to do it one more time." His voice is pinched, as if he's enduring the pain with me. One more douse of the torturous liquid draws out a weak mewl, but I hold back the real expletive I would like to hurl to the heavens. I count to ten and look to him when the heat of his breath soothes the sting.

"Better?"

"Yes," I whisper, bewildered by his proximity.

I lift my head from the back of the couch and our lips are a whisper apart. Neither of us moves. His gaze strays to my mouth as our breath mingles together in an excruciating invitation to unite.

I want him to kiss me. Badly.

His eyes flash to mine and back to my mouth as his tongue strokes his bottom lip, and it's nearly my undoing. My nipples pebble beneath the lace of my bra and I moan. I do—a desperate, bleating sound that rips from my lungs. I'm drawn to this man: this powerful, strong, elusive man, and I want him to kiss me. Closing his eyes, he leans toward my mouth, inhaling deeply, breathing into me not once but twice. Two long, deep, intimate breaths.

"Colin." Even to my own ears I hear the desire hanging in the word, yet I'm surprisingly not embarrassed.

"Charlie." A flush spreads up my chest at the intensity with which he says my name. "I can't."

Wait. What? He drags his gaze away from me to grab the butterfly strips he laid out prior to cleaning the cut. And just like that the moment is over, my lips cold with the undeniable air of rejection. With deft fingers he closes the gash, setting bandages along the jagged line in perfect congruity. He finishes by wrapping it in white sterile gauze.

"You shouldn't get your hand wet for a few days; let the wound begin to heal before you do. Re-bandage it tomorrow and look for signs of infection. If it's inflamed, swollen, or deep red, you need to go to the hospital." I hear him, but I can't answer. I've been repeating his decree over and over again: *I can't.*

"Charlie?" His voice is firm, compelling my eyes to seek out his.

"Why can't you?"

"It's complicated."

"Do you have a girlfriend?"

"No." He hangs his head and pinches the bridge of his nose. "I don't have a girlfriend. I have a difficult past. You deserve more than I can give you."

"Shouldn't I decide what I deserve? What I want?" I think he's stopped breathing, and I wait for him to say something, the silence ramping up to uncomfortable the longer it continues.

"I can't," he whispers finally.

I flush with anger: anger at myself for pursuing him when I know it's a bad idea. And irrational anger with him for his ability to disregard the very clear invitation I just laid none too delicately at his feet—or more accurately, at his mouth. Is it possible I'm completely imagining the intense electricity that's all-consuming when we're together? Yet after a moment's thought I know he couldn't be more right. Colin isn't the only one with a past that will prevent any sort of future.

A knock on the door breaks the tension and Evan pops in. "Rick Scott is waiting on line one." He looks to me. "You okay, Charlie?" His smile is keen until he focuses on my face and then he glances at Colin.

"I'm fine," I say, scrambling to stand. I have a sudden need to flee, and escape this place that Colin drags me to every time we're together. With a last glance in his direction I stare into his eyes. They've darkened to mask any emotions, a perfect poker face.

"I'll leave you to your business. Thanks for this." My hand is not the only thing aching right now.

The only acknowledgement to my statement is his brusque nod, effectively dismissing me from his presence. Turning, I practically lunge for the door, knowing I'm not wanted. Colin McKenna doesn't want me, and I'm not sure how I feel about that.

FOUR

"I CAN'T BELIEVE I let you talk me into this," I say, turning in front of the mirror. "This dress isn't appropriate for the bedroom, let alone a cocktail reception for a presidential candidate. It's indecent."

It's true. This plunging black satin number leaves little room for my breasts and not much more anywhere else. I should have left my hair down for modesty's sake, but it's twisted and pinned in a loose knot behind my head.

Turning the corner, Molly gets her first look at me. "Shit. Tim will be panting when he sees you."

"Then get me something else to wear. That's the last thing I need," I say, rolling my eyes.

A change to my original itinerary has allowed me three weeks to enjoy Indiana. Molly is fun, and after working alone for so long it's nice to be surrounded by people. Tim, on the other hand, has presented a challenge. His invitation on my first day has transpired into an insistent appeal to dine with him at lunch, and sometimes a dinner invite. He's nice—Molly thinks he's cute—but absolutely not for me.

And the sad part is I may see him tonight. Four hundred supporters are attending a cocktail reception in Colin's honor; my excuse as to why I couldn't attend was derailed by Molly. I didn't come prepared for socializing with the elite, but she's generous with her wardrobe. It looks more Nordstrom rack than closet; she'll take silk, satin, and sexy over a T-shirt any day.

"Look at these!" I say, poking at my cleavage. "They'll enter the party ten minutes before I do." Cringing, I pull at the plummeting neckline to draw the fabric over my breasts, but they pop back out.

"You look fantastic. Stop adjusting. It's supposed to look like that."

Turning from the mirror, I accept my fate. I'm going, I'm going in this dress, and I'll just have to figure out a way to get comfortable with it.

"I'll never get another opportunity to attend an event like this. Never in my lifetime, Charlie," she pleads. "You have to go with me. I need your support."

"I doubt that. You could have fun at the ob-gyn with your legs in stirrups." I grab my clutch purse before slipping into stiletto heels, also on loan. "Okay, I'm ready. Let's get this over with."

She whistles at my final product. "You clean up nice, Charlie Carter. You're going to steal all of the men tonight, and I was hoping to meet my future husband."

"You can have them all, even Tim."

She pulls on a thick velvet cape, covering a sparkling blush tease of a dress. No doubt men will be eating out of her hand as soon as we walk in. "How about a certain smokin' hot senator? God, the eyes and pouty lips are bad enough, but that body," she says as we walk out the door and get into her car. "Just imagine what's under the suit. He's Superman, Charlie, and I think you may be his kryptonite."

I suppress a groan—from the vented blast of cold air, not the image of Colin McKenna's bare chest. At least, I tell myself that. My nipples have beaded, brushing painfully against satin. It's the cold, bitter cold, the frigid air, it's not him; nope, not the sexy chiseled line of his jaw or the muscles so prominent their outline is visible against cotton.

"Let it go. There's absolutely nothing between us," I say for the millionth time, my heart constricting as I do. Damn heart. I need a new one; this one is defective. It keeps breaking into pieces each time I see him or hear his voice. I'm still reeling from the imprudent feelings my traitorous body insists upon. I can't seem to forget his piercing eyes, and the butterflies merrily dancing in my stomach each time he's near.

"Let's get real. I've seen the way he looks at you."

"Yeah." I watch the streetlights blur, one after the other, as Molly maneuvers through the city. "As if I have two heads."

She laughs. "Redheads must cause him to drool then. If it makes you feel better, you're the complete opposite of the last woman I saw him with."

Jealousy peeks her head in to say hi. I'm not happy to see her. "And who would that be?" I ask with as much practiced patience as I can muster.

"Raquel Meyers."

"Who is she?"

She shrugs. "A local socialite, who spends her daddy's money. Her family made a fortune in public storage and she's made a career out of spending it."

"Are they together now?"

"I work on rumors, Charlie, so I don't know what the truth is. I heard he broke it off and Raquel's been persistent about getting him back. That's why she's throwing the party tonight." Molly looks out the window as she pulls around a circular drive to the valet.

A renovated warehouse has been revitalized with large floor-to-ceiling windows. Inside, bright lights hold the night at bay and allow arriving guests a peek at the metal-and-wood industrial interior.

"How beautiful is she?"

"Come on. You can see for yourself."

THERE ISN'T ENOUGH ALCOHOL in the world to prepare me for Colin and Raquel Meyers. Her arm is draped across his back, guiding him through the room, close to where Molly is vying for a life partner. She's an expert at flirtation and the four men surrounding her are lapping up every sound of her voice, every coy tilt of her head, and every sexy flip of her hair. All the traits I'm seriously lacking, and each of them I wish to possess right now.

Colin is stunning in a black suit, the lines hugging his tight, muscled frame. Blue eyes, white shirt, slim black tie, and I'm speechless: caught off guard by the herd of elephants galloping in my chest. He is devastating, as each woman here could testify to, including me. Damn him, and damn my traitorous heart.

It takes a monumental effort on my part to drag my eyes away. I sidestep behind the defensive line that is our quartet to hide, but I can't not look.

Peeking out from behind a beefy bicep, I ogle Colin's stunning date. She's tall and slim—as in, supermodel skinny—the neckline of her red silk dress dips to her waist. Her dark hair is sleek and straight, shining past her shoulders. With eyes as dark as her hair, she exudes sensuality and an unparalleled provocative elegance wraps around her like a snake. Raquel Meyers is as perfect as he is.

An illogical surge of jealousy rips through my abdomen at the sight of them together. It's ridiculous. Of course he would be with a woman like her. There's no comparison between Raquel and myself; I'm simple and unsophisticated, far from the stunning creation gracing his arm.

My breath catches and before it expels with some ravaged form of I-am-woman-hear-me-roar, I smile and nod toward the bar as if I'm headed there for a drink. Molly winks her understanding and then I beeline for the exit. I need air. But the second I'm swallowed by the monotony of four hundred people, I collide with Evan.

As he lunges forward, I grab his arm. "I'm so sorry. Excuse me."

"Everything all right, Charlie?" His eyes narrow as he gives me a cursory look.

"Yes, absolutely. I'm just headed outside to clear my head from the champagne."

"Do you need me to hold your hair?"

I laugh. "No, thanks. I can manage."

"Okay, but you'll let me know if you need anything?"

"Sure, yeah," I say, already turning to go.

When a burst of February wind sweeps through the lobby door, I decide to take my chances on a stroll to the opposite side of the building. A long hall opens into an art gallery. Old machine parts are blackened and hang on stark white walls; photographs of the factory during its prime, along with the people who worked here, are suspended beside them. It's easy to get lost in the past, and I do, until a shiver runs up my spine.

I hug myself, rubbing my arms, but the chill becomes persistent and somewhat energetic. I tense; only one person has ever caused this reaction from my body and I was hoping to avoid him all night. The soft silk of his suit coat drapes over my shoulders, and a wave of sandalwood highjacks my brain. *God, he smells good.*

"In the early 1900s these buildings were built to make equipment that farmers used throughout the entire country. We're standing in what used to be the main offices; behind us is a portion of the manufacturing plant." His voice is a soft caress laced with dirty promises. He could recite the encyclopedia Britannica and I'd have to change my panties after the first page.

Colin isn't touching me, but he's standing close enough that his breath moves through the loose curls framing my face. My heart stumbles and I'm sure he can hear the thunderous thump when it starts again. I try to steady my breath, the volatile pulse of it a definite giveaway of the effect he has on me.

"You're a history buff?"

His shrug moves the outline of his shadow. In the dark we're united perfectly, an enticing illusion, and I have to look away. But the real thing is just as tempting. *Why does he have to be so damn beautiful?*

"History is important; it's what led us to the present and will see us through to the future. I've studied the past, believing it will guide me to the right decisions." After a short pause he shifts toward me, close enough that my head tips back to keep hold of his eyes. "I endeavor to understand every detail to ensure an appropriate outcome."

Electricity thrums between us, confirmation I didn't imagine the strange connection.

"How's your hand?"

I had almost forgotten; it happened so long ago. Lifting it palm up, I show him the puckered pink wound. "It's fine."

The shiver becomes a tremor when he runs a finger along the scar, warming the skin below it. "I'm sorry you were hurt." I don't know if he's referring to the injury or his dismissal.

"You don't need to apologize. I'm used to it anyway."

"You're used to it?" His brow draws down into three lines.

I shrug and smile. "It's par for my course. If it's possible, it will happen to me. I don't have the best luck."

And that's how we get stuck, eye to eye as the seconds tick by and the air grows thick with a palpable energy. Neither of us is willing to break the deepening silence, but eventually thoughts of him with another woman burst from my mouth in a moment of unrestrained frustration.

"Where's Raquel?" I ask. Crossing my arms under my breasts, I square my shoulders and ease toward his tall frame.

His gaze darkens and flashes over my chest as he weighs his answer. "She's just a friend, Charlie."

"You don't owe me an explanation."

"Somehow I think I do."

"I get it, Colin. Your words were crystal clear. You *can't* with me, but you can with her. She's bewitching. I applaud you on your taste."

"Don't put words in my mouth. That's not what I said."

"Then tell me what you really mean. If you don't give me the true story, I'll make it up on my own, and right now it's ending with you and Raquel Meyers."

He steps closer, taunting me with the heat radiating from his chest. "You don't know me. You have no idea how complicated I am, how complicated my life is," he says, holding me firmly with his gaze while our bodies remain a millimeter apart. "For some reason I can't stay away from you. I've tried, Charlie. I have, but each time I see you I'm drawn back in even though I know I should stay away. You deserve more than me."

His head dips and my knees weaken. Without thought, I reach for his hair. The silken length slips through my fingers and I fist it. *Oh, God.* I pull, drawing him closer still, and the connection feels… *right*, like my hands were meant to live in the soft waves. A low rumble vibrates into me and he lowers his lips to hover directly over mine. He inhales deeply, slowly and methodically, taking my breath into him as if I'm the last whisper of oxygen to fill his lungs.

Moving a fraction, his lips brush against my cheek and my heart gallops. I can't think; the only thing running through my head is *please, please kiss me*.

"Charlie." He murmurs my name as his nose runs along the line of my jaw, rubbing delicately against my skin. His hands, which have remained by his side, move to my nape. His fingers dig into my hair to hold me steady, but even without them I wouldn't move, I couldn't move. Everything is so soft, light, a teasing need. He's on a slow, deliberate path, tracing his lips and nose along every inch of my face, breathing in every minute detail as his thumbs draw a delicate line along my lips.

"Colin, please." To my horror I've whispered it out loud, and although it was barely spoken the words seem to echo throughout the room.

For the briefest moment he presses his lips against my forehead, holding me tighter than he ever has before.

"I'm sorry," he says, pulling away. My hands fall indelicately to my sides, empty and wanting. "My focus has to remain on the campaign. This… us… can't happen." His lids fall closed for the briefest second, as if the words hurt him as much as they do me.

I'm shocked. Once again, in the matter of a second, he's transitioned from hot and welcoming to cold and detached, spiking my anger. "You need to figure your shit out, Mr. President. Don't toy with me," I hiss. "Go play with Raquel if that's how you operate. I don't do drama, and frankly that's all this has been."

He flinches. "I shouldn't have come in here, I know that. I was telling you the truth when I said I'm drawn to you on a level I don't understand. I…." He grabs his nape and hangs his head. "I'm not trying to hurt you, Charlie. I can't stay away from you and I don't understand that. I've not encountered feelings like this before."

I pause, knowing his thoughts are exactly my own. I can't stay away from him; I know I should, but for some unfathomable reason I can't.

"Well, you seem to be doing a good job of reeling me in and casting me back out. That's not okay with me. How's that for an understanding?" I rush until words are gone and the ache is back. It comes out in a whisper. "Don't do this again, Colin. If you don't want to hurt me, then you need to stop offering a glimpse of what it's like to be with you only to push me away."

He nods just at the moment voices enter the room. I slip off his jacket, handing it to him. Our fingers touch during the transition and the sharp unexpected pang of lust, desire, or whatever the hell it is travels sharply up my arm.

"I feel it too," he whispers, finding my eyes. His are confused, bewildered almost, and for a second I understand him. I'm the unknown factor. He had his life planned out; a very specific path lay before him, and not anywhere on his road to travel did Charlie Carter exist. Yet here I am, and his struggle is one of diversion. Should he divert from the path he's meticulously planned, digress for an unknown draw toward a stranger, someone so unlike anyone he's met before? I'm not anywhere near the social category of the women within his circle, further complicating his struggle.

"Colin, there you are." Raquel's voice is smooth, high-society syrup. When I glance toward her I notice Evan hovering at the outskirts of the room. "Oh, how sweet. Who is your little friend?"

I roll my eyes. I'd rather verge on adolescence than be her kind of brilliant.

“Impeccable taste,” I murmur to Colin. “Thanks for the history lesson.” And with that I head out the door to find Molly and her boys, bypassing Evan without so much as a glance. He catches up to me with a hand to my shoulder in the empty hallway.

“Charlie, I’m sorry—”

“What is it with everyone and their *I’m sorrys*?” I stop and turn, exasperated. “And exactly why are *you* sorry? For telling Colin where I was in the first place, or taking Raquel back in to save him from me?”

He growls and shoves a fist in his pants pocket. “I’m trying to help him. And not because it’s my job; he’s my best friend and I’d like for him to find some modicum of happiness.”

“And I’m the key to his joy? Is that what you’re saying?” He doesn’t respond so I keep going. “Listen, Evan, I don’t have casual relationships with men and I’m not interested in starting one now. Don’t use me as your pawn. I won’t let him play with me. I know for certain I deserve more than that.”

He nods and I slip back to the party, sidestepping Tim, who’s waiting near the entrance—hoping desperately to get swallowed by the crowd to become invisible.

FIVE

VOICES IN THE HALL startle me awake. The muted browns of the hotel room are slow to click into focus, as is my brain. And then it does and my new reality slides into place. For the unforeseen future, I'm on the campaign trail. From private plane, to private car, to private room, I've been secluded in luxury while adjusting to the hectic pace sure to hit tomorrow.

Up until now, I've been managing social media content with information funneled to me from Evan. But the day after I said my piece to Colin, I got the call confirming the date I'd join them in New Jersey.

Here I am, hopping down from the ginormous king bed to enjoy my very own vodka cranberry, compliments of the mini fridge. My cocktail company is an overstuffed chair and a rapid-fire text battle with Ali and then Mom, both drilling for details on hot senator and my new locale. As I pop up for drink number two, a knock barrels through the room.

Latch in place, I pull the door open three inches to find Evan's smile.

"Hi, Charlie. Settle in okay?"

"Everything's great, including the full selection of baby bottles." I tug the lock free as he nods.

"Your head's in the game already. I like that. I'm on my way to the lobby bar; come get the full sixteen ounces before they start carding at the counter."

"Last time I looked I was eight years past legal, but thanks for the compliment." I peek down at my silk cami and jeans and then back to him to assess my gut feeling. I've never gotten anything but good nature from Evan, and he has to be better company than the chair. "I'll meet you there in a few."

"Sure. See you—" His phone rings and he waves before stepping away.

I head to the bathroom for a fresh check: brush teeth, wash face and pits, add mascara and lip gloss. One minute to inspect the manic mane of flaming curls and another to tame them in a ponytail and then slip into my black leather jacket. "Not too shabby," I say to the final product in the mirror before grabbing my clutch and taking the first step into a new adventure.

It's how I'm approaching the next two hundred days. I'll see Colin. The inevitable heart pitter-patters will follow and maybe some of the aching emptiness when he walks one way and I move in another—but that's been the story of my life. I can appreciate him from afar and also that he's not playing me as he could. If he was a lesser man, and more like the politicians making headlines for who's-yanking-their-chain, I may have already made it into the been-there-done-that-pile. I'll figure out how to work with him, casual and cool.

Right. Two steps into the bar I need another fresh check. It's not because of the three men at the side table who turn when I enter, or the bartender who stops washing glasses to stare, it's Colin. And not only because he's relaxed and leaning against the counter in jeans hanging so low they're begging to come off. But because of how he looks at me. The minute our eyes connect, he's the lion on the hunt, watching and circling—hungry. Danger bristles along my nape. And then the mask falls and he allows me in, a glimpse at the man behind the political persona, and I find his vulnerability speaks to mine.

A painful memory tries to fall into place, but I'm quick to put it back on the shelf. Those are for another time, not this one, with Colin watching me walk into the sophisticated bar with dark floors and chrome fixtures. Not while his eyes rake over my body and a simmering ache makes me want something I'm not sure how to ask for.

As I approach him, I search for the perfect words. Something to compete with the smooth nonsense women use with him every day, but all I come up with is "Hi."

A smile spreads across his face, digging a dimple into his cheek. "Hi, yourself."

After our last encounter tension should creep in, but it doesn't. I'd like to wrap my arms around his neck and, hip to hip, listen to him recap every second of his day. Instead I sit and order a drink from the waiting bartender.

Colin leans on an elbow, relaxing with his back to the counter and a long leg kicked out before him. Relaxed looks good on him—really, really good. So does the white shirt open at the collar and the pushed-up sleeves.

"Did you have a good flight?"

I roll my eyes. "How could I not? Your plane is the bomb. I lounged on the couch and watched *Judge Judy* on repeat."

His eyebrow skyrockets. "*Judge Judy*?"

I nod. "It's now programmed as a favorite over CNN. Try it; it can put your problems into perspective. My neighbor borrowed a couple of eggs for the eleventh time in as many weeks. But Judge Judy? She had to put the smack down on taking the car without returning it."

A laugh rumbles through his chest. "I'll keep it in mind."

His gaze is ripped from mine when Evan slides next to him. "Is he telling stories already, Charlie? Don't listen to him; I didn't do half the shit he accuses me of in college."

Colin swallows down his disagreement and beer. When he can talk, he says, "I'm quite certain all of your misdeeds are labeled correctly in the Dean's office. You only received an invitation for Christmas dinner after spending half of freshman year in his wingback."

Evan smiles and signals for a round. "Not true. He couldn't stay away from my winning personality. I'm infectious."

"That's what she said," I add, and bite my lip.

Their back-and-forth stops and they turn, a slow-motion twist to look at me, and then Colin throws his head back and laughs. "Tell me a story, Evan," I say, in hopes I can see that complete abandon on Colin's face.

He shakes his head. "I was a saint."

"Bullshit," Colin says. "What about Tina Austin?"

"What about her?"

His brow arches as he answers, "Spanking her ass in the library staircase before chem lab ring any bells?"

Evan grins. "Only the sound of her voice as she begged for it."

I giggle and think he sounds a lot like Ali. Falling into their history becomes easy. Colin laughs as I haven't seen him do. His buttoned-up persona is gone; this is the peek at the man behind the campaign I've wanted to see.

I envy their friendship, the closeness that extends beyond them and into a group that remains tight to this day. My friends tended to be Ali's because I don't do deep. Opening up and sharing the ingredients that make me tick is not my thing. Boyfriends and the latest fashion trends fell flat, so I engaged on a superficial level. Parties in college saw me on the outskirts of the room, watching as Ali commanded attention: women want to be her and men want her. As Colin and Evan share their history, I become more aware of mine and the truth I will never tell.

"Excuse me," Evan says, and pulls his ever-ringing cell from his back pocket.

When he steps away I switch gears. "Why did you choose this life? It must be hard. Every minute and movement examined under a microscope by millions of people."

Colin tilts his head, contemplating me as I do the same. With the dimmed light shining from above, he's pitched into sharp angles. His cheekbones, jaw, even his lips find a straight edge as he sinks into serious thought and leans closer to me.

"I don't remember a time when it wasn't my purpose. As a child I saw President Reagan at a public rally. He was passionate; he believed his position could affect positive change. And he did, Charlie. His administration saw the States into the most prosperous period of the century. Even more than that, relations throughout the world eased under his leadership," he says. "I can bring us back to that point and beyond. I wouldn't have given up everything if I didn't think it was true."

The spark in his eyes fades and he's lost in himself for a moment. But then his gaze slips to my mouth. *Yes, my mouth, remember it?* I want to ask. *Because I would like mine to touch yours and see if fireworks explode behind my eyes. I think it's a real possibility.*

"Why do you hate politics so much?" he asks, and then takes a long drag from his bottle, watching me as he does.

"Because of its false face. I've come to appreciate authenticity and the political arena doesn't seem to know what that is. Whatever happened to what you see is what you get?" Hypocrisy gets stuck in my throat but I swallow it down. We're not talking about me.

"Who are you? Tell me." The intensity behind his question reaches me and insists on forgoing caution.

"What do you mean?"

"I…." Three lines appear between his eyes. "Good coffee puts a smile on your face, and with blueberry pancakes, a small satisfied sound erupts from the back of your throat when you swallow. It seems to surprise you every time, as if you weren't expecting the pleasure. I want to know you. Do you like a 6:00 a.m. start to your day or ten? What do you wake up for every day and look forward to?"

I choke on my laugh. He's studying me as if I'm a difficult equation and he must find a method to determine if the statement is true or false. The scrutiny is overwhelming and remarkable at the same time. He's been paying attention—and I'm only half-afraid of what he'll find.

"I like a reason to stay up late. A good book I can't put down or a movie I feel as if I'm a part of. At night I leave the room cold so I can pile on the blankets. But I don't like spiders or cold showers. My favorite thing is my family and how they love."

"Are you happy?" The question is a rough whisper that grinds on my nerves.

My lids flutter as a snowball rolls down my spine and into an avalanche of emotion I rarely let myself feel. It settles in my stomach as a pile of scattered regret. I shake my head as if not wanting the words to slip free. But here they are: "I want more."

Day-to-day is supposed to be enough, but in a moment of desperate self-awareness I know it's a truth I've never admitted to myself. "There has to be more for me somewhere."

Blinking out of my daze and into the face of the lion, I grab my clutch.

"It's getting late," I say.

As I slide away from my seat, he catches my hand. I look at the connection; sizzling zaps of electricity poke at me in a daring game of *do I stay or do I go*? His eyes darken to a dangerous blue.

"You don't need to hide from me."

But I do.

I should run, bury myself under the years that have slipped by. But the new whirlwind of opportunity his hold offers is enticing the prey from her hiding spot. From the moment I met him, the deep rumblings of a different future struggled to the surface, aching for release. I want to run with him and feel the wind streak through my hair and drown all of my senses in the bright light of living.

"Come," he says, making the decision for me.

He tugs me behind him to the elevator as my pulse pounds in my ears. The air is thick when we're closed inside the four-by-four cell. He's impossible to ignore: tall, silent, almost brooding with the clench of his jaw. I have never before felt anything close to the longing building deep within my heart, and it frightens me.

He says nothing as we climb. Floor after floor flies by and I stay locked tight in my mind with only his steady breath keeping track of time. In seconds we're racing down the hall until he stops to swipe a key card that opens his suite. One minute I own my mind and in the next, I'm pushed against the back of his door and under his control. It's that easy.

He's got my waist, holding it, sinking his fingers into the pad of flesh that curves into my ass.

I gasp.

He draws closer, staring at my lips, and I run my tongue along their length, moistening them while they remain parted in wait. A delectable shiver runs down my spine as his mouth hovers over mine.

"I breathe you, Charlie." The murmured words are barely a breeze and I wonder if they were really said at all.

But he takes me in one breath at a time. Long deep drags, as if I am his lifeline and without me he couldn't survive. My knees weaken at the intensity and I lean in to him.

Oh, oh, God. Lips touch and retreat, a light gift before he pauses and does it again. Sweet and savoring the second time, we taste and learn the flavor of our compatibility. Goose bumps spring up on my arms. Any ideas I had of what his kiss would feel like were wrong. In the gentle press of his lips, I hear his secret, and it speaks to a longing I had never known until it became apparent I missed him. That somewhere we had met before, and although time kept us apart, it was no match for two souls that remembered what is was like to find their other half. *It's that good.*

And then we're crushed together. Hot and demanding, just like him. His erection grinds against me and I melt into a pool of need.

It's perfection and I'm at peace. Feelings of inadequacy and insecurity from a past I can't let go float away until there are absolutely no thoughts of them anywhere. I'm free, for the first time in fifteen years. I'm free from pain, and it's because Colin is where I'm meant to be.

I suck his tongue, hungry for everything he offers. He groans and his tightly bound control slips as he licks and bites into my mouth, driving pleasure from the piercing sting until my cry rebounds against the walls. I'm at his mercy. With his silent insistence, I accept my fate and dive in. Wrapping my arms around his head, my fingers plunge into his hair and I pull him closer, matching him need for need. We're stuck together in a frantic, pleading kiss.

A knock on the door startles me and I make to pull away, but he holds tight. He continues to nip and pull at my lips, his tongue dipping to touch mine seductively. After another moment, he gentles, as if he can't pull away cold turkey. It's a slow, sensual descent from heaven to earth.

Another knock at the door, more urgent this time, and he breaks contact. "I'll be right there," he calls in a grating voice. Glaring at the door, he turns back to me. His hands move to cradle my nape and his gaze softens when it finds mine. *Holy hell.*

"I should go," I pant, stunned by the intensity of what just happened between us. He straightens to his full height, releasing my body, yet his hold remains in place.

Stroking his thumb over my bottom lip, he whispers, "So beautiful."

Another knock fractures the strange pull between us. Finding my voice, I loosen my grip on his hair and say loud enough to be heard in the hall, "Thank you for the information, Senator. This will be a great addition to the website."

Colin releases me, the soft swell of his lips downturned as he does. He studies my mouth and then my cheek and hair, as if he's memorizing the moment. With one last look at his ravaged hair I turn, pulling the door open to find her evil highness glaring at me.

He sighs. "What do you want, Ella?"

I slide out of the room. "You have an early day tomorrow. I'll leave you two to talk. Good night," I say lamely, and then hightail it down the hall.

Moments later, my back is pressed against my door and I trail my fingers over my tender lips.

Holy shit. What just happened? I made out with the hottest man on the planet, possibly the future president of the United States. I don't make out with anyone. I've never really wanted to, too scared by my past to let men get close.

He's running for president. I'm no good for him. Actually, I could harm his campaign; scandal is the last thing he needs. My head falls into my hands. I can't let this happen again, not with Colin McKenna.

SIX

I CAN'T STAY AWAY. As soon as I saw him waiting in the lobby my eyes were glued to his, and then to his perfectly sculpted ass when we walked to the waiting car. I couldn't stop staring at my hand where it was swallowed up in his while he helped me into the SUV. My heart raced at an embarrassing pace when I thought about how firm his lips were when he was needy, and how they softened to enjoy every morsel of my mouth.

Colin McKenna is a drug and I'm a thousand percent addicted with no hope for rehabilitation. Hell, I don't even want to check myself in for treatment.

The man is smart. During the twenty-minute drive, I listened to him spew off facts about environmental policy and healthcare reform as if it's everyday dialogue. He's also busy. From a manufacturing plant to a hospital and then on to meet the governor for dinner, his day is full.

I stick out like a sore thumb in the gray metallic walls of the factory. A green silk blouse and pencil skirt are a veritable flag waving amongst the sea of men. That and my flowing red hair is screaming "woman" to the predominately male audience gathered to watch the senator speak. Ella is the other standout, and she's behind him. But I like to think of her as a she-devil because the death stares she comes up with are otherworldly. It grinds me that she's the depiction of elegance in a snappy silk ensemble that mirrors his. So I ignore her.

But the media doesn't. Colin and Ella make a picture-perfect pair and the press is taking them in as if they'll walk into the White House hand in hand. She sneers in my direction and my blood boils.

With camera in hand, I act as my own photographer. My singular subject doesn't disappoint. A navy three-piece suit is tailored to the sculpted lines of his body and with a red tie, he's very patriotic and sexy as hell. The lens hides my ogling. I can gawk without being obvious. At least I think so until he stares directly at me with a damn smirk that tests the endurance of my lace panties. *Damn man.*

I walk off to the side of the assembly. The machines groan, voices hum from the many employees in various stages of work production. It's a huge warehouse with conveyor belts, moving parts, and people all operating in sync. I stop in front of a large robotic arm, or more like a crane, picking up a huge steel plate for two men who bolt it in place. Colin's speech ends. On his way into the factory with the owner, he glances up and catches my eye. His poker face is intact, but his gaze scorches with intensity. A flush steals down my chest and the smirk is back, tempting the corner of his mouth into a full-out grin.

He's playing with me and my pulse likes the game. I turn away to recover, watching the robot pick up another plate.

And then life moves in slow motion.

Panic sets in with the staff when the arm swings away from them, when it should have moved forward. It's wobbling as if the steel is too heavy a burden for it to carry. I realize too late the load is swinging in my direction, recognizing in an out-of-body experience sort of way that everyone is running away from me, yet I'm the only one incapable of escaping from it. The crane teeters, screeching out a warning.

Sparks flare when the steel hits the concrete and the robot's arm breaks away. I feel the impact, but it comes from the wrong direction.

Colin rams into me. The velocity he uses to push us both out of the way sends us flying to the floor. My butt and shoulder take most of the shock, yet my head snaps back with an echoing thud.

The room blurs. He's searching, hands, fingers, running up and down my sides, frantic.

"Charlie!" he screams.

Then there is black.

JUST WHEN I THOUGHT the day couldn't get worse, it did—the emergency room physician insisted on a head CT to rule out brain trauma. I couldn't be more embarrassed. From EMT to the ambulance and then the hospital, I tried to tell them this is how I always act. Sarcasm comes naturally, testing is not necessary. But caution won over my assurance.

Colin wouldn't leave. He demanded to stay with me and I ordered him to his scheduled engagements. The battle ended in compromise when they brought me to the same medical center where he planned to speak.

And speak of the devil; he peeks around the curtain to find me in bed. I'm too tired to react when he scans over my prone form, braless and in a hospital gown. He makes it up to my eyes and I hate that I see worry in his. I wave him in.

He sits in the chair next to the gurney, staring at my hand lying by my side.

"A little headache is the only souvenir I'll leave New Jersey with," I tease, but his sullen mood doesn't lift. "How was your meeting with the hospital president?"

No response. He leans forward to rub the white sheet covering my legs between his fingers. Minutes pass and finally he whispers, "Fine."

"Hey," I say, touching the top of his hand. The light connection holds so much weight my pulse accelerates. "This was the best press you could ever get. You're a hero. Honestly, I have no idea how you were able to get to me so fast."

His head snaps up. "I couldn't give a shit about press right now," he growls. "You could have been killed." He grabs my fingers, pulling them against his heart and the frantic beat underneath.

"But I wasn't. I'm okay, because of you."

The atmosphere changes, his eyes transitioning from ferocious to bewildered. "I don't know what you're doing to me, Charlie," he mumbles. Before I can reply, he rises and leans in so close our breath mixes. Closing his eyes, his lips find mine; slowly at first, a gentle exploration.

"I'm not broken," I murmur into him, and then my hands are in his hair. Pulling him from tentative to certain, he becomes insistent and pushes against me.

Soft and firm all at once, he takes his time to taste me in long licks, groaning as he does. My head doesn't hurt so much as the empty ache between my thighs. This man, with his wicked tongue and beautiful mouth, one arm propped against the wall so he can arch over me while freeing his other hand to skim the outside of my breast. A featherlight touch that I feel everywhere: a pang in my heart and a tempting pulse in my clitoris. *Oh, God.*

The hospital is not the place, nor is this the time to explore the sexual attraction that apparently neither of us has the strength to ignore. Slowly we break away, my fingers trailing down his jaw, which he clenches as they rake over his cheeks. Pressing his forehead against mine, I hold him close while our breathing slows.

The physician arrives and Colin snaps up, moving to the corner of the small room.

Addressing both of us, he says, "Ms. Carter, your CAT scan is clear. You have a small concussion, and the headache will continue for a day or so." He directs the next comment to Colin, somehow suspecting he'll care for me. "Watch for dizziness, blurred vision, and worsening headache. If that happens, get her back to an emergency room. She'll be tired and sleep is fine, but I recommend waking her every few hours to ensure coherency. I'll send the nurse in with discharge instructions."

Colin nods, the pink in his cheeks fading to pale. Geez, it's not like I'm dying over here. It's a headache. I'm not even sure why he cares so much; we met just weeks ago. Sure, we've had two steaming-hot, heart-pounding, let's-get-it-on kisses, but it's not a marriage proposal, for God's sake.

Colin thanks him as he moves past the curtain. Turning to the shelf in the corner, he grabs my clothes and returns to my side. "Here, let me help you."

"No." I draw the line. "I'm not an invalid. I can dress myself." My lion is back. He's studying me as if we're going to wrestle to find a victor for this battle and then I remember his schedule. "You have to leave! The governor is waiting!"

"I'll reschedule, don't worry about dinner. Let's get you back to the hotel where you can rest. You'll stay in my suite."

What? My heart almost explodes from my chest at the thought of being in his bed. "No way, on both counts. You're not missing an important meeting because I bumped my head. That's just plain stupid. And I don't need a babysitter—my brain is fine." I push him off the side of the gurney. "Go!" I point to the door.

He smiles. "Are you kicking me out?"

"Yes, most definitely, go. I'll take a cab to the hotel," I say, and fall back to the pillow, energy zapped.

"I'll leave Evan with you; he's been camping out in the waiting room."

I don't know what to say. It's nice, so nice to feel cared for. Colin moves forward once more to press his lips to my forehead. He lingers for a moment and then slides down to my ear. "You will be in my bed, Charlie. If you're not in it when I arrive, I'll find you and drag you there myself."

Holy.... Pinching my chin between thumb and forefinger, he tips my head to find my eyes: his flare like a comet burning through a midnight sky.

"Yes, sir," I whisper, enjoying the prickle of anticipation light up my skin. "I'll be there."

He nods and with a parting look, he turns and walks from the room.

I DARE TO OPEN one eye and then the other, curiosity winning over the devil in my brain. Morning light streaks through the open window, casting a glow on the beige paisley rug. The suite is quiet. Colin woke me throughout the night with a soft caress to my cheek each time. And then he'd ask me a question, like who is president of the United States. Of course I said him, but he didn't send me back to the hospital. He just smiled and kissed my forehead. When my headache was on the verge of creeping back in, he had pain relievers and water ready. I feel the pulse of it now, and sure enough, there are two pills waiting for me with a glass of juice on the nightstand.

I gobble them up and slip from the sheets to look through the hospital bag. My heart sinks. The Nikon I used the last of my savings on didn't make it. It's in pieces and the lens is crushed. *It could have been me*. No sense worrying where the next one will come from, it is what it is.

Washing away my sour disposition becomes my focus and I'm pleased his suite has the mack daddy of all bathrooms. A shiver strikes when I step in to see the white marble beaded with droplets of water. He was here—naked—when I was asleep in his bed. *Oh my God*. I strip and step in to three shower heads. At first I'm chilled when I turn them on and then the heat eases the ache in my shoulders. But it also loosens my jumbled thoughts.

Colin McKenna wants me. The feeling is reciprocated. Yet there is one thing, one thing I'll never tell.

I'll never get beyond it. I may be able to live with myself and the decisions I've made, but with a sinking certainty I know Colin won't be able to forgive my past. Not Mr. Perfect-in-every-way.

A part of my brain is screaming to run. It's a compelling argument: my past, Colin's complications, and our disparate lives have very little chance of successfully merging. Then the other part, and a frighteningly large part of my heart, is insistent I stay, follow the unknown road ahead. That's what scares me the most: the unknown. I love the tingly feelings and the ease simply *there* between us. But the path we're taking is blurred. How is it possible anything between us can end well? That frightens me, but I know without a doubt I'm not strong enough to walk away; not now. This part of me is winning the battle, so I'll focus on the present. One day at a time.

With a leisurely pace, I finish and then take advantage of the hotel amenities: toothbrush, lotion, and spa-quality hair products. Clothes would be nice, but instead I wrap a soft towel around my chest and open the door to find something to wear. I stumble to a stop. Colin is standing by the bed. Neither of us moves, nor do we say a word. My heart thumps so loud I'm sure he can hear it as it tempts me to take a step forward.

He stares and remains statue still with his eyes on mine. "Charlie."

I shudder at the sound of my name on his lips. His voice is sensual; warm, caramel smooth with a rough grate on the undertone. My body responds. Suddenly the cotton is coarse against the tight buds of my nipples, and my blood pulses at the apex of my thighs. *Lord, have mercy.*

"Colin. Good morning."

He's not subtle as he pores over every inch of my flesh, stalling on my breasts spilling over the top of the towel. When he has his fill, his eyes move to mine, a small smile touching the corners of his mouth.

"I had your things brought from your room." He waves toward the armoire.

"Thank you."

He takes a step forward and my lips part. *Don't stop. I want more than your kiss—let me feel the slow drag of your fingers along my bare skin, please.* But he hesitates and shakes his head a fraction. A rush of breath deflates my lungs when he steps away and closes the door behind him.

I collapse on the mattress, gulping in air and waiting for my pulse to come down to earth. Not fair; it's so not fair he works me up to my boiling point and leaves me needy and aching all over. After a minute,

I look toward the plastic sack on top of my bag. Curious, I roll over to grab it and then snatch it closed.

He didn't.

I think he did.

I pull apart the box like a five-year-old on Christmas morning and know that he did. He bought me a camera ten times better than what I'd depleted my life savings on.

It's perfect for upcoming events and I'd like to thank him. I race to get ready: a quick blow dry, a cashmere sweater that hugs my curves, and a pencil skirt that does the same. When I walk into the living room he's on the phone, staring out the window toward the river behind the hotel. I'd blame my spinning head on the concussion, but I'm pretty sure it's because of those low jeans. Damn, the way they sit on his hips, and the open-at-the-collar button-up. I fan myself just as he turns to catch my uninhibited gawk.

His eyes take on a tornado effect. I wonder if there's a law against causing a person's heart to race, because if there is, he should be arrested. Talk about a health hazard. Motioning to the buffet, he offers up the coffee. Not waiting for further invitation, I practically dive for the cup.

"How do you feel?" he asks as he ends his call.

"I'm perfect," I say, looking up through my lashes.

He licks his lips and I can feel it as if his mouth was on my neck biting a path to my ear. "A gift from the gods sent to ruin me," he murmurs in the tone that sets my blood on fire.

I still, coffee halfway to my mouth. "We should talk, Colin. What is this?" I motion to him and me. Parameters are good and he should set them.

But he strides toward me with a single-minded purpose. Setting down my mug, I back up. He's not deterred.

"This is a kiss, Charlie." *Oh.* One hand to my nape, the other just above my ass and he hauls me against him. The solid lines of his chest collide with my breasts. "I'm going to show you how good we are together."

If it's possible to melt, I do. My insides liquefy and I grab his arms to stay upright. It becomes easy to let the past disintegrate into nothing at the first pass of his mouth. A barely there brush and then he tastes my top lip and then the bottom, teasing with his teeth. I groan and close my eyes, giving up the intimacy of watching for the relief of feeling.

My hands roam; steely biceps ripple under my touch, broad shoulders are just as rigid when he tightens his hold. His mouth is warm, minty fresh and destructive. Long, provocative licks of his tongue render me speechless. Questions turn to need and I dive into his hair to pull him even closer while I stroke back into his mouth.

His growl rumbles between us. I love the slow squeeze on my ass, and that he grinds his erection into me. How does he do this? How can he make me so overwhelmed and desperate to attach myself to every part of him?

I can't think; I can only feel. He's everywhere. His body and mouth command my response and I do by nibbling and sucking on his lips. We play until he breaks away to nip my chin and neck. "You're delicious." He presses each word into my flushed skin.

A shiver sings down my spine as he kisses a wet trail along the opening of my V-neck sweater. His mouth closes over the swell of my breast and my nipples tighten in anticipation. But he moves in the wrong direction, sucking and licking his way to my lips—sensual and slow once more.

I gulp in a breath when he tucks his nose beneath my ear. My thoughts are scattered, just like my heart. We hold tight as if we'd crumble if one were to disentangle from the other. And maybe that's the truth. *Maybe that's our truth.*

Finally he straightens to his full height with an adorable shy smile. Taking my hand, he pulls me to a couch in the middle of the room, where I fall to the cushions, sitting on one leg to face him.

"What would you like to talk about?" he asks as the sweet smile turns to a devilish smirk.

I study him while my pulse slows. The ridge of his jaw, every angle of his face and the thick rows of lashes lining his eyes. It doesn't do much but ramp up the antsy feeling crawling under my skin. Whatever this is—I'm in deep. His beauty is just the tip of the iceberg and I want to explore the depth of what it is he's offering.

"Colin… I…." His smile grows while I stumble for words. Damn man. "What the hell is going on with us?"

He laughs, a hearty rumble in his chest as my eyes narrow with irritation.

"Oh, Charlie," he says, reaching over to caress my cheek from temple to chin. "I don't know."

Ugh. "Not knowing isn't working for me. I don't have a lot of experience with relationships, or with men in general, for that matter." I sigh, embarrassed by my admitted naiveté. "You're brilliant, insanely gorgeous, vying to be the most powerful man in the world. You can have any woman you want; why me?" It's the million-dollar question. Why Charlie Carter?

He looks at me like I've grown two heads. "Why not you? Your beauty is more than ivory skin and emerald eyes. It's woven in the fabric of your essence. From the moment we met there was something. It's something undeniable and so strong it pulled me into the fabric of your life over and over again. I tried, Charlie. I tried to stay away because my world is hard, *I'm hard*, but when I lie awake at night, I see you; when I close my eyes, I see flaming waves of red hair spread over my pillow. Your voice whispers in my ear and I can't deny I want you with every breath I breathe." He plays with my fingers, still entwined with his.

"What I see in you, Charlie, is the burgeoning light of innocence giving way to desire. And I'll be damned if I'll let any other man foster that need. I want you to crave me and to need me inside you. It's as simple as that."

Wow. A tingling sensation has sparked in my groin, confirming I want that too. I want him to be the one to fill me with new memories and to burn away the old. But then his light changes. The sweet joy that softened his features turns hard and his nostrils flare.

"I don't have much to offer you."

My mouth falls open; I stare at him like *he* has a second and *third* head. "What are you talking about? We've just gone over a list of your attributes."

"You misunderstand me. Yes, I have money and stability, and I'm confident I'll take the oath to lead this country. But that's it. I have nothing to give. I'm a shell of the man I once was."

He drags in a breath. "I meant what I said, Charlie. I enjoy being with you. It *is* that simple, but that's all it is. I can only give you one day at a time. There is no future with me." He brings the back of my hand to his mouth and brushes a kiss over it while capturing my gaze. "I told you I would always be honest with you, and to that I hold true. I will not lie to you, so believe me when I say this: I want you. I want to be with you. I want to touch you and feel you next to me. I want very badly to be inside you." His lids flutter closed and he swallows as if contemplating the prospect. Goose bumps dance on my arms as he opens to find me. "But it's all I can offer: my body, a physical connection."

Damn. I'm speechless again, not sure how I feel about this. Honest, yes. Straight up, he's proposing sex. But can my fragile psyche accept his offer? I can't ignore my reaction to him. I've never experienced it before and I don't want to return to drab days where I felt nothing but living minute-to-minute. My mantra pops into my head: one day at a time. This, I know how to do. Today, he's offering himself to me.

I turn, climbing to my knees to place a very gentle kiss on his mouth. He doesn't respond. I pull back, ever so slightly opening my eyes to look into his brilliant blue stare, a silent offering of consolation for his pain. "Breathe me, Colin," I whisper before leaning back into him to place a light pressure, my lips to his.

He groans and takes my mouth with a repressed aggression that speaks to the control he's shown up to this point. This is different—

this is a man in need. One hand snares my nape and the other grips my waist to pull me into him. The desperate lashes of his tongue claim me as his.

The feeling is mutual, and so he knows my thoughts, I grip his shoulders and straddle his hips.

He moans when I grind into him and he grows hard beneath me. I shiver from the heat of his fingers sliding up my calf and over my knee to push up my skirt.

When he finds the lace edge of my thigh-highs, he growls "Christ" and drags his mouth from mine. He looks down and we both watch as he slides the fabric higher, baring my pale skin from the waist down. "Charlie," he whispers on a soft sigh.

The evidence of my arousal is painted on my white satin panties. I flush. Gripping his hair, I bury my head in the crook of his neck to hide my embarrassment. But with every breath, I take in the subtle hint of sandalwood and my clit throbs harder.

I whimper when his thumb runs the length of me to find the swollen nub. "Colin."

"Do you want me to touch you?"

I groan when he does, rolling his thumb in expert circles. I couldn't say no if I tried; this man has me under his spell. I was bewitched the moment we met in my dream. "Yes."

But instead he takes my chin, in the way he does to get my attention. I lift out of what could very easily become my favorite place to find his eyes darkening to a dangerous depth.

Never releasing the hold he has on me—my hips, my gaze—he pulls me onto his erection and rubs. When my mouth falls open on a gasp he takes it in, tempting me with just the tip of his tongue. And through it all he thrusts the hard ridge up and down in a rhythm meant to drive me mad.

"Go, use me, Charlie. Take what you need, I've got you," he says, moving faster to spur me on.

God, he feels good. I hang on to his nape and arch my back to ride him, unashamed that he's making me fall apart. This connection, this unfamiliar yet extraordinary connection, is absolute perfection.

"Please," I beg.

"Let go, let me see you come," he says, rocking into a faster tempo.

His phone startles us both. Quick to send it to voice mail, he doesn't miss a beat with his hips, but it immediately rings again—an incessant wail.

No, no please.

Glaring at the screen, he lets out a long sigh and stills. "McKenna." His tone when he answers could curl straight hair.

Shit. I moan inwardly, trying to steady my pulse and the throb between my legs. Our rhythm broken, his free hand lingers on my thigh, kneading gently. I can tell by the cadence of his words he has to take the call.

His eyes find mine just as he moves to cradle my cheek. I lean into the warmth of his palm and grin. The smile that burns across his face is so stunning I kiss it. A sloppy, teeth-touching, giggle-inducing kiss that's quick to turn hot and needy as his mouth works over mine. My heart leaps before I pull back to hide in the crook of his neck, panting. I fall into a daze and breathe in his musky male scent. Happiness may be packaged in a crisp oxford button-up and low-riding jeans. And right now, I'm tempted to hump his leg to finish what he started.

God, this is crazy. I sit up and climb off his lap. His eyes track my progress to the bathroom. I need time to recover from the latest mind-boggling morning with Colin McKenna.

SEVEN

"HEY, AL. WHAT ARE you up to?" Tucking the cell between my ear and shoulder, I fluff the messy waves cascading down my back. I miss Ali. Not that we've seen each other often since she started medical school, but I'm antsy for a face-to-face instead of daily calls.

The paging system announcing a code falls silent on the other end. She's at the hospital. "Charlie! Bow-chicka-wow-wow. Tell me everything."

I laugh. "You're insane. Skip the pediatric rotation and jump right to psychiatry. You'll have fabulous relationships with the patient population."

"Hmm, you may be on to something, but alas, I have to complete them all to graduate. Besides, the kids think I'm funny and you do too. Now give me the scoop."

I hash out the funky fall at the factory, the flight to Albany we took this afternoon, and everything up to the black-tie dinner that starts in minutes—minus some of the feel-good moments. *A girl has to have some secrets.* "I like him. He's a little bit broken and I can relate."

"I can tell you do."

"How?"

"Because your blush is coming through the radio signals from New York to Washington, and even if I didn't know you're the color of a tomato, your voice is as thick as molasses. Love is in the air."

"If you start singing, I'm hanging up."

"Not a chance, I need more deets. What are you wearing to this shindig?"

Where are Molly and her closet when I need them? I've done my best with a floor-length black wrap dress; the plunging neckline and high split add an air of elegance to an otherwise simple design. Paired with a gold necklace and matching stilettoes, I'll make the grade. "It doesn't matter. Colin won't be looking at me. In public my role is different. I've spent the whole day studying him and gathering information for the blog, and the only way I got through it was to hide behind my camera."

"My best advice: stop staring at his ass. That's a sure giveaway to the press."

I swallow a lump. "The media is everywhere he is. It's a crazy life."

"It is, and you're about to live it."

"Me?" I choke on incredulity. "I'm not living anything different than what I was two days ago. Colin was clear. We're nothing but behind the scenes. I just didn't know it would be hard to focus on business."

"Find your balance, Charlie. This is the first time you've fallen for someone and he happens to be one of the most prominent faces in America. Don't get swept away in the emotion of it."

"Not possible. I can't get attached, but the way he makes me feel is nice."

She laughs. "Just wait, sister. Nice isn't going to be the adjective of choice when he really gets his hands on you."

"Hmm. Speaking of hands, what happened to the surgeon you went out with last Friday?"

Ali doesn't hold back. Shy doesn't fall into the arsenal of terms one may use to describe my sister. In her anatomy class she volunteered to be a 3D interactive dummy her fellow students could use to map out the human muscular system. It was all in the name of higher education and because she had a crush on Tommy Hanson, a fellow classmate. I laugh so hard as she recants her disastrous date, I have to reapply liner to regain the smoky eye effect.

"He sounds charming. I'm sure he didn't mean to talk about his ex-wife."

"Only hello and good-bye didn't include the name Deirdre, and I think that was just to impress me. Why can't I find a normal guy? You know, one who'll shower me with spankings."

I hide my giggle behind my hand. "I'll send you a picture of Evan. He's exactly your type, pretty with a side of dirty."

"You do that. I've got to run. A seventeen-year-old junior light-weight took one too many to the head and is in intensive care. Tell your man to outlaw boxing. Bye, babycakes. Call me tomorrow."

My man. Not quite, but the thought makes my pulse skyrocket. "Be safe."

Ending the call, I check out the red numbers on the digital clock—quarter to seven. With my camera case slung over my shoulder, I head from my room and down the stairs for a night filled with Colin McKenna.

THE PARK ROYALE IS the oldest hotel in town. A grand staircase empties the second floor into the first and it's on my way down that my eyes spring from watching my step to Colin. He looks as powerful as his position demands. A wide stance, the lines of his finely fitted tux stretched across his shoulders, with one hand pushing his jacket aside to sink into his pocket. My heart likes him as much as I do. It gallops faster, as if to drive my feet at the same pace.

People mill about in sparkling dresses and black ties, yet all I see is him. Relaxed, he stares out of the lobby window to the street beyond. But then he tenses, straightening his spine before turning.

His gaze singes my already frazzled nerves. One heartbeat, two, and then in his imposing gait he moves forward to meet me as I hit the marble floor. He attracts the attention of everyone as he stalks across a foyer three times the size of my apartment. I can see the headline now: "Second Time Insanely Hot Senator Rescues Redhead." This fall would be caused by my pulse as it revs to meet the speed of an oncoming cardiac arrest.

"Charlie." My hand is in his, and just as he did this morning, he brings it to his mouth.

And then he looks at me through his lashes.

Death by Colin McKenna is a gift.

A rumble starts with his smile, it stretches across his face and then he throws his head back in a laugh that draws a multitude of stares.

It's catchy and I can't help my grin when he rubs his chest. "Did I miss something?"

He bites his bottom lip and I would like to replace his teeth with mine. Damn, this has to stop. The intensity, the feels, the tingly sensation lighting up my spine, all of it, so I slide out from in front of him and head in the direction of the ballroom. He manages to stay with me, his hand on the small of my back to guide me past the entry and through a less populated passage of the hotel. Everything is buffed to an ancient-bronze sheen.

"You're stunning," he whispers, low enough for my ears only. Deep enough that I'm instantly aroused.

"You look pretty amazing yourself. Nice tux." I keep my eyes centered on the now empty hallway, but I can sense his smile. And I'm pretty sure it's ending with a dimple that would break hearts everywhere. "So, is this what you do every day? Fly around in private planes, talk it up with fan girls who want to hand over their panties and drink Champagne?"

He chuckles and stops as we come to a door. Looking in either direction, he takes advantage of the silence and presses me against it. "To clarify, Ms. Carter, as I know facts are important to my esteemed journalist." Intensity builds in his eyes as he pulls me forward and against every hard part of him. "When I look into the crowd, there is one woman I see. And it is only with the strength of a thousand men I continue on, when all I can contemplate is if your inner thighs taste as sweet as your lips."

Oh, Lord. His hands slide up to caress the sides of my breasts and I want more than anything for their full weight to fall into his palms, to feel his skin next to mine, for him to pull the tight tips between his fingers. I moan at the press of his hardening length against my stomach. He leans down to nip my jaw and then he draws the tip of his tongue along my bottom lip, tasting the gloss I added to brighten them.

"Cherry," he murmurs into my mouth.

"Colin," I whisper as his hands find my hair and tug, pulling so my neck is bared to him.

"All I see is you, Charlie," he says, the heat of his breath warming a path as he speaks into skin. When he licks my collarbone, I wrap my arms around his waist, beneath his jacket. His muscles contract under my roaming fingers.

For all I know, I could be opening Pandora's Box. But my body wants him and I do too. I'll stay on the right side of the line emotionally and delve into this physical connection that is so alive between us. I can do it and if I can't—I'll leave.

"Did you wait for me?" I ask. "In the lobby, were you there for me?"

He tightens his hold and my breath explodes from my lungs as he lifts up to find my eyes. He's so intense, jaw clenching as he almost growls, "You know I did."

All of a sudden my dress feels like sandpaper. I want it off, I want to rip his shirt open and press myself to his hard naked planes. "I can't stop thinking about you touching me."

His features soften, but his erection does not. "I know."

"Will you do it again?"

The side of his mouth pulls up. "Here?"

I fight the blush heating my cheeks and turn my head to stare at the floor, embarrassed because I have absolutely no idea how to seduce a man, let alone one like him.

Taking my chin in hand, he brings my eyes back to his. "Don't look away from me. I like what I see; a strong, clever, independent woman." His voice is deep, the warm caramel that soothes my stiff spine. "Don't ever be ashamed of how I make you feel, or to ask for what you want, because I have the same thoughts."

My lids close and I lay my cheek to his chest, his racing heart evident under my ear. For a moment I drown in the sweet hint of sandalwood that is now forever synonymous with him. I still have my arms around his waist and I squeeze until I think he smiles. His fingers run through my hair and then down my back to cup my ass.

"I don't know how to do this," I whisper.

"I'm going to show you the way."

I swallow a sudden ball of emotion that wells in my throat. Colin McKenna is bigger than life and he's going to seduce me. *Done*.

Pushing against his chest, I say, "Let's go before I need to route back to my room for a quick change."

"Your dress is beautiful." He smirks and my cheeks stay pink.

"Don't play coy, Mr. McKenna. You know exactly what I'm referring to." And to prove my point, I squeeze my thighs together to alleviate the constant throbbing between them.

His eyes darken as he watches my show. "Later, Ms. Carter, you will find out what it really means to be wet."

Holy cow. My heart races so fast it's in a new time zone, but he just takes my hand and pulls me behind him. The other side of the door reveals a short hall. Mingled voices rise as we draw near the end. It opens to a narrow room filled with shadows as campaign staffers move in front of and then around small lamps hanging on the walls. As soon as we hit the perimeter he tightens his hold on my fingers for a second and then releases me.

The loss of contact is an anchor. My feet slow down as he slips into the crowd and forgets about me. And why shouldn't he? I'm an employee, just like everyone else here. We work for him; our main focus is to see him to the steps of the Capitol where he'll take the oath of office. Evan is by his side, pointing out the logistics of the event. John Montgomery steps in. He's tall, his short hair completely gray, but his features remain handsome even though he's older than my father. He's elegant in the way he moves until he spots me and his eyes narrow.

I fall back into the mix of staffers. Every other employee is doing their job and my panties are soaked from a hallway encounter.

I bite my lip. *An employee*. This is the straight line I have to walk and to ensure I do, I turn to retreat in the same way I came in. It only takes a minute to hit the lobby. Following the lead of guests, I enter the grand ballroom. Two-story walls and a balcony surround the entire perimeter. A stage is set at the very end and I think Colin must be behind it. Crystal chandeliers cast a glow on constituents who paid thousands of dollars to attend this five-course meal, with their presidential hopeful as the appetizer.

Everyone has a place and not surprising, mine is at a table in the far corner. When the senator appears by way of the double doors, the hum of the crowd expands into excited chatter as he progresses into the room and finally to his seat. I've never attended an affair as formal as this, one where small talk is expected and charm a requirement. I'm a vessel of the campaign, so I mimic Ali and her natural grace in all things social. I must be doing something right. The man to my right keeps staring. Brown eyes that have more than a splash of red track my glass as I bring it to my mouth. He reminds me of someone you'd see in an advertisement for cheap cologne, and he smells a lot like it too.

When he smiles it does nothing to me. No tingles or feels, no energy. I grin and it only encourages him into an introduction.

"Joel Reeves," he drawls, as if I should recognize the name. "Owner of BGG Communications."

"Charlise Carter. Nice to meet you." I offer my hand and he holds it for seconds too long. I have to pull it away from his grip.

"You have no idea who I am, do you?" he asks, in a husky tone that has hair on my nape bristling to attention.

"Should I?"

He winks and I find myself growing uncomfortable under his blatant scrutiny. "Maybe not, but I'm going to enjoy telling you."

And he does. It's easy to let his constant chatter fall to the background, and I poke around each course, more interested in the champagne than food or Joel what's-his-name.

After dessert is served, the lights dim, one spotlights Colin as he takes the stage. It gives me a new focus. "Excuse me," I whisper, and head into the shadowed perimeter of the room with camera in hand. Hiding under the balcony and behind a column meant to hold it up allows for an unhindered stare. Here is the centered man that commands attention and holds it as everyone waits with baited breath for each word. I take a few shots and mentally map out a blog post, jotting down key points on the notepad I stowed in my case.

A sound scrapes behind me. An old door creaks at the hinges somewhere in the darkness. I turn. No one approaches. My pulse kicks up a notch, but I resume watching Colin. And then it happens again, followed by the scuffle of footsteps growing near. I squint into the recess next to the stage, only to find uninterrupted blackness.

The crowd explodes in applause. I jump, hand over my mouth to hold in a scream.

Jesus, Charlie. I curse and bolt back to my seat for more champagne and to calm my racing heart. As the standing ovation ends, a quartet takes Colin's place on stage and I sit. Joel takes up where he left off. I keep drinking. My eyes stray to my obnoxious neighbor, who is so high on himself it's revolting, and then to the gloom nestled in the faraway corner. But more often than not, I'm centered on Colin and his tablemate, a platinum blonde who tosses her hair over her shoulder every thirty seconds until dessert is cleared. When her hand lands on his bicep, an antsy energy pushes me to my feet.

Joel hops up at the same time. "Dance with me."

My eyes narrow as Colin leads frosty onto the floor that's filling with couples.

"With pleasure," I say and take his hand.

But I regret it the minute his arm wraps around my waist, smashing my breasts to his chest. I swallow down my nausea and glare at Colin as he winds his woman in graceful swirls. He catches my eye.

His jaw sets in a rigid line. As if on automatic pilot, my hand snakes around Joel's neck. My partner is fluid enough to make me look like I can dance, but smarmy enough to lick his lips, and I realize my mistake. What I meant to be a taunt at Colin was taken as an invitation by the wrong man.

Joel's nose presses in my hair. His damp breath hits my ear as he whispers, "I'm in 505, meet me there in ten minutes."

What? No! I suck at jealousy and everything that has to do with men in general.

"Thank you, Joel, for keeping Ms. Carter occupied." Colin. A shiver rakes down my spine at hiss sharp tone. "We have business to attend to, so if you'll excuse us for a moment." I catch a glimpse of Joel's fallen brow in a what-just-happened-here expression before Colin has his hand on my lower back.

"Now, Ms. Carter," he says, loud enough to spur my feet into action. It takes a minute to clear through the ballroom and I keep my back straight when I notice more than one set of eyes tracking us. We hit the edge of the dance floor and he grabs my hand, taking over the lead to pull me along and then up a hidden staircase to the balcony above.

"Colin. Slow down."

He doesn't acknowledge my request but for a low rumble. His anger radiates in waves but he takes shorter strides until we're tucked into a dim alcove far away from curious gawkers. A mask of uncertainty clouds his expression as he backs me against the wall.

Leaning down, his arms brace on either side of my face. "I'm new to this, Charlie. The reactions you elicit are… unfamiliar, and I don't do well with uncharted territory. But I do know I won't share you, ever," he says through his teeth. "Hear me when I say this: I don't ever want another man's hands on you—never again. Tell me you understand."

Surprisingly, I'm not afraid of the depth of his reaction; in fact, I'm attracted to it. The evident passion in his voice and his actions are something I've unknowingly longed to have, to feel within myself.

For so long my life has been about living to get through the day and into the next. With Colin, the deep-seated emotion is enticing, and it makes me want him even more. The opportunity to taste any level of this type of intensity has become a necessity.

He grinds into me, and as soon as I open my mouth to respond, his lips take mine in a desperate kiss. When his tongue sweeps into my mouth, I moan and grip his hair, pulling myself flush against the lines of his chest. His hands knead, touch, and roam over every inch of my back while his mouth continues its devastation. God, he tastes good, like champagne and something new, something that's been out of my reach until now.

I vaguely hear Evan call his name, but I don't care. I grip Colin harder, kissing him longer. This is what I want; this is what I've wanted since his damn phone interrupted us this morning. I'm on fire; every muscle in my body is attuned to his. My groin clenches with delicious need. When Evan's voice grows louder, his hold loosens.

"Don't stop, please," I beg into his mouth. Diving into me once more, his tongue slays me, erasing every thought of the outside world until I'm breathless and we have to break away to drag in air.

He cradles my cheeks, drawing his thumb across my bottom lip. I close my eyes and fight the emotion churning behind my lids. Finding a balance is going to be harder than I ever thought possible.

"I'll come for you in an hour, Ms. Carter. And if I wasn't clear before, let me spell it out for you now." He kisses me, a hot crush of his mouth against mine, before he pulls away with my bottom lip between his teeth. "Your night will begin and end with me."

EIGHT

THE SUBTLE HINT OF sandalwood clings to my skin and if that isn't enough reason for my dopey smile, the sight of Colin's retreating backside is. I watch him until he disappears down the stairs and then I realize I'm all alone and swallowed by shadows. The chandeliers hang below the floor of the balcony, so it's only lit by the tops of their iridescent glow.

It's obvious the balcony is used for storage as I walk around stacks of chairs and unused tables. The thirty feet from wall to railing allows for plenty of room to peer below without being seen. A perfect reprieve to think about our agreement and his wife and baby, the reaction to Joel.... He's as complicated as a pint of Ben and Jerry's Salted Caramel Brown-ie Ale. A mouthwatering mix of complex ingredients that's easy to devour. And I want to. Whatever *this* is, it makes me burn in places that have remained frozen under an arctic tundra. I'm ready to shed the parka and get naked with the hot senator.

Even though no one is here to see it, I giggle behind my hand. Dancing continues, and my silly grin remains when I find Colin is not amongst the participants. Frosty pouts her injected pucker and then slithers up next to him. He doesn't acknowledge her but for a handshake and a nod before moving on to the next person waiting to engage him.

An awareness creeps over my skin. Someone is watching. My heart rate sprints as if to confirm it. At first I'm stuck, unsure what to do. But then I turn, because I'm psyching myself into a panic that's senseless. It's probably an employee of the hotel sent to retrieve a packed-away item.

"Hello?" Other than a solo by the violinist, there is no response. "Is anyone here?"

The sad truth is, I know fear well. It's been a long time since I've felt the effects, but here it is prickling at my nape.

I step forward and deeper into the shadows, winding through desks and lamps. A crash draws my attention. A man turns and I catch a slice of his features between piled-high boxes that are coming down on top of him.

"Who's there?"

He bolts.

Sprinting forward, he jumps over hurdles in his way and races to the opposite end of the balcony.

I follow.

I don't know why, other than I have a something-familiar feeling rolling around my stomach. Picking up my skirt, I do my best to catch him in four-inch stilettoes. He flings open a door. When I reach it, it reveals a dark stairwell. I take my time—it's a tunnel of terror for the clumsy. The last step dumps me in the bright lights of the kitchen. Employees turn from watching the man dash out of an exit on the far wall to me rushing after him and into an alley.

Cold wind stings my cheeks. The latch clicks closed behind me with a definitive clang. Tires rumble on the street in front of the hotel and the loud thump of my pulse echoes in my ears. Whoever was watching me is gone, as is the tickling feeling of being watched. I turn to open the door, but there is no handle. Rather than bringing more attention to myself by knocking, I cross my arms to hold in heat and head in the direction of the cars. I assume I'll find the hotel lobby, but instead I slip on a patch of ice.

Throwing out my arm isn't enough to catch my balance and I land with a loud *oomph* and an aching hip. "Lovely." My mumble is lost in a freezing gust that pushes through the narrow opening.

I stand to brush off my pride and gravel pebbles from my backside. A shiver claims my shoulders but it's more electric than frigid, and I freeze.

"Charlie?"

Colin. *Oh, for the love of God.* Of course he would find me panting in an alley with a dirty ass.

A glance behind me confirms it's him. His features are impassive, other than the brow that shoots up as he draws near.

"I, uh…." He shakes his head as I stutter. "Thought I saw someone I knew."

"In the kitchen?"

My cheeks burst into flames. "Maybe, yes. How'd you know I was outside anyway?"

He chuckles. "Rumor spread rather quickly that a redhead was terrorizing some poor man in the bowels of the hotel."

"And you naturally thought of me."

"It seems trouble has a way of finding you, Charlie."

"You don't know the half of it," I mumble as he takes me by the elbow.

"Come," he says. "You can tell me what happened upstairs."

"Upstairs?" I squeak. But my heart races to catch up with my imagination and what we could possibly do in his suite.

TWENTY MINUTES LATER COLIN knows everything, which is very little. In hindsight, I think I chased a stowaway from his hiding place in the balcony. Poor guy is probably freezing in a box on the side of the road as we speak.

Colin is reclining against the back of the couch. I'm in the chair at the small side table, ten feet separating us. I've had enough brandy to warm Iceland. Or, maybe the heat is from the way he tracks me with his eyes. From the tips of my toes, that are now freed from heels, along the line of my legs, one crossed over the other and bared by the long split in my skirt. And then to my breasts, now rising and falling with my heightened breath. All from a damn look that has my nipples pebble to sharp points. I should stare at the floor, his shoes, not his quads that are hardly contained in black pants, or his biceps bulging as he crosses his arms over his bulbous pectorals—muscles. Every single muscle on this man is tight and thick.

I squeeze my thighs together and he growls.

He growls.

I do it again and he stalks forward.

From couch to chair, he's on me in a second. My head snaps back as his hands grip me above my waist and he hauls me up. I'm plastered against him with my fingers in his hair—every luscious silk strand. His mouth slams into mine.

My God.

Hot, sweet like wine and sexy as hell, his tongue sweeps in to taste me. Deep lashing licks to shorter strokes, and my heart leaps into next year. Something is going to happen between us. I want it like I've never wanted anything before. I'm taking a new path and he's at the end of it. No matter what happens between us, he will become a part of me and I'll take him with me forever.

He breaks away, breathless and pleading with his eyes.

"Tell me to stop, Charlie." His chest heaves beneath my hands as I run them all over him and then his shoulders, feeling the rippling veins on the side of his neck and up to his jaw. I hold him as a struggle plays out on his features and in his gaze. "Talk to me," he whispers.

I brush my lips against his. "I want this."

He groans his agreement and tugs on the belt holding my dress together. It billows open and his thumbs help it from my shoulders and then down my arms until it falls to floor. Left in lace lingerie, I wonder what he's thinking. I'm more buxom than bony and for the first time in my life I care that my hips are round and my breasts are big.

Stepping away a foot, he says, "Take off your bra."

I hold my breath; no one has seen me naked before. Not like this. My vision blurs as I reach back to the clasp.

He inhales at the same moment I feel the chilled air against my skin, confirming my vulnerability. "Charlie," he breathes, lifting a hand to feather his fingers down the side of my body, stopping on my hip bones. "Look at me."

A cry is lodged in my throat. I'm afraid of what I'll find when I do. I need him to kiss me and make me forget the insecurities in my head, and the past that swirls along with them. A bleating whimper escapes when I find his hungry eyes, and he says, "You're gorgeous."

I launch myself at him, kissing his chin, his cheek, nipping on his jaw. "Make me feel everything. Make me feel so good the only thing I'll remember is this night and you."

The last word is lost in his mouth. He sweeps me up as if I weigh nothing and holds me against him. In seconds we're in his room and then I'm on his bed.

"Lie back." It's a soft command, but a command all the same. I scoot to the middle of the mattress and drop from my elbows as he pulls his belt free. Need rushes between my thighs and he watches me squirm. One button and then the next; by the time he frees his shirt and bares his chest, my clit is throbbing and I'm wet, so wet and panting with anticipation. His pants and boxer briefs follow. The man has no shame. He stands stock still, hand stroking his hard length as I take in my fill.

Holy Shit. He *is* a god among men. There's nothing soft about him. His abdomen ripples with dips and shadows. A small smattering of hair frames his erection. And oh my, it's—I swallow a lump—it's more than I thought it could possibly be.

Pain. The thought beats into my mind. But I want this. I want him so I push the thought away.

I fist the comforter on both sides of my hips and he reaches for his bag to pull out a condom. He tosses it on the nightstand. At the same time, I say, "I'm on birth control," and then heat shoots up to my cheeks.

But he doesn't hesitate.

Climbing on the bed, he presses his lips to my ankle. He kisses and licks his way up until he's groaning, sucking and tasting my inner thighs as he spreads my legs wide.

"Fuck, Charlie." He growls my name and then he's the lion eating the lamb.

Through my panties he licks my slit. My cry breaks free just as my head slams into the mattress. I squeeze my eyes closed. He sucks my clit through the lace, lapping and teasing with his tongue and then teeth. I bow into his mouth and with a groan, he peels me free of everything. I'm bare. My lips part, but I can't speak. I can only watch and feel and breathe through the pulsing ache in my core while he kisses me everywhere.

This is different than I imagined; I'm different. I've never given myself to someone in this way—without doubt or sorrow, with freedom to welcome every touch and explore in return. I'm consumed with knowing him, finding the smallest places and where the lightest stroke elicits the rush of his breath or hunger to flare in his eyes.

It's more than I ever thought it could be: the bunch of his muscles beneath my hands, the heat of his skin and the long drag of his tongue as he savors every inch of my body. Nuzzling the sensitive dip behind my ear and along my neck, the side of my breast and down to the curved indentation at my waist—he cherishes every part of me.

I grab his erection. Silk and steel, he melts into my hand. "Charlie," he hisses, and tucks his nose beneath my chin. I hold him, pushing from tip to base and pulling back, rubbing my fingers over the end in a caress. I run on repeat until he's panting and flexing into my grip.

"Enough." Pinning both of my arms above my head, his mouth crushes mine, sucking my tongue into his mouth, and now I'm squirming and begging for him to touch me. *Touch me, please.*

And he does. Oh, God, he does. While one hand holds me prisoner, the other grabs my breast, pulling the tip. I cry out and look at him.

"I'll make you burn for me, Charlie; only for me." *Oh, I am.* I'm on fire. His fingers leave a burning wake just as promised, moving down, down to the most sensitive place nestled between my thighs.

A low moan from the back of his throat settles in the air as he dips between my folds. "Open your legs. I want to see you." *Oh, God.*

I let them fall apart, and he weighs one down with his knee. He rubs around my clit. Slipping to where I'm the wettest, he gathers my heat and teases me with the slickness by painting it in tight tiny circles, but never where I need him the most.

"Please, please, please," I beg. I beg and scream when those damn fingers slide into me. "Holy, *oh.*" I groan, loud and shameless, as he reaches in and tips forward, pumping and rubbing me into a full-out cry. He feels so blessed good.

"So tight," he says in a pinched voice, as if he's on the precipice of finding the Holy Grail. But that's me and I bow from the bed.

"Please." I beg for something, anything. "Make me come, please make me come." I try to move. Pinned down, my only recourse is to flex and roll my hips, bring him deeper, faster, and take in his growl as he crushes his mouth to mine.

He grinds his palm into my clit and it's my undoing. I scream and explode into a million pieces as I come and come all over his magical hand.

When the haze clears he's raised up on his elbows staring down at me. His body is a protective and possessive frame as he nestles between my thighs and his tip spreads me open.

I find his eyes, so blue and questioning. I'm not afraid. I want to give him everything I've held within myself for so long. "I want you," I whisper, latching on to his shoulders.

"Charlie, baby." As the words pass his lips he slides in another short measure and then he rears back. Rocking his thick shaft into me inch by glorious inch, he only pauses when he hits my core. His forehead falls to mine and we lie connected while my body adjusts to his size.

"You fit so good, so full," I say, even though it's not enough. I want more; I want him to move, so I roll my hips.

His shoulders shake with the low rumble of his laugh. "Give me a second, baby, or this will be over before we both want it to be." Taking my sigh into him, he focuses on my mouth, kissing me until I'm breathless.

Our connection deepens as he rises onto his hands. I clench around him in response, and his nostrils flair. My fingers trail along his shoulders and down his arms, following the definition of his muscles as they flex beneath my touch.

"I can't get enough," he says. "Even being inside you is not enough. I need to own every part of you."

He throws his head back as he pulls out, and I know we both feel the glide, exquisite and necessary. Lifting my hips from the bed, I try to force his reentry, but he's entirely in control. Waiting another heartbeat, he slides in again. I groan when he pulls back and finds a gentle rhythm, moving in and out. He licks his lips and I drape my arms around his neck, using them as leverage to lift up and kiss him.

"So good. It's too good...," he mumbles against my mouth. And it is. So intense and so good my toes curl as I wrap my legs around his backside. I'm close to overwhelmed; the feel of him buried in me, knowing I'm really here in this moment, with his voice whispering in my ear to *hold on, don't hold back, give me everything....* I almost can't hold on, falling deeply into every sensation and losing myself in them.

I've never done this with someone and felt connected in every possible way, not just physically, but emotionally. A rush, a warmth spreads out from my chest at the realization that this is my beginning—a spring in the middle of winter, the ending of a chapter and the start of another, with Colin as the central character. Right here, in his bed, clarity reigns as his mouth claims mine again, teasing out a moan so he can claim that too. He owns me. I would give him anything. Take it, take all of me, take everything and anything. And he does, wringing out every ounce of pleasure. He knows where to touch, how to extract the smallest whimper and the largest groan. I could never tire of being with him, with him over me and in me, pushing, pulling, driving, and devouring until the ache becomes a need. A need so intense and all-consuming, I begin taking from him. Calling out unabashedly to *move faster, go deeper, push harder*. Don't stop, never stop, never stop making me feel this good and needy and so, so full. *Please*, I beg. Pleading with him, pleading for I don't know what….

Pushing off his shoulders, I fall to the bed and he follows, his head dipping to my nipple. Taking me into his mouth, he teases with his tongue and bites down, hard, only releasing me when I gasp and clutch his hair. But I don't pull him away; I hold him in place. I want more. He does it again and this time I go a little wild, raking my fingers down his back and bucking my hips to meet the increased pace of his.

Everything he's doing is magnified in the pulse between my thighs. It started as a slow flutter when he first entered me, but it's built into a steady cadence. I focus on the feeling of him. I'm climbing high, fast, and he's coming with me. Throwing my head back, I relish in our connection, kneading my fingers into his back, his muscles flexing with control as he pushes me to a place I've never known, didn't know existed.

I can see the moment when he loses it, loses himself as I have done. Gone is the controlled restraint and in its place is a wild abandon. Giving in to my demands, his hips thrust with a determined pace, driving forward, pushing harder until each strike elicits a guttural grunt from him and an exacting cry from me. Sweat pebbles on his brow, beading and rolling, dropping to my chest where it slides between my breasts. I watch, fascinated, as his eyes follow it down and the black of his pupils blur into the blue with a need so powerful it would scare me if I didn't feel the exact same way.

My mouth finds his, licking and sucking and tasting. Who am I, but a needy, hungry woman begging for the only thing that can save me? Colin. Only him, it will always only be him. I give myself fully, joining him in the freedom to feel beyond good, beyond words.

"Don't let me fall." Sudden panic overtakes me as my body threatens to tumble from a cliff.

"I've got you, baby," he whispers. "We're going to fall together. Come with me." The whisper turns to a demand, forcing me to hold on and together, we dive headfirst into an abyss of pleasure so deep and plentiful we drown in it, breathe it, and live through it.

Falling, his full weight presses me into the bed, and with his head cradled in my neck I savor his pulsating body. I have never felt this good. I didn't know having sex could feel like this, could make my body respond in such an uninhibited, glorious way. With trembling muscles I squeeze my legs, holding him close. In a minute he lifts his head, a small smile touching his lips and his eyes.

"Hi."

My heart free-falls and I grin in return. "Hi, yourself."

His mouth finds mine, an endearing connection, our tongues gentling as they meet in a sweet duel. After a moment he pulls out of me. Wincing, I close my eyes at the loss. It felt so perfectly right to have him inside of me.

"Are you okay?"

I smile. "Perfect." Because I am. Tonight with Colin, this was my first time. This was the first time it's felt good, and true, and beautiful. This is the first time I've made love with a man and I'm perfect, absolutely, astonishingly perfect.

Planting a quick kiss on his shoulder, I run my nose against his skin, inhaling his scent. He is beautiful. Rolling over, he pulls me with him, tucking me into his side. I lay my arm over his stomach and snuggle into his length. We remain this way for a long time, not speaking, just basking in post-orgasmic glow.

In time, I wiggle down, resting my palm on his abdomen and my chin on top of that. He's awake.

"I've never felt like this before, Colin. That.... It was... well, it was super fantastic. Will it always be like this with us?" I watch him and how he's concentrating on me. A sliver of light slices through the doorway, just enough to illuminate his eyes as he searches mine, penetrating the depths of them as if he can see into my soul. I thought he might smile, but I was wrong. A mask slowly settles in place. Picking up a section of my hair, he fans it between his fingers and then drops it back to my shoulder.

"Go to sleep, Charlie. Morning will be here before you're ready for it, and when it comes, maybe you'll find the answer to your question."

Hmm, I bet he'll be my wake-up call. I smile as the night stretches before me. Sliding my cheek against his skin, I burrow down and let the darkness fall.

I STARTLE AWAKE, ALONE. The bed is cool next to me, as is the air as it settles over my skin. My body aches in all the right places. I smile through my stretch, hands above my head and toes pointed. If I let myself, I could get lost in the hotter-than-hell memories of Colin McKenna's hands on me, and his lips, and the way his body fit perfectly into mine, but I'd really like to find my missing person and entice him into bed to recreate the perfection. I grab his shirt from the back of the chair and slip it on while walking into the main part of the suite.

His skin is burnished gold by the small lamp glowing on the desk where he sits, reading through a brief. He's pulling at his lower lip with his fingers. I stand in the doorway, watching the rise and fall of his bare chest in complete awe that I'm with this brilliant man.

He looks up. "Did I wake you?" I frown at his rigid jaw and his tone—affectionate Colin is gone, Mr. President is securely in place.

"No, I.... You weren't there when I woke. I missed you."

His eyes fall back to his papers. "I'm working. Go back to sleep."

"But I'm cold without my thermals or you," I tease, walking behind him. Bending down, I grin into his neck and slide my hands down to rub his nipples. He tenses and his quick intake of breath tells me I have his attention. "Come to bed, please."

Pinning my fingers between his, he snaps, "Leave, Charlie. I don't have time for you."

Right. That hurt. It hurts so much I can't breathe. My heart plummets to my stomach. I yank my hands away and wrap them around myself. He doesn't move. And before he has a chance to, I dart to the bedroom and throw myself on the mattress, head buried in the pillow. Last night meant nothing to him when it meant so much to me. I've been dismissed. I can see it now; I'm the errant employee he'll fuck when it pleases him and crush when it suits him. His words are crystal clear: *I have nothing to give. I'm a shell of the man I once was.*

I can't do this. It's one thing to have unattached sex; disrespect is intolerable. I won't allow him to treat me like shit because he's a broken bastard. I deserve more than that.

Dragging myself to my feet, I find and slip into my bra and panties. My dress is a lost cause on the floor in the living room, and even though it's mortifying, I'm taking the walk of shame in his shirt so I can clear out of here in a hurry.

I know when I'm not wanted.

Rushing through the suite, I only pause to grab my camera case and key card. The door shuts behind me with a definitive clasp.

I run, trying to leave it all behind. The memories, the feelings, the experience I wish I could take back. My room is stale and dark, but I fling myself onto the bed and take up a new chant. *I will not cry. I will not cry.* I won't; tears are for fools. They don't wash away pain or free me from it. A long time ago I began to see them as a weakness, so I haven't allowed myself to cry since I was fourteen. I will not be weak. But my lids burn even through my motto. For the first time in years I want to howl into the pillow.

What have I done?

NINE

THE MORNING LIGHT COMES all too soon, as does the recollection of last night's events. I groan, rolling onto my back. My entire body is sore, as if I've worked out for eight hours with an Olympic wrestler. I stand corrected—like I worked out with Colin McKenna. Tears coat my eyes when reality weighs in, crushing.

A ring startles me, and I give the phone a death stare Ella would be proud of. There are only a few people it could be, and none of them are at the top of my people-to-chat-with list, especially Colin.

Propping up on my elbow, I grab the receiver and growl, "Charlie Carter." I should at least pretend I'm a tough-as-nails bitch.

"Charlie."

Oh shit, it's him. "Yes?"

"We need to talk. I'll be down in five minutes." He doesn't ask, he demands, and it pisses me off even more.

"No, Colin, you won't." The chill in my tone could freeze over Miami. "I've forgotten last night, as you did the second it happened. There's nothing more to discuss as it relates to that topic. For the immediate future, I will continue on in my position. Should that become too difficult to manage with boundaries, I'll submit my resignation. Thank you for the call." I slam down the phone.

Fuck off, Mr. President. I fall back, breathing hard. Tears fill my eyes and I struggle to get them under control, the hard-bitch façade cruelly letting me down in my moment of need.

I need a plan; I can't stay here. *Shit.* If I give up this assignment I have no work to go home to. Rolling to my stomach, hurt floods through me and escapes in slow-moving tremors. The last few weeks become overwhelming all at once: missing my family, the travel, the fall at the factory, and Colin, mostly Colin.

I'm startled when weight shifts the mattress and I know it's him. My eyes flare open just as he sets a room card on the nightstand. I should have known he'd find a way to get one. Evan manages the reservations and must have the second key to all of the booked rooms. When his fingers rake through my hair, anger simmers in my stomach until it boils over as a roar into the pillow. I don't want him to see me like this.

I crawl to the opposite corner of the bed from where he sits and turn toward him. His face falls, three lines digging into his brow.

"I'm so sorry."

My pulse hammers in my throat. "You have no right to be in my room. Get out."

He flinches as if I've slapped him, and a part of me wishes I had the satisfaction of doing so. "Charlie, I—"

"Let me make one thing clear." I cut him off and stand; aware that I still have his shirt on. Oh well, I'm too pissed to stop this tongue lashing. "I can understand not having a heart to give; I've probably got you beat in that category. But what I don't understand, and will never accept, is being treated like a whore." I drag in a quick breath and keep going, each word louder than the last. "It has taken me more than fifteen years to repair myself to a level at which I can successfully make it through the day, and I won't let you destroy my precarious hold on my self-respect. Don't tell me you're fucking sorry!"

I straighten my back and tug my hair behind my ears, trying to find some level of dignity. Arms crossed over my chest, I make my stand. "I'd like you to leave."

Colin rises, cautious in his approach. Even through my anger I can appreciate his beauty, in fitted black pants, and a white T-shirt stretched across his chest. His nipples are visible through the fabric and I have to make myself look at beige herringbone wallpaper—plain, just like my life before he walked into it. He stops in front of me and his eyes blaze with smoldering need.

"No," I cry, stepping back and into the wall with a thud. He's on me, closing me in with his arms and then his mouth. For one second I relax into relief at the stroke of his tongue, but then I rip away, forcing my head to the side, panting. His rock-hard leg is pressed between my thighs, rubbing against my sore and swollen parts and it feels so damn good. I don't want to want this, but my body responds with a gluttonous flush. "Let me go."

He sighs. "Ask of me something that's possible. Charlie, please." His nose sinks into the crook of my neck and he breathes me in. "Forgive me."

My heart plummets to the floor and I know it's going to get trampled on, but I can't resist him. I sink my fingers into his hair and he groans. Circling his arms around my waist, he stands to full height and my feet leave the floor. God, he tugs on all of my emotions—the good and the bad. But I won't let him treat me like a throwaway; I'll end up resenting him and hating myself for accepting it as my value.

"I may be naïve, Colin, yet I know what this is. I'm fine with our arrangement, it works for me. But I don't want to feel like garbage every time you've had your fill."

"I'm sorry," he whispers, pressing the words into my skin. "It's the truth, Charlie. I want to be with you. To do that, I have to work through my emotions without hurting you. Last night was a big lesson for me." Dragging his forehead to mine, he forces eye contact. "Please forgive me. It won't happen again, I promise you."

"I want to believe you."

"Give me a second chance."

So much sadness is in him; it's in me too, yet I wonder if it has to be that way. This is new territory for both of us, and we'll have to work together to figure it out. I brush my lips against his.

"I may be a fool, but I will."

We stay stuck to each other for minutes, and then he walks us to the bed, dropping down so he's lying on top of me. I run my fingers over his back while he nuzzles my neck.

"Don't you have a meeting this morning?" I ask on my way to complete distraction.

He glances at the clock. "I have thirty minutes to show you just how sorry I am." He nestles between my thighs and I giggle, sinking my hands into his silken hair.

COLIN'S PLANE IS THE bomb. In the main cabin, a couple of recliners face a sectional and just behind them are two-by-two leather seats with tables between the rows. It's also got a conference room in the back and a full kitchen in the front. The most amazing addition is Mrs. Brenner, a stewardess who may as well be a pastry chef.

"God, the chocolate truffles this woman makes are to die for," I say to Evan as he refines Colin's speech for tomorrow's rally. "Here, taste one." I push my plate closer to where he sits on the couch, and then wash the temptation off my tongue with the latte she also produced.

He shakes his head. "Thanks, but no. I don't do crack."

My giggle is interrupted by Ella, who tugs open the back room door. She files out with her nose in the air and then slides into one of the chairs. As she buckles in, John follows her out and then the senator of my dreams is just behind him. The man makes me blush every time he looks at me like he is right now. Blue eyes darkening to the color of midnight gaze intently through thick rows of lashes. My pulse takes off and it doesn't help that he sinks down into the chair where he can continue to make my panties melt.

He smiles, broad, decadent, and ending in a dimple on his cheek. *Damn man.* Of course I lick the chocolate from my finger—long, thorough strokes of my tongue—and find some satisfaction as his grin fades. His nostrils flare as I suck the evidence of my snack from each digit.

The mood is crushed when the she-devil catches on and whips her head around to singe me with her death stare. I shiver from her vehemence. She really hates me. The sharp rap of Colin's voice as he calls her name breaks the tension apart, and the three of them finish their business.

"Don't let her get to you, Charlie," Evan says. "Ella wants Colin to suffer with his grief for the rest of his life, or be with her as his only other option."

"I don't get it," I whisper, staring at my lap and my coffee cup. "She's such a bitch; why does he put up with her?"

"Listen," he says, and I look up to find him staring at me. "Colin is in deep with you. Don't worry about the Montgomerys. The two of them know how to run a campaign, and that's why they're here. John's been pushing him into the presidency since he started dating Abby." Finally, I have a name for the wife who haunts him. "They've got a hard-on to get Colin into the White House. We're so close to the goal now, they're worried he'll get distracted with you; that's all it is."

My heart sinks. "And what do you think?"

Evan's smile is kind, if not a bit sad. "That you're the exact diversion he needs. Charlie, he's devoted every minute of the last five years to this run and the fifteen before that were calculated steps. After Abby," he draws in a breath, "after the accident, there wasn't anything for him to do but focus on his career. In my opinion it was unhealthy, but no one has brought about the balance he's needed. Until you."

I pull up my knees and hug them to my chest as if in protection from the answer that awaits my next question. "But why me?"

Evan shrugs. "Colin likes redheads."

My brow falls and my gaze slices through him like a laser beam. He holds up a hand as if in surrender, chuckling. "You hold your own, when most women go Stepford, as if that will get him into a chapel to pledge vows. It's the epitome of annoying."

I laugh, but it's strangled and tight coming out. "So he's not into submission?"

"God, no, not like that. Keep giving him shit, Charlie. He needs it and he needs you. Colin is good at what he does, the best, but you compliment his demanding personality. That's not only good for him, but for the campaign. You've lightened his perspective. Hell, he's smiled more in the last week than he had through the last few months. People need to see him as a man, not just the commanding Senator who gets things done. All facets are important."

I gulp down my anxiety with my latte. Evan goes back to work and I stare at the object of my fascination for the few minutes it takes us to land at JFK International Airport. I'm surprised as we disembark that two vehicles wait on the tarmac. Colin steers me to the second one. "Dinner," he mumbles, helping me inside. My seat becomes his lap as he pulls me over to straddle his thighs. No talking—just kissing. At some point his hands find their way under my shirt as we make the most of the half hour ride into Manhattan.

When the town car stops, he sets me aside so I can catch my breath and straighten my clothes. He looks perfect of course, damn him, but he just smiles at my scowl and tugs me out of the door and into old world charm. Two-tiered crystal chandeliers bounce light off walls, which hold pictures of an Italian family, from birth through graduations and marriages. What's most amazing is the aroma; a perfect blend of spice and fresh air, growing the vegetables on the vine.

The host beams as if he's known Colin for many years. "*Buona sera*, Senator McKenna! *Come sta*?"

"*Molto bene, grazie. E lui, Signore Rosa*?" Colin replies as they shake hands, Signore Rosa using both of his.

Transitioning from Italian to heavy-accented English, he says, "It's been too long. We're so happy you found your way back to us."

"Signore Rosa, my friend, Charlise."

"*Benvenuta, Signorina Charlisa! È molto bella*." His eyes brighten as he appraises me. "Please, I have a special table for you." He motions us into the restaurant.

Colin's arm lingers on my lower back as we follow. Candles flame and sparkle against the white cloth dressing the tables. At the far end of the room a wood hearth is burrowed into a rock wall. Behind it is an even more intimate space. Signore Rosa waves us to a booth hidden behind a chest-high wall separating it from the rest of the guests and plunging us into our own private bistro.

Before I have a chance to sit, a petite woman with streaks of gray in her otherwise black hair enters. Her Italian is quick. Colin doesn't appear to have any trouble keeping up.

"*Mamma Rosa, cosi bello vederti.*" Her small frame is dwarfed in his embrace, but she squeezes him and he laughs. When they pull apart she kisses him affectionately on each cheek.

"You stay away too long," she admonishes. When she spots me her eyes round and then narrow. Mama bear protecting her cub.

"*Una ragazza*?" she asks him.

"*Un' amica.*"

She tilts her head, studying me. I must pass inspection because she smiles, squeezing both of his cheeks. Without another word she waves us to sit, rattling something off in Italian.

I slide into the center of the circular booth and Colin follows, sitting so close his leg is pressed against mine. He brings my hand to his mouth, brushing his lips over my knuckles and my heart constricts.

Our waiter appears from around the corner. "*Buongiorno*, my name is Anthony and I'll be serving you this evening."

Colin's eyes never stray from my face as he orders a bottle of chardonnay.

"You come here often." I state the obvious and watch his brow fall, adding a grim nod.

"It's been years," he says, looking around the small room as if to remember the long-ago visits.

"Tell me," I prompt.

It's takes a minute, but finally he sighs. "My wife and I would eat here when we were in New York. It was one of my favorite places...." He trails off, and his eyes reconnect with mine.

I stare, not sure what I should say or how I feel about it. "Will you tell me about her? What was she like?"

"I...."

Anthony saves him by returning with bruschetta and wine, which he pours in front of us. "Is there anything more I can get for you?" he asks.

"Nothing at the moment. Thank you," Colin says, rubbing his forehead as if it hurts.

I sip from my glass, spicy with a hint of vanilla, and watch him above the rim.

"Charlie," he starts again, "I didn't bring you here because I want to talk about her. I haven't been to Rosa's in a long time; they have excellent food. I thought you might like it too."

"I want to know you, Colin. She's a huge part of who you are: the love you had for her, the time you spent together, your loss, they've all shaped who you are today."

The mask settles in place, the expressionless expression, as he unlocks our hands. Elbow on the table, he sighs. "Abby. Her name was Abby." His head drops and he focuses on the empty plate in front of him. "I knew Ella from college; we both volunteered to work on a local campaign. She invited a group of us to a fundraiser sponsored by her family. Abby was there. I thought she was different from everyone else. She didn't cave to her parents' high-society social demands; she was more of a free spirit. John always considered her a rebel." He laughs, a hard, brittle sound.

"Go on," I prompt.

"What else do you want to know?" he snaps. "It's in the past; she's gone."

I don't want to push him, but I have questions. "How long were you married?"

"Two years."

"How did she die?"

He blows out a breath. "In a car accident."

"I'm sorry." And I am. I know his anguish. I've felt it and lived through the years it takes to recover into a new reality after someone is forever gone.

"Abby is a difficult topic for me to discuss," he admits. "I don't want to bring her into our night together, please. I really did bring you here because I like it, not because she did."

"Is she the reason you're complicated?"

His mouth pulls up at the corner. "You could say that. I feel like my whole life is complex. My marriage is certainly a contributing factor, and then there's my career. Both of those things make it nearly impossible for me to have a normal relationship." His voice houses a certain level of hopelessness I deeply wish I could erase; yet I don't understand why these two things hurt him so much.

"You equate the complications of your life to your ability to have a relationship?"

"A normal one," he clarifies.

"What's normal?"

He shrugs. "A wife, a dog, 2.5 kids, living in a subdivision in Middle America with a minivan and a white picket fence."

I laugh. "So, why can't you do normal?"

"Charlie," he levels his eyes at me, "this is exactly one of the reasons why I'm drawn to you." He finds my hand again, squeezing it against his thigh. "You see beyond pretenses, but in this case there are truths that can't be overlooked or forgotten. If all goes as planned I'll reside in the White House for the next eight years. There is no subdivision surrounding 1600 Pennsylvania Avenue. That's a big complication."

"So you're missing one out of seven; a wife, a dog, and kids are all possible. In technical terms, Middle America refers to the territory between the East Coast of the United States and the West Coast. So if we go with that definition, The White House is a part of it. And I think you could put one hell of a white picket fence up around the lawn. You would be, after all, the president of United States, with the most absolute power. I have no doubt you could make a new fence possible. Don't let that be an obstacle to the life you want to live."

His mouth splits into a beautiful smile. "In the matter of a minute you have been able to simplify what I thought was one of my most complicated challenges. Thank you."

I love how his face lights up and that I can make it happen. But his reason for it saddens me. "Are you serious? Do you really doubt you'll ever find love again?"

He sobers immediately. "I doubt I'll ever trust enough to fully love again, Charlie. That's the crux of many of my complications. I know this statement doesn't make sense to you and it's not something I'm willing to go into detail about. I can only tell you for years the women in my life were more interested in what I could offer them versus who I am."

"Raquel?"

He nods. "Yes, like Raquel. Her infatuation was with a United States senator who would one day seek the presidency, not the man behind the job."

I can understand now why he feels hopeless, if this is the type of women he's surrounded by.

"You're being awfully open tonight." I'm rewarded with another stunning grin.

"I meant what I said this morning; I want to be with you. For it to happen I realize I need to open up. I'm hell-bent on doing that and getting to know you too." My pulse hammers in my throat. I want to interpret his words as a reassurance that we can have more than just one day at a time. But that's impossible and I suck down a gulp of wine to move past the silly burst of hope.

"Now it's my turn; I want to know about you," he says, tilting his head to find my eyes. "Tell me about your family and your childhood. I want to know everything."

Hair on my nape bristles. "Everything?"

"Yes, details. Where did you grow up?"

How do I start? So much of my life is vague and undefined. "I lived in Brighton until I was eight. Just me and my parents, it was the three of us. Our house was small and white with green shutters on either side of the front window. I'll never forget that." I clutch my stomach as it turns over. I very rarely let myself fall back into these memories. "We didn't have much. My dad worked on the assembly line. I think the only new thing he ever brought home was a Buick LeSabre. My mom was proud of him, and how hard he worked to get it," I say quietly.

"You're close to your parents?" It's a question, but it's said almost as a statement.

"Yes, my whole family. I wouldn't have survived without them." I cringe, knowing right away I've said too much.

His brow draws down. "Explain."

I close my eyes and breathe through a replay I struggle to put back on its mental shelf. Claustrophobia and the grating crunch of metal crowd my mind. "The mom and dad I have now adopted me when I was fourteen. My biological parents were killed by a drunk driver. In the new car, we went for a ride…."

Shit. I drain the rest of my wine and Colin fills my glass as soon as it's on the table. The accident is one of the memories I buried, very rarely contemplating how it shaped the rest of my life. "I spent the next couple of months in the hospital. When I was healthy enough to go home, there wasn't a home to go to; I had no relatives to take me in. I spent the next six years as a ward of the state." Muscles in my neck strain with tension as I mention foster care.

"The Carters had two biological children, my brothers Ian and Sammy. My mom always wanted a large family, and after Sammy was born she couldn't have any more babies because of complications during his delivery. They began to foster children. That right there places them in the saint category, if you ask me. They had a few different babies, who were short-term placements. It was heartbreaking for my mom to let them go when their families were ready, so they decided to look into adoption. Ali was placed with them first and she begged them to take me too. Ali can talk anyone into just about anything; she's very persistent." I laugh at such a huge understatement. She was told by more than a handful of teachers she wasn't smart enough for medical school, that she would never get accepted to one program, let alone every one she applied to. Challenge Ali and she will win.

"So that's it. The Carters took me in, they loved me and I fell in love with them. It didn't happen overnight; there were some rough patches along the way, but they are the best thing that has ever happened to me."

Colin leans in to brush a kiss on my cheek and then he whispers, "That was hard, I know. Thank you for sharing a piece of yourself with me."

I grab his lapel, holding him close for a moment longer as emotion clogs my throat. *There's so much more.* It's on the tip of my tongue, but I stay silent and cling to him. His mouth finds mine, light at first, sweet. But it changes to a hard, biting need. I grab his neck as his tongue lashes against mine, deep licks, and then he releases me, panting. Our foreheads rest together.

"Charlie," he groans.

I smile and pepper kisses against his mouth. "That was the best distraction."

His hand lands on my thigh, fingers digging in and kneading.

"Tell me something else. Ali. She's special to you?"

I lean away. "Life becomes lonely when there isn't a constant person to hold on to, to talk to as you're bumped from family to family. Ali and I met when we were placed with the same foster family, and we became inseparable. She's confident, outgoing, funny, and gorgeous." I get the warm and fuzzies as I think of her. "Ali protected me then and she supports me now."

"Where does she live?"

"She's finishing her residency program at Georgetown Medical School in DC."

"You miss her."

"Very much, but she's found her passion. I'm proud of her for that."

"What's your passion, Charlie?" His voice turns into warm caramel, smooth.

I've never thought about it before. My life is traditional, boring to most, and it happens like clockwork. Laundry on Monday, dinner with Gram and Mom on Tuesdays, video games with Sammy and Ian on Thursday, Sunday dinner with the whole family, and working in between. Stability has been enough for a long time. But I keep coming back to *more*—something just for me. "Finding happiness. For a long while when I was a child that was a struggle."

"Are you happy now?"

That's the second time he's asked me this question. "For the most part, yes."

His brow digs into three lines between his eyes. "You live alone?"

"Yes."

"No boyfriends?"

I laugh. "No, none."

"How is it someone hasn't persuaded you to enter into the fine constitution of marriage, Charlie?"

"Easy," I say with a smile. "Because I haven't fallen in love."

Our eyes lock for what seems like an eternity. I have never been afraid of the future, because in foster care it didn't seem like I'd have one. When I was adopted, each day became my focus, not what might happen tomorrow. Now, with Colin, the future beckons to me. I know the odds that he'll be a part of my forever are slim to none, but in a way he's already included. He will always be in my heart as the first man I've opened myself to. So, while I look into the deep pools of blue, I let him see me and a glimpse into a fairy tale I never hoped to live. I dream of my own picket fence and the possibility of a relationship where I'm loved and I give love in return. I let him see how just the possibility of it flushes my cheeks.

He watches the impossible fantasy filter through my mind, never looking away. Eventually he opens his mouth, but he says nothing, only tilts his head and remains contemplative.

After a minute, he leans forward. “What’s your favorite color?” A grin spreads, digging a dimple into his cheek.

“Hmm.” I smile. “Magenta.”

“Magenta.”

“Yes, a cross between red and purple; it’s beautiful.”

Lifting his wine glass, he watches me above the rim.

I can’t help the shiver spreading down my spine. I’m amazed he can seduce me with a look, a hot, sexy, shiver-inducing, dark-eyed look. It makes me giggle and he motions for Anthony so we can begin the next part of our night.

TEN

NEW YORK CITY IS strangely quiet, with only a few pedestrians racing by. Fat snowflakes fall, layering a white blanket over the muted gray tones of the city. I stop to look up at the sky, wondering at the beauty of the moment and at the heavens for creating it.

Colin is slow in his approach. He grabs me by the hips and stares down into my face. It's easy to be with him, and so is my smile when he leans down to press his mouth against mine. Closing my eyes, I focus on his touch, the soft fullness of his lips, and the heat radiating from beneath his coat.

He becomes more persistent, forcing his tongue inside my mouth in deep lashing licks. I groan and rake my hands through his hair. A chill shakes my body and I can't be certain if it's from his kiss or the cool air.

"Let's get you inside," he murmurs. In another block we're received into the warmth of the lobby. It's a welcome haven from the snow that, if the bellboy standing next to me can be believed, will disable the East Coast for the next twenty-four hours.

It's a good thing our luggage is already delivered because Colin glares at the poor guy and he shrinks away. He's quiet on our ride to the eleventh floor and then to his suite. I wish I could climb into his mind, understand what takes him from light and fun-loving to the troubled, introspective man standing next to me.

How easily the road traveled has led to a shared room. My bags sit close to his with an assumption we'd be together. Laying his coat on the couch, he walks to the bar for brandy. Tipping a glass in my direction, he says, "It'll warm you up."

I nod and turn to the fascinating winter wonderland coming to life outside the window.

In seconds I have my drink, the heat of his chest is at my back, and my pulse races. My eyes move to the amber liquid, the same color as the unique sliver in his left eye. I sip, and moan as it goes down. It sears a delicious molten path to my stomach, a lot like Colin, warming all over.

And then it's gone, ripped from my hand. He sets the glasses down and I'm in his arms. My gasp is muffled by his lips and I want him with an instant urgency.

Once in the bedroom he loosens his hold on my legs, but my hands are nestled in his hair and I cling to him, feet barely skimming the floor. Colin's touch is tempting, seductive as he removes everything between us—nothing separates him from me and we come together, skin against skin. Enfolding me in his arms, he worships my mouth with his; my body heats under his touch as he caresses every whispered shadow.

He captures my groan, taking it in to mix with his. I whimper as he kisses across my cheek to my ear and down my neck, nibbling at the hollow above my collarbone.

My hands move: they're everywhere, his shoulders, arms, running over the hard lines of his back. Everything he does taunts the wicked pulse between my thighs.

Without warning, he pushes me to the bed, but he doesn't follow. His breath falters as he gazes. Slow and deliberate, his inspection is thorough and his voice rough. "God, I want you. Just the thought of you gets me hard."

I can't help but stare at his rock-hard erection. His hand follows my eyes, stroking up and down. "Seeing you naked in my bed, wanting me as much as I want you, is almost too much," he whispers and his eyes change. The passionate need is replaced with veneration, a worshiping glint as he drinks me in.

"Charlie," he breathes into the silence, my name a prayer on his lips. Slowly he lies with me, bringing a hand up to cup the full weight of my breast. Closing his eyes, he leans in so his mouth hovers over mine, not touching, just taking. It's so intimate, but I want to kiss him.

"Colin," I whisper and the word breaks the spell.

When his eyes open, a devilish gleam replaces the adoration. He pinches my nipple, pulling it until I moan. The sweet sensation drives straight down to my groin, a sharp, inescapable fluttering. He smiles, a slow, beguiling grin as I writhe beneath his dark stare and the attention of his fingers.

"I'm going to taste you, baby. Lick and bite you until you scream my name."

My mouth forms a perfect *O* but I say nothing, paralyzed with anticipation. I watch as he dips down, taking me into his mouth, laving thc elongated tip of my breast with his tongue before teasing it between his teeth. I lean back into the bed, reeling from the pleasure his mouth brings. One at a time, he plays with my breasts until I'm wet and hungry for him.

"Please," I beg for I don't know what. For him to continue, for him to touch me, for him to bring an end to the burning need building between my thighs. Slowly he moves, his nose trailing along my skin, teasing a path until he presses into the small patch of hair, groaning as he breathes deeply. Eyes trained on mine, he pushes my thighs apart.

"You're intoxicating." His voice is hot, his breath hotter as he blows against me. Looking up through his lashes, he asks, "Do you want this, baby? Tell me you need this as much as I do." I'm speechless, so he blows against me again. "Say it; I need to hear you."

"Yes," I barely breathe out before his head dips, the tip of his tongue swirling around my clitoris. My body arches off the bed at the sweet carnal sensation, and I moan loudly. Closing my eyes, I focus on him, and the tormenting flicks of his tongue.

Wrapping his arms under my hips, he becomes impassioned, groaning as he lifts me to his mouth. I can't move, my only outlet the incoherent words falling almost soundlessly into the still air. Clenching my hands into the shccts, I surrender to the beautiful intensity, panting.

"Colin," I cry. His lips close around my clitoris in response, sucking and rolling it between his teeth. I arch and instinctively move with him, a wicked, slow dance. The music is his mouth, playing artfully, and all I can do is wait, longing for the crescendo. Releasing my death grip on the sheets, I grab the soft silk of his hair as his head sways between my thighs. He looks up, eyes scorching and erotic, his tongue insistent and hot, teasing but not taking me over the edge.

"Please," I whisper, begging for the push from the burning plateau.

His answer is to slide a finger inside my welcoming body. I groan again. The longing and desire build, the friction of his finger along with his mouth take me higher, faster than I thought possible. I writhe against him, the dance becoming feverish. I need; I want.

"Don't stop." Two fingers plunge into me once, twice, his tongue flicks and rolls again and again, and he launches me beyond the brink. I explode, screaming out in awe as the crescendo hits violently. Waves of pleasure crash through my entire body and I bow into him once more. His mouth and fingers continue moving on me, in me, pushing my orgasm on and on.

When I can stand it no more, I tug his hair, pulling him up to me. Diving into his mouth, I taste myself on his tongue, relishing the feel of his lips stroking over mine. Without thought, I grab his bottom lip between my teeth, sucking on it, mimicking what he just did to me. Drinking in his low moan, I spur him on for more.

"What do you want, baby?"

"I want you."

"What do you need?" he taunts me again.

"You, always you—now," I say, pulling him to me.

In one swift move he enters me and I cry out as my body acclimates to the invasion. Before I can form a coherent thought, Colin rolls so I'm on top, straddling his hips. His erection reaches inside of me in a new way, a full tormenting stretch. We groan together when I rotate my hips, deepening the penetration. Our eyes lock, the intensity staggering.

Leaning down, I place my hands on either side of his face, cradling him tenderly. My mouth hovers over his, not touching, just taking. Taking him into me every way I know how. His breath, his body, we become one, and I begin to make love with Colin McKenna—sweet, beautiful, passionate love. I feel it all. I feel all of him. My hips move, rounding gently at first, pulling him in and out at a taunting, tortuous pace. Our breath mingles together, held tight against us as our bodies join, again and again, over and over.

In time I push up, sitting on him fully so he sinks in further, a new humbling depth that has us both groaning again in unison. Our rhythm changes, needing, wanting, an inexplicable desire to come together we move passionately. The joy in this moment, in us, is achingly sweet.

"Colin," I whisper as our eyes meet, his a deep blue, mine bewildered by the staggering emotion I feel toward this man. This man, who has unleashed years of unknown, pent-up desire. My thoughts scatter, frayed with unbridled tension, and I dissolve around him, mind and body surrendering to the mystifying connection.

I cry out as his hips push me higher, rocketing with him, trusting in wherever he takes me, and I come. I erupt around him, vaguely hearing his cry as he joins me. We are one; we are us.

My breath shattered, I fall, splayed out on his chest. His hands wrap into my hair, holding me tight as our bodies calm. Eventually he pulls my lips to his, kissing me gently. We breathe into each other, sated.

I DON'T KNOW HOW long we lie wrapped together. My limbs are like jelly. Incapable of holding myself upright, I stay snuggled into his side. Colin rubs my back, his fingers soft on my bare skin. Finally I look up, gauging his reaction to make sure I don't lose him to dark thoughts like I did the first time. His eyes are closed and he looks relaxed. His cheeks are soft, his jaw isn't clenched as it sometimes gets when he's tense. He opens one eye, smiles, and opens the other to fully look at me. Before I can say anything he grips under my arms to bring my lips to his.

I lean back to look at him and slip my hand through the wayward curls disheveled from my grip. Brushing my mouth against his, once and then again, I snuggle back into his arms, but I'm not cocooned in his warmth for long. He slides out from beneath me; leaning on his elbow, he stares while I lie flat on my back. I immediately cover my breasts, but he stops my hands.

"I want to look at you," he says, smiling. And he does, every curve and inch of my body. "You're so beautiful, a work of art created just for me." Sliding the backs of his fingers from my temple to chin, he trails a blazing path down my neck, following the contour of my breast and circling my nipple. It grows taut from his now familiar touch. My breathing spikes. His eyes seek mine, watching my reaction when he pinches it.

I groan. "You're driving me crazy." I mean it, too; the slickness between my thighs is a testament to the fact.

Colin chuckles, a sexy throaty sound, and says, "Don't move."

He cups the fullness of my breast, weighing it in his hand. "So soft, so perfect," he whispers, squeezing and kneading.

Moving to my stomach, he draws a circular path around the planes of my abdomen, getting lost in his own thoughts. His fingers come to a sudden halt.

I grab his chin, forcing his gaze to meet mine. "Hey, don't go anywhere. I want you to stay with me." For the briefest moment his eyes widen. There's vulnerability within them and then he's gone. He becomes blank, shutting down and shutting me out.

I sense his internal struggle against falling back into his comfortable pain. Clenching his jaw, he rolls onto his back and breaks all contact with me. His lids close tight and my heart lurches in my chest; I know his pattern now. As soon as he lets go, gets close to me, he withdraws or tries to push me away.

I'm not going to let that happen so I scramble onto my knees beside him. Grabbing his chin, I mimic his stern tone, "Colin, look at me." He doesn't move, his chest moving up and down evenly. He lifts his hands to press the palms against his eyes, long fingers covering his forehead, reaching into his tousled hair. "Talk to me."

It's heartbreaking to see such a strong, passionate man splintered in this way; unable or unwilling to move beyond the misery he's convinced he should live with. After a moment of silence I lose my patience. "You are an obstinate, confusing man!" I think his lip lifts in hint of a smile, but I can't be sure.

"I'm going to be honest with you, and if you get mad so be it. I'd rather fight for you than let you slip away with a ghost. Abby is gone." Her name stings my tongue. "Her death was tragic; I can't imagine the pain you endured. She died five years ago, Colin; you were thirty-one years old. I can only presume to know the love she had for you, and with that, Abby would not have wanted you to suffer her death your whole life. You loved her; it's okay to let her go."

His brooding silence slices my heart with each passing minute. Getting frustrated, I pull against one of his arms and he allows me to move it easily, lifting his other so his wary eyes can open. Kneeling naked by his side, I grasp his hand and wait for him to speak.

"It's much easier not to feel anything," he says finally, "rather than put trust in myself again." His jaw clenches as he contemplates his thoughts. "It's hard for me to let go of what happened, forget the past and trust what I feel when I'm with you. I can't relive the pain I experienced; it almost broke me." On a sigh, he continues. "When I'm with you, Charlie, I forget about everything. I forget about Abby and what happened. I feel alive again."

I wish I knew how to help him. "I'm not Abby." My voice wavers when I say it. "What happened to her isn't going to happen with me." Longing to touch him, I gently stroke down his cheek, running my thumb along his full bottom lip.

"You deserve to be happy, Colin."

He winces. "I need to learn how to count on someone again; I haven't allowed myself the opportunity to get close to anyone in a very long time. It's not something I ever thought I would willingly do. It's easier not to feel than to risk feeling pain at the level to which I was injured with Abby."

"I'm not the woman you fell in love with ten years ago. My future is not tied to Abby, just as my past is different from hers. Maybe it's time to take a leap of faith. Believe in me." I sound desperate even to my own ears. For an inexplicable reason, I need him to believe in me.

He remains silent, considering my words for a long moment. "Remember what you said to me?" I have his attention now; his brow furrows in question. "You told me you could offer me one moment, one day at a time. Well, I want tonight. Will you give me tonight, Colin? All night?"

He sits up, his chest an inch from my breasts. Digging his fingers into my hair, he holds me still, his thumb rubbing over my bottom lip. Our eyes remain connected as he answers me with a sweet kiss. I lean in, parting my mouth to accept his tongue. Falling back to the bed, he takes me with him, covering his body with mine in a blanket of heat.

CONSCIOUS THOUGHT INVADES MY dream and brings the morning with it. Colin's breath warms my ear. His head is tucked into the crook of my neck, as if he fell asleep kissing me. The blanket is pushed below my waist by his arm lying across my stomach. Closing my eyes, thoughts of the night flood in and flames burn my cheeks. His mouth tasted every part of me. He gave me everything and more than I thought possible.

I still don't quite understand why this breathtaking, gorgeous man wants to be with me, but at this very moment I've decided not to care. If we can manage to be together privately then my past won't interfere with his future and we can love through the night and work professionally in the day. A frown mars my perfect morning as thoughts drift to the reality of that possibility. The *reality* is I'm no good for him. I've gotten lost in all of Colin's complications and forgotten my own. So what if he learns to trust me, when I'm keeping the secret of a lifetime? I could destroy him and his long-sought position. I can't lose sight of that again.

One day at a time, Charlie, I repeat my mantra. If I have to I'll leave to save him. I won't be the reason he isn't elected president.

Muted light filters in through the window, so I'm unable to gauge the time. I slide out of bed, slipping his discarded shirt around my shoulders as I cross the room to push back the curtain. Holy cow, it's still snowing. Now it's falling at a forty-five degree angle, heavy sheets of winter white marring visibility. The streets are empty, the city brought to heel by a blizzard.

Warm arms slide around my stomach, pulling me into a wall of muscle. *And good morning to you too, Mr. McKenna.* I smile as he leans in, kissing my neck while my hands smooth over the bare skin of his hips. Oh, I like naked Colin.

"Mmm," I murmur, rolling my head to his shoulder to open myself to his lips and teeth. It's so nice to wake up with him. Who am I kidding? It was so nice to spend the night with him. I giggle as he turns me around.

"Something funny?" he asks, his right brow lifting.

"I was just thinking about last night," I say, my smile faltering as his eyes darken.

Crap, did I wound his ego? "Last night was *funny*?" He pushes his growing erection in to my abdomen.

"No, I would never...." I can't think, let alone form words, when he does it again.

"I'll show you just how funny I can be."

And he does, twice. Once on the desk and then bent over the back of the couch. For the love of all that's holy, the man has stamina and mad skills.

Still breathing heavy with his chest to my back, he says, "Jesus, Charlie. You make me crazy...." Kissing across my shoulders in a pattern known only to him, he grips my hips. I moan as he rocks into me and mumbles something about starting the day.

He slips free and I immediately miss the fullness, but he tugs me up and leads me into a huge bath with three showerheads. The water runs to hot before he pulls me in behind him.

"Wash my back?" His smile is sweet as he offers me the soap and turns to grab the shampoo.

"With pleasure, Senator." As he starts on his hair, I lean on my tiptoes to kiss his shoulder, resting my cheek there as the spray cascades over us. It's amazing how my life has changed in one week. I'm strong and sexy and happy. Happier than I'd ever thought possible. I smile and wrap my arms around his waist, squeezing.

I don't know when he finds time to work out, but his body is proof he does. Releasing him, I wash the round and defined muscles on his shoulders and then around to the hard expanse of his chest. When I rub his nipples, he growls and I smile. I spend more time than necessary washing his hips and the sleek planes of his ass, just because I can.

"Like what you see, baby?" He chuckles while I keep washing.

"Mmhmm," I murmur. To stop his laughter, I reach around to his abdomen and sink further down. His head tips back on a sharp inhale as my fingers run over his length and down between his legs. I don't tease him for long, falling to my knees to wash his legs.

Standing when I'm done, I murmur, "Mission accomplished," into his skin and hug him tight. Colin turns. I reach for his hair and pull him down for a kiss.

As he begins to break away, a last-minute decision has me jumping up and wrapping my legs around his waist. He laughs into my mouth and grips my butt to hold me so I don't fall. I smile too, kissing him again and then his chin, moving to his rough cheek.

"Do you really have to go?" I pretend pout, my bottom lip pushing out like he does sometimes.

He leans in and takes it between his teeth. "I do, for a little while this morning to meet with John and Evan. The weather has changed our plans so we need to get our schedule adjusted." He pinches my ass. "Then I'll come back to keep you company."

Knowing I've been defeated and he's going to leave, I hold on and drop my legs. "Come back soon," I whisper in his ear.

"You can be sure of it, baby. I'll order breakfast while you finish up." He kisses me on the lips and I pout, for real this time, when he gets out of the shower. I watch through the glass door as he towels off, first his hair, rubbing it with both hands, and then his body. Everywhere I touched, the lucky cotton does the same. If he could see my eyes now, they'd be pathetic pools of envy. Damn towel.

When the show's over, I find renewed vigor to join him. Hair shampooed and conditioned, and body washed, I rush to dress. Because I'll be alone for most of the day I wear just my panties, a long sweater, and the moisturizer smoothing my legs into a high shine.

Colin's on the couch, laptop open in front of him on the coffee table and phone to his ear. He's casual in a pair of jeans, with a white T-shirt molded to his chest. I try not to get lost in the visual stimulant that is Colin McKenna, moving to the fresh coffee brewing nearby.

He tracks my progress and I smile as he does. It's invigorating to know he finds my body attractive. I've never thought of it as sexy, and I love that he does.

Pouring two cups, I deliver one to him. There is a certain amount of sweet contentment in his eyes, yet they always house the slightest hint of sadness as if he's never quite whole. I wonder about this; is it because of Abby? The baby? Just as I'm about to sit with my coffee, a knock sounds at the door. I jump to open it.

"Charlie!" he says, as if in warning.

I expect room service, yet Ella Montgomery's hostile gaze greets me instead. She looks over my wet hair and her lip curves in a snarl as she meets the end of my sweater and the beginning of my bare legs.

ELEVEN

"YOU THINK YOU'RE special, don't you?" Ella spews in her hateful tone. "Don't fool yourself; you're no different than any of the others. I told you to stay away from him; obviously you're not a very good listener." Taking another glance at my body, she seethes. "You'll never be able to hold him; even you have to know that. Look at him and look at you." She chuckles under her breath. "You're nothing. Absolutely nothing. "

"That's enough." Colin's voice is rough as he cuts Ella with a biting glare. He softens when he finds my eyes, trying to end his call. I glance away when John Montgomery follows his daughter in. Holy shit, I didn't know breakfast was for four. Humiliation paints me pink. I feel it burn up my chest as I stand half dressed in front of the two people in the world who find me repulsive.

"Excuse me," I mutter, and stumble toward the bedroom. Closing the door behind me, I pay little attention to the muted voices on the other side. Staring wide-eyed, I let the floor blur as I wait for the commotion to quell and consider what to do. Should I get dressed and return? *No thanks; I'll save myself from that bit of torture*.

How quickly my light mood crashes around me. I absently rub my palm where the sliver from the coffee mug sliced through. Colin's world is so complex and mine is not. I once told him I like simple things: beer and baseball games. His life is filled with wine, tuxedos, and the people who go along with them.

"Charlie?" He hesitates at the threshold of the room.

I stay still as he sits next to me on the bed. Taking my chin in hand, he lifts it so I have to make eye contact.

"Don't worry about Ella. She's not used to seeing me with someone."

"Why didn't you tell me they were coming here?" I whisper.

"I didn't know they were. I only knew it couldn't be room service because I had just placed the call."

"I'm embarrassed." My voice trembles. "I don't want them to hate me and I can't understand why they do."

He sighs. "They don't hate you. John and Ella don't understand why I'm with you."

"Isn't it the same thing?" I ask incredulously.

"No, it's not. For their own reasons they're unwilling to allow me to move past Abby."

"I don't think that's it," I interrupt. "They don't want you to move past Abby with me. If they approved of who you were with they would support you."

"That's not true."

My anger is tipped. I rip my hand from his and walk to the other side of the room. "Yes, it is, Colin; don't lie to yourself. You can't tell me if you were fucking Ella she wouldn't be shouting it out to the nearest newspaper, publishing it on your website. Ella soon-to-be McKenna would be flashing in neon lights."

His brow furrows with his own anger, but I'm not sure if it's aimed at me, or the accuracy of my words. He knows it's the truth. Standing, he moves before me, grabbing my chin once again. "I'm not with Ella."

"Were you ever with her?"

He pauses and I know it's true. My heart sinks before he confirms my fear.

"Just once and it was a mistake." His voice is low, as if he wishes he could take it back; the confirmation or the act itself, I don't know.

"When?"

"Just after Abby died. I regretted it the minute it happened. I was in a very bad place."

"Do you want her now?" I choke out the question.

“God no, Charlie. I have no desire to be with her.”

There is a certain amount of relief from his words, yet I know she wants him and it’s why she hates me. I have him now and she does not. “Tell that to her,” I bite out. “I don’t expect warm and fuzzy, but I do expect civility.”

I can’t compete with women like Ella Montgomery; she was right about that. Colin once told me he has little to offer, which I would dispute at every turn. On the flip side, the truth is I don’t offer him anything other than a secret mistress only a select few will ever be aware of.

My eyes connect with his; worry laces his brow and it makes my anger subside. “I’m not afraid to have this conversation with her; I just want to have pants on when I do it.”

He chuckles, leaning down to kiss me. “I’ll take care of Ella and John. Keep your pants off, baby; I like you just the way you are.”

I only hesitate a second, his mouth is too tempting to fall victim to my wallowing. Just as we dive into each other, there’s another knock on the door.

“Breakfast,” he mumbles against my lips. With a brush of his mouth to mine, he leaves me wishing for something more.

HOURS PASS AND SNOW falls, taking my optimism with it. With Colin gone, I’ve written my blog piece, updated the schedule from information Evan sent via email thirty minutes ago. Pictures followed. Working at the desk reminds me of Colin and more often than not, my eyes stray to the blinding white light pouring through the window to think about the current state of affairs. My vision blurs as do the lines defining what *this* is. For me, not him.

Separation and boundaries are harder than I thought. Colin has more experience, a wealth of knowledge to help him separate real feelings from sex, not a relationship, fucking, not love and maybe not even friendship. A strange state of intimacy and a new vulnerability is confusing me. I want to belong. To him? Not possible. But with his people, in the world he lives in. Maybe. I'm familiar with insecurity and staring from the outside in. Foster care does that. A quick succession of families and as many schools didn't grow attachments, it drove me into myself until I was the definition of introvert. I existed.

Each year post adoption, I found more of myself and bit by bit put the pieces of Charlie Carter together. Although I still like to watch and assess, I'm involved, maybe not bursting with happiness, but content as I step through life. I don't open doors to anger like I did this morning. My well-thought-out and planned adult path has become a roller coaster, a thrilling ride I've enjoyed. But now I've hit the slow crank as I near the peak of a steep climb, one minute notches into the next and I'm afraid of the downhill slide I'm about to take.

Ella hates me. So does John for that matter. A veritable fountain of animosity oozes off them with every interaction. The question gnawing at me is why do I care? It's important for Colin to respect me, casual or not, but the family he used to belong to shouldn't affect me. Yet the message his former sister-in-law spouted is hard to part with: *you're no different than any of the others.*

As one of or *the* most eligible bachelors in the United States, Colin is a wanted man. Women desire him, including me. I've joined the ranks of Ella and Raquel Meyers. Both of whom want him back. When he walks away will I? Months from now I'll be relegated to Michigan with a loaded bank account and memories. Because she's right, I'm the latest in the lion's food chain with many more meals to come.

I mull on that as the sky unloads its own burden.

Moments pass as an ache takes up space in my chest. *I don't belong here.* Nothing but a deep craving to fill up my thoughts with something other than the truth moves my fingers to type Facebook in the waiting search engine. When it opens, I flip through the long list of comments on Colin's page. Most are positive and the others pose questions about campaign stops. I work on answers and updates and then notice a message in the inbox which is strange because I thought I'd disabled the option to do so. The internet connection slips and it takes a minute for the mail to pop up. An unknown sender, Sara Abbott, presents a simple statement.

I know who you are and what you did.

My heart thrums out of control just like my thoughts. Me or him? It's Colin's page but an account I created for him. And what could he have done? Mr. McPerfect is squeaky clean. Or is he? I don't know much about the man who I lie next to at night. Only what he shares because true to my word I haven't researched him. I've let him feed me information pertinent to his campaign, his beliefs, and the man behind the presidential persona. Colin wants me to know him for who he is, not what the media has created. I get that. Actions and words are interpreted by each person through their own filter and beliefs.

I gulp down a lump and fight my hammering pulse screaming *it's me*. The realization prickles at my nape. But more probably it's an opponents' supporter submitting a scare tactic. It may have worked. The once crisp edges of a simple sentence fade as I get lost in the fog of *I don't belong here*. Time seems to cease, one moment blends to the next and a cold sweat breaks out on my forehead. It's a familiar numbness.

A crash in the hall snaps my eyes into focus. Voices, laughter, the giddiness of happy strangers snowed in, jars me awake. I click on Sara Abbott's account and find it's clearly a pseudonym, with no attached personal information. The account was created the same day the message was sent. I take a screen shot and then delete it from the page.

Standing, I stagger my way into the bedroom, jamming my shoulder against the doorframe as I enter. A sharp breath scrapes my throat. The pain reverberates down my arm and I massage the sting away with my eyes closed. Behind my lids the gap between Colin and I grows wider. We're on opposing teams, he the refined millionaire vying for the highest seat in political office. Intense, confident, brilliant and poised, Colin McKenna didn't ask for my feelings to get involved. But they are, they're winding up and around his legs in a vine of *please let this be the more I've been waiting for*. I recognize the clinging necessity, the desperate connection; it's similar to when I found Ali but bigger. A deep tug that says this is exactly who I need.

"Damn, damn, damn," I cry to the empty room and sink to my knees.

I open to find all of the clothes Colin stripped from me the night before strewn around my legs. The silk camisole slides through my fingers and images of last night spark in my mind like a slide show: dinner, falling snow flakes, his mouth, the color of brandy and the dark sky, his hands, his grip, my heart as it explodes when he makes me come. But more than anything, it's the sick sense of completion I have whenever I'm with him. I laugh, a crazy brash snicker. So foolish, juvenile really, to have dreamed up this fairytale link with a man who told me we have no future together.

But knowing it doesn't stop me from grabbing his worn T-shirt from the floor. I shove it in my face like it's the antidote to the poisonous apple the wicked sister-in-law tempted me with this morning. My eyelids flutter while gluttonous drags of air soothe me in sandalwood and Colin.

I don't want to go, but I don't know how to stay.

Not when I know *this* will end with me rocking in a corner as fifteen years of pent-up-tears rip my soul in two.

"Charlie?"

Fuck, my pulse explodes and a scream jams in my esophagus.

"What—" Colin crouches to bring us eye to eye. His brow crumples as he takes me in, panting from his sneak attack with his shirt pressed to my nose. "Are you okay?"

I blink away his worry and drop my chin, smothering myself in white cotton and hoping he gives me a moment to formulate a response.

Tension seeps into the silence and grows each second until he demands, "Talk to me."

God, this is hard. And so is his face, when I peek from behind my shield: rigid lines of muscle tense as he grinds his jaw. "I don't belong here," I whisper.

He shakes his head, as if this is a surprise. "Why would you think that?"

"We come from different worlds. You're Ivy League, and I'm bowling league. I can't compete with women like Ella or Raquel." Pushing to my feet, I leave the piece of him behind and step to the far side of the room. Distance, it's what I need to think and purge the impulse to throw myself at him and hold on for the rest of my life. "I'm not strong enough to do this, be with you without caring, to give you my nights but not my heart. I thought I could." My voice quivers as emotion closes in, tears are not too far behind the runaway thump battering my ribcage. "But I was wrong."

He stands. A million miles could be between us but I would feel the weight of his stare, determined, verging on dangerous as he stalks forward. My head tips back as my hands come up to stop him a foot away.

"If I stay I'll get hurt, and so will you. I can't take that chance," I whisper.

Pain slices across his features before his mask falls into place and I want to take it back, press rewind and rework the words. "You believe I'll hurt you?" Incredulity clouds his tone.

My shoulders slump. "Not on purpose, no, but Colin," I reach for his hand and it's a bad idea. The strength in his fingers, the soothing heat as he wraps them through mine is as natural as the sun rising, weakens my message. "This morning with Ella, I realized I will always be the woman hiding in the bedroom you have to explain away to someone who's been in your life forever, the people who belong there. I don't. I'm a girl from Michigan playing mistress with a powerful man. I don't have the confidence needed to survive in your world and not be broken when it's time for me to leave it."

"Do you trust me, Charlie?"

My skin tingles all over. "You know I do."

He crowds into me, wrapping my trapped hand behind my back and bringing us hip to hip. Enveloped by his heat, and all things Colin, I sigh and relax into his embrace. "I want less Ivy League in my life." He tries to smile, but the curve of his mouth falls before it reaches anywhere but sadness. "I don't want to lose you. Give me time, I'll try." He licks his bottom lip and then he tugs on it with his teeth. "I'm not perfect, baby, and God knows I've already hurt you. But I'm willing to put the effort in to make this work. Thoughts of you rise to the top of the thousands of things I have left to do. You're important to me."

Crap, my knees weaken. I wiggle my hand free and then wrap them both around his neck. He tries on a grin and it breaks into a small dimple that vanishes as his grip tightens on my waist. "You asked me last night to take a leap of faith, and today I'm asking for you to do the same. Give us time."

Emotion wells in my eyes and a hot tear bubbles over and slides down my cheek. He groans and catches it with his mouth before it can fall free. And then he kisses my jaw, lips, nose, and finally he breathes against my forehead, "We'll find a way."

"Oh, Colin." I tilt back so he can find my mouth and he does, scorching me with the intensity in his kiss.

Damn it. It's too late for second thoughts. Right or wrong, I want to be with him more than anything in this world. I only hope I'm not proven a fool because of it.

TWELVE

May

THE LAST THREE MONTHS are a wash of hard work and sex. I giggle. What a terrible introduction to my current article. No truer statement has ever been made, but the American people don't need to know how my thighs ache or that I can't stop smiling. Colin outdid himself last night. I fan myself thinking about his masterful mouth. And the same man who makes me scream all night long is well on his way to becoming president of the United States.

My favorite thing is when we're just Colin and Charlie. Whatever state we're in, he finds something special for us to do, a quiet dinner at an out-of-the-way restaurant, or a walk in a park, or sneaking off to the show and making out in the back row.

I set my laptop down as he moves into the main cabin of the plane. I've seen and touched the naked contours of his entire body and his elegance still catches me off guard. He's obscenely attractive. My heart beats double time as a smile spreads into a dimple on his cheek.

Seconds later, he pulls me up and onto his lap as he sits on the couch. I've separated myself from Colin completely when we attend events. If he's on one side of the room, I'm on the other and I only look at him through the lens of my camera. It's my only hope to keep our relationship, whatever it is, away from public scrutiny. One glance at my doe eyes and the media will latch on to our flaming-hot affair.

Tonight is different. The Kellys, friends from Notre Dame, have invited family and his closest supporters to their restaurant for a benefit in Colin's honor. His mother and father have flown in to see him—

that makes me nervous. But I've no time to think about them as he cops a feel through my thin sweater.

"Behave."

He throws up his hands. "Not doing a thing."

"I know what you're doing, Mr. McKenna, and I'm very nicely asking you to behave yourself."

"Or what? Will you punish me?" The devilish smirk is in place and I want to nip it from his lips. And why can't I?

I laugh and look around. Evan is dozing in a far seat, eyes closed, and the Montgomerys are hidden in the conference room. I latch on to Colin's hair and pull his mouth to mine. He takes over and I take in his tongue and then his groan. Deep, long, and too much for our current location, I ease away and suck on his bottom lip.

But he's not done. I'm flat on my back with his hand palming my breast. Even through the sweater and bra my nipple springs forward. I hold back a cry when he pinches it, knowing we're not far from being caught. At the same time, I want him to ease the need growing between my thighs.

Reason checks in and I push against his chest. "I'm sorry, please," I beg.

"For what?"

"Sorry I got you going."

He smiles. "It doesn't take much with you, Charlie."

Touching his cheek, I repeat my earlier missive. "Behave."

"Yes, miss." He sits up and takes me with him. "How may I help you?"

"I'd like to go shopping for a new dress when we land."

"Charlie, you could wear a potato sack and be the most beautiful person in the room."

I roll my eyes.

"You really have no idea how gorgeous you are, do you?" Shaking his head when I don't respond, he says, "You're a stunning, beautiful woman." He pauses as if time will form the connection between his words and my brain.

"Your skin is creamy, translucent perfection." Running his fingers down my cheek, he travels along my throat to the open V-neck of my sweater.

My breath hitches.

"Your body is a tantalizing plane of dips and valleys, tormenting even the saintliest of men." His voice is hot, his stare hotter as his hand roams over the curve of my breast, blazing over my stomach, hips, and finally my thigh.

"And if all of that wasn't enough, your face is exquisite. Full, pouting lips." He groans and closes his eyes while he says this, opening them again to continue. "I love to kiss those lips, suck and bite them."

Oh, my dear Lord, I'm going to combust; he is so unexpected.

"Your decadent almond eyes are the color of the Emerald Isle on a bright, clear day. Men would cross oceans to be with you; I would cross continents and swim raging seas to be with you." He kisses me, light, teasing with his tongue.

"That was the most beautiful thing anyone has ever said to me," I whisper.

"It's the truth, baby."

We're interrupted by the captain announcing our approach. Colin stands and then helps me to my feet. Dropping down into the recliner, I slip my seat belt in place. Then our fingers link across the span of the chairs, and he studies me from where he sits.

I close my eyes as the jet's engines rev for landing. The pull of the plane slows and my stomach sinks as we do. How is it possible for us to end with a happily ever after?

I STARE AT THE reflection in the mirror, mollified by the person before me. My hair was a willing partner and it falls in Veronica Lake waves down one side of my face. A thick coat of mascara to go along with the dramatic brush of black eyeliner, and I'm a verified fifties bombshell.

With barely there cap sleeves and an open oval neck, my dress is reminiscent of the era too. It plunges in the back to a deep V, ending at the curve of my waist. What makes it unexpected is the black leather. It skims my curves in a pencil skirt ending just above my knees.

Colin did more than have a car ready to escort me to a boutique. He sent me to a spa where I was pampered and fussed over for hours. Now, a limo is waiting to take me to the fundraiser, where I'll meet him and his parents and a slew of his friends.

"Ms. Carter?" As I grab my clutch, a knock sounds on the door to my dressing room.

"Yes?" I open to find Rebecca, the owner, who saw me through my indulgent day. She hands over a bag.

"This is the last surprise," she says. "Your driver is ready whenever you are. Enjoy your night."

"Thank you," I whisper, and peek in the sack.

Inside is a small gift, a card tucked in next to it. I rip it open.

Dearest Charlie,
You are incomparable, unparalleled in beauty and honesty.
When I'm with you I leave aside my doubts and mistrust.
Don't ever leave.
Colin

Honesty. My heart thumps in my throat, a hard uncomfortable beat. He wants me to stay, of that I'm sure; but as what, as we are now? There's no mistaking the red box and gold scrollwork. *Cartier.* I pop the lid and gasp. The cuff is a panther, the head and body of which are completely encrusted in diamonds. *Holy wow.*

It's gorgeous and confusing at the same time. The day-to-day aspect of our relationship blurred for me months ago, but he never set new boundaries, never said his feelings had changed or grown. Behind closed doors we're closer than ever, but in public we remain separated. Maybe he's rewarding me for it. Damn, that thought burns a hole in my stomach. I don't want to be his paid-to-be-silent mistress, but I slip the bracelet on my wrist because he obviously wants me to wear it tonight. Tomorrow we'll talk about what all of this means.

STANDING AT THE ENTRANCE to the restaurant, I'm drawn to Colin. Everyone else falls into shadow. He's standing, turned toward the door as if in wait for me. The McKennas are more relaxed, sitting before him in two plush chairs. One of his hands is in the pocket of his black slacks, white shirt tucked in with a belt wrapped around his waist. A silk magenta tie is pinned in place. He's perfect.

My chin falls to my chest and I take a deep breath, focusing on my nude stilettoes. When I finally look his way again, his casual stance has changed. His eyes are no longer light, but deep and smoldering as he drinks me in. My body responds, and I squeeze my thighs together to alleviate the twinge. And then I'm immobilized. Barely breathing, I watch this lithe, outrageously sexy man move my way, still in disbelief that his hunger is for me.

Colin very deliberately, very slowly studies every inch of my body. My heart thuds when his gaze stumbles and sticks on the bracelet.

Finally he's here, holding out his hand to steady me as I take the three steps to enter the bar. He brushes a sweet kiss against my knuckles, in direct opposition to the heat radiating out of his eyes. There is nothing sweet about this look.

"Charlie," he whispers.

"Colin."

"You are absolutely stunning." He leans in; I think he's going to kiss me but instead he whispers in my ear, "You have no idea how badly I want to be that dress right now, cupping your breasts, stroking every inch of your satin skin. I will have you tonight, take you for the torture you'll inflict upon me for the next six hours." His lips glance over my cheek as he pulls away.

I stare, unmoving.

"I promise you."

Yes, please. I like his threats and I like his promises even more.

"Come, I want to introduce you to my parents."

I tug against his hand before he can move me from the spot, his brow rising at my delay.

"Thank you for the bracelet, but—" His finger hovers over my mouth before I can continue.

"Don't. I'm not very good with words or expressing myself."

"That's not true; you do it every day."

A sad smile pulls at the side of his mouth. "That's in a different context. With you...." He stumbles for words, in effect making his point. "I want you to know you're different, special to me in a way I can't articulate. Please accept my gift and know I want it to be yours, more than any other." I tilt my head in confusion. He wants me to have it *more than any other*?

He brushes his lips against mine. I wish we were alone to talk—who am I kidding—so I can have him now.

"Later, baby. I promise." Oh Lord, his look and his promises have my pulse sprinting and my groin aching.

"Come." I stumble behind him as he leads us the short distance to his parents. When we arrive, he pulls me over to his side in the same spot he stood moments before. His hand rests on my waist, leaving mine open to greet his parents but as I wait for introductions their focus is on his fingers kneading my hip. I blush, and consider moving away, but his touch stifles my nerves.

The McKennas stand, his dad an elder version of Colin with bright blue irises, tall and handsome.

"Charlie, meet my father, Michael, and my mother, Colleen." Her hazel eyes flare, struck by something I'm not aware of. She grins, but it's tentative as she tries to inconspicuously glance over my hair and dress. When she spots the diamonds dancing on my wrist, she can't quite hide her gasp.

I bite back a question that would appease my curiosity and instead say, "I'm pleased to finally meet you after all Colin has shared with me." He smiles, hanging his head as if embarrassed, but I can't figure out what it might be from. I force my gaze back to his dumbstruck parents.

Colleen is the first to snap out of her stupor. "Charlie, it's wonderful to meet you as well; although I'm afraid we're at a disadvantage. Colin has kept you a well-hidden secret." She glares in his direction.

"I was keeping her to myself, Mom."

And with that, he orders a round of drinks from the passing waitress and then motions for me to sit next to him on the settee opposite his parents. I'm surprised when he pulls my hand onto his leg, rubbing my knuckles with his thumb. Apparently tonight I'm not going to be a well-hidden secret. I slide closer, drawn into him as I squeeze his thigh. Colin is my favorite place; wherever life takes him is where I want to be. It's a stunning realization. One day at a time is impossible to manage. I swallow the lump in my throat.

"Charlie," Michael says, pulling my attention away from my thoughts. "Since Colin has kept us in the dark, you'll have to help us catch up. How did you two meet?"

We talk over cocktails. Colleen and Michael McKenna live in a suburb outside of Boston and have only a hint of the telltale accent, something completely missing from Colin's dialect. They're proud of their children. Ryanne, their younger daughter, lives nearby. Over the course of our drink, more guests arrive and the restaurant and bar begin to fill.

Just as we stand and the McKennas excuse themselves to mingle, a booming greeting jars the steady hum of voices. Colin laughs.

"There he is!" I swing around to find the man causing the ruckus. He's ginormous. A burly lumberjack stuffed into a suit, he grabs Colin by the arms and then swallows him in a hug. As they slap backs, the man glances in my direction and his eyes narrow to slits. A ripple of anxiety runs down my spine as Colin introduces me.

"Charlie Carter, you say?" The giant looks to Evan, who pops into our small circle.

"She's the magician working on our social media campaign," he says with an easy smile. "It's a huge success."

"Huh," the lumberjack says while staring at my hair so long I run my hand down the waves to make sure it's not sticking straight up. "Well, then. If you like her, I like her. Blake Kelly," he says, holding out a hand. Mine is lost in the warm mitt for a second.

"Don't let him intimidate you, Charlie," Evan says before sipping from a glass of Champagne. "He's more teddy bear than ogre when you get to know him."

"Watch your tongue. Who saved your ass on campus more times than I can count? How about when you slept with Dean Harker's girl? That man wanted blood."

"They broke up," Evan qualifies.

"Two days before you had her in your backseat."

I'm distracted from Evan's response when a beautiful raven-haired woman steps to Blake's side. She doesn't stay put for long, reaching for Colin to place a kiss on his cheek.

"It's so good to see you." Her voice is melodic with a hint of an Irish accent. She glances at me, tilting her head as she rakes over my face with her clear gray-blue gaze. Her perusal isn't unkind; it's thoughtful and curious enough to prickle at my nape.

Finally, she smiles and looks away. "Colin," she says, "your future is bright indeed." I wonder if her eyes flick toward me for the shortest of seconds.

As strange as I find her comment, it stiffens his shoulders. To ease us through the moment I blurt out the obvious. "You're from Ireland?"

Carla smiles. "Yes, long ago. Blake couldn't live without me, so he stole me away to the States. And how did Colin find you?"

My brow sinks. "I don't know that he found me. He asked me to work for him and I agreed."

She looks to Colin with another question and I think he shakes his head as if to drop the topic.

I'm stuck in a state of *what just happened here* when a booming laugh interrupts Colin's glare. A second lumberjack walks in. But this one is red-faced and his ruddy hair is anything but flat. Draping an arm around Colin and Evan from behind, he smacks a kiss on each of their cheeks. A laugh bursts out of my throat before I can stop it and he turns his attention to me.

"Well, now, who is this wee lassie ye brought with ye?" he says, getting closer to me with each word.

Colin growls, "Aiden."

But he disregards the tone and takes a quick look up and down my dress, a slow whistle resounding as he does.

"Well now, Colin, looks like ye found yerself a fine bitta fluff." Aiden grins, holding his hand out. I take it and he squeezes, surprising me as he leans in to kiss first my right cheek and then my left.

"That's enough."

"Oh now, don't get yer feathers in a bunch, Senator. I was only sayin' hello to your fine-lookin' woman."

Blake takes him by the back of the neck and smiles. "Play nice, brother."

Aiden's grimace speaks to the tightness of the grip. "I was just having some fun."

"Well, you can do it with someone else or Colin may flay you before dinner." Blake winks at me. "We'll see you shortly," he says and drags Aiden away. Carla waves and follows as they slide into a group who, based on their towering height, could only be more Kelly's.

Colin gathers me into his side as a young waiter approaches with Champagne. He takes a glass for me first, grabbing a second for himself. Evan stares across the room and my gaze follows.

The restaurant is huge and open. Windows line an entire wall that looks out to an open field. A soft glow spreads across the room as paper lanterns hang from the rafters and candles flick feverishly on top of each table.

But based on the sour look on Evan's face, I don't think he is appreciating the ambiance. "I see Alex Miller weaseled an invite out of Aiden," he says.

Colin whips his gaze in the same direction. The muscles in his neck flex as the hand on my hip pulls me closer.

"At least you know the Kellys have no id—"

"Isn't that Samantha Billings?" Colin asks, drawing Evan's attention to a leggy blonde across the room.

Evan sighs. "I think you might be right. Excuse me." He tips his head in my direction.

My thoughts are jumbled. The McKennas, the Kellys, their reactions, the bracelet and Colin's note, it all hurts my head. I'm thankful when Colin is distracted by more visitors and he gets into a discussion about addressing natural disasters.

"Excuse me," I say and then whisper in his ear, "Ladies' room."

He tightens his grip for a second before letting me go. It's a quick trip and more about space than anything else, but when I return the room is so full I can't find Colin. And I think that's probably a good thing. I mingle on the outer edge of the restaurant, watching men and women exchange animated greetings, and circle to the bar for a drink. So many people stare as if they know me. Hesitant smiles, hands lifted in half waves, and I feel like I'm in the twilight zone.

As I edge up to the bar, the man Evan referenced earlier appears by my side. He's cute, but it's his honey-colored eyes that make him interesting.

"Hi." He holds out a hand that I shake. "Alex Miller."

"Charlie Carter."

"Have we met before?" he asks. "You look so familiar; I just can't place you."

"No." I smile, because at least he's asking and not gawking like half of the people here. "I don't think we have. I'm new to the group."

"Yeah? Well, you look like you belong just fine."

"Thanks," I say, and then order a drink from the waiting bartender. "How do you know the Kellys?"

"From Notre Dame."

"Oh, then you're friends with Colin too?"

He hesitates for the slightest second. "Yes, Evan as well."

"It's nice of you to show your support."

"I wouldn't miss it for the world." With his drink in hand, half-way to his mouth, he scans the room. "So you're a Colin McKenna enthusiast?"

I almost choke on my drink. "Uh, yes. McKenna for president." I laugh and pump my fist.

He smiles behind his glass. "And you, how did you come to know Colin?"

My heart skips a beat. "I… um, I work with him on the campaign."

He nods, contemplating my answer. But I know he doesn't buy it when he looks at me through his lashes, flashing his eyes over my chest and hair. "I assumed the two of you were together when I saw you with him earlier."

"Oh, I…." I don't know what to say. It's the first time I've been asked to explain our relationship and I'm at a loss for words. Uncomfortable with the topic, I decide to bail. "Would you excuse me, please?"

Not waiting for a reply, I flee from the unpleasant feeling of not knowing where I stand. Colin was very clear he can't offer me more than one day at a time, yet today he presents me with an expensive gift, introduces me to his parents, and is displaying affection in public. All these things are in complete opposition to our agreement, and right now none of it makes any sense to me.

In my haste to escape from Alex Miller, I've run into Colin. He's entangled with a stunning brunette. Her arms squeeze too tight, hold him for far too long to be just friends, and then her eyes deepen with appreciation as he pulls away. The sudden burst of jealousy proves to be another uncomfortable reaction.

Our gaze connects just as I turn to leave. He grabs my hand, a gesture sure to confirm Alex Miller's suspicions.

Colin comes up with some excuse for his new girlfriend as to why he's got to leave with me, and then tugs me behind him, through bodies and down a long hall. Once we're tucked away in Blake's vacant office, he turns to face me with guarded eyes. "What's wrong?"

"Nothing, everything's fine," I try for believability with a fake smile.

"Charlie, I know you well enough to discern when you're upset, and I can tell you are now. I'll ask once more, what's wrong?" When I hesitate, he snaps, "Tell me," and my temper flares.

"I don't know how to explain to people why I'm here and who I am to you. It's confusing. I've tried to say I'm a part of the campaign, but it's not believable when I can't take my eyes or my hands off you." I hold up our entwined fingers as evidence of the problem.

"Don't complicate it. Just be honest."

"Sure, great. Problem solved. I'll tell everyone I'm fucking their presidential hopeful. That should go over well."

"Why would you say that? It demeans what's between us."

"What?" I'm flabbergasted. "Isn't it the truth, Colin?" I wait for him to acknowledge it and when he doesn't, I continue. "You know it is. We were clear with each other when this began: we're day to day. If I recall, you said *there is no future with me.* So I'm not speaking out of context when I say it's hard to explain to your family and friends I'm a temporary fuck buddy."

I yank my hand from his and turn to walk away. He grabs me before I can leave, pulling me around so our faces are inches apart. "Charlie, I don't know what brought this on, but right now, right here is not the time nor place to have this conversation." His tone holds an ounce of condescension I don't appreciate. "Given we're at a fundraiser with my family and friends, this can wait for a more appropriate time."

"If you don't want to know how I feel then don't ask the question," I hiss.

"For the love of God, what do you want from me? I'm in the middle of a campaign. I can't do this, it's not what I want—" He stops to run fingers through his hair.

My heart explodes. But I nod and step back, because out of everything that's happened today, that makes the most sense. I repeat it so we're clear. "You don't want me."

THIRTEEN

"CHARLIE, NO." COLIN SHAKES his head. "No, that's absolutely not what I said. I need you." He tries to draw me in, but I stand my ground. "I don't know what you want me to say. I've been honest with you. What do you want me to say?" He fumbles and my frustration returns full force.

"Nothing," I seethe. "I don't want anything from you." As I say it I know it's not true. If I was honest with him and with myself I would tell him I want his heart, not his goddamn diamond bracelet. "I haven't asked you for anything and certainly not this." I hold up my wrist.

His mouth parts, like he's stupefied by the comment. "You don't like it?"

"I don't understand it. It's beautiful and very, very expensive. Why would you buy this for me?"

"Why wouldn't I?"

"Because it's an extravagant gift to buy a short-term mistress. It's all very confusing; I can't wrap my head around any of this."

"Charlie, please...." He struggles to explain himself, just as he did before. Resting his hands on my waist, he stares at me with so much vulnerability I crack just a little. "I want to give you something, a piece of me, if you will. It's the only way I know how...."

I have no heart to give. His words haunt me. Colin can't give me anything but a fucking diamond bracelet and his body; days and months of starving affection lie ahead of me. My eyes well. For as long as I'm with him, this is what the future holds: gifts that will never fill the void, the longing for real affection growing with each passing night. His tender, gentle touch, sweet words, and romantic gestures are the closest I'll ever come to having something more. This is the reality of our situation.

For a moment I let him hold me, comforted by sandalwood and all things Colin. Eventually I lean away and place my finger over his lips to stop his heartache. "It's nothing."

My fight is gone as quickly as it came; there's nothing more to say. "I didn't realize I would find it difficult to explain myself to others, that's all. I'm not asking for anything more from you, Colin. I know your limits and for now it's fine."

He cringes, licking his lips before saying, "I don't want to lose you, Charlie." We stare at each other for a moment, because I can't promise him he won't.

"You're right; this isn't the time or the place for this conversation. I'm sorry I brought it up." With my palm to his cheek, I force him to look at me. "I don't want to ruin our night; you've been looking forward to this for a long time. Let's go enjoy your friends." I tug on his hand to move him away from this topic. I regret that the ease he held earlier is gone, replaced by his clenched jaw. "Please, let's have fun." I turn and pull him after me.

It takes a while, but his mood seems to lighten and I force myself to relax for his sake. Our fingers remain entwined as he speaks to more people than I can keep track of. The odd stares are second nature by the time friends from college appear, insisting he reminisce and do it bellied up to the bar for old time's sake. I wave him away, smiling.

Alex Miller approaches as soon as he's gone. "Charlie, I want to apologize. I think we got off on the wrong foot, and I'm hoping we can start over. I didn't mean to imply or put you in a difficult position."

"No, not at all, Alex. I'm sorry I vanished. I just needed some air."

He nods. "If you ever need to talk…."

Colleen and Michael find me then and Alex slips off without another word. Michael glares at his retreating figure.

"Do you know him?" My question draws his attention.

"Not well."

"But you don't like him?"

Colleen answers, "Alex was friends with the Montgomerys, Abby and Ella. There's some history there that injured Colin. Because of it, we're not fans."

"I was wondering about the Montgomerys; why aren't they here?"

"Most of Colin's friends aren't enthusiastic about that family, and neither are we. It would've been uncomfortable for everyone if they were here." Her lips press together as if to keep herself from saying more. What is it about the Montgomerys no one wants me to know?

I find Colin with his friends and smile. I love to see him happy. His eyes are drawn to mine, and even though they're alight with mischief, a layer of uncertainty remains from our earlier conversation. It saddens me we haven't moved past it. Raising my glass, I let him know I'm fine. His grin acknowledges me before he turns back to join the group.

I swallowed the last sip of my gin and tonic and Michael offers to get refills, leaving me alone with Colleen. Seconds after he leaves, she says, "I'm so glad Colin has finally found you, Charlie," she says. Caught off guard by the swing in topic, I can only nod.

"I want him to enjoy life again, and he is with you. I haven't seen him smile like this in a very long time." Grabbing my hand in hers, she says, "I'm thrilled you're together."

I don't know what to say other than the truth. "I am too. He means a lot to me, Colleen."

She laughs. "That's easy to see. You can't look at the two of you without knowing you're in love with him and he with you."

My pulse goes crazy. Love Colin?

Slipping free from Colleen's grip, I swallow down my angst and think about him—and it's not a long stretch. *I wake up thinking about him*. He's my obsession. We haven't spent a night apart since New York and when he's gone, my heart hurts. My groan is lost to the hum of the crowd. What I thought was a heavy dose of lust is more than infatuation.

I love the damn man. My anger about the bracelet and with him earlier makes sense now. We're at an impasse. He wants me to stay; there's no doubt of that, yet his feelings haven't changed.

But I want the *more* to come now.

More. It's an enticing thought, and also problematic; my past is currently the biggest complication we face. I promised myself I would leave, protect him and his career from the truth. Has the time come?

I look up to find him stalking toward me, slowly, watching intently. In seconds he stands inches away and he tips my chin. He's truly a beautiful man. But beyond the chiseled godlike masterpiece of his face and body, he's the real deal. Under the suit lies a sweet vulnerability that the world doesn't see, but I do. And I know now that I love him when he's demanding and when he's smooth, forceful and gentle. Looking into his eyes, green to blue, my heart shreds into pieces because the truth will destroy us. *My* truth will ruin the possibility of more with Colin.

"Charlie," he sighs, reaching for me. I fall into his chest and my nose meets his neck. Breathing sandalwood and him, I melt into his hard lines. "Don't leave me."

His whispered words are a mirror of my thoughts.

I might not have a choice.

MIDNIGHT: THE END OF the day and the beginning of another, one more chance to get it right, to start over.

In foster care I would sit up all night to protect myself. At midnight I'd pray the morning would bring something different. I never expected a happily-ever-after, but anything would have been a step up from hell.

The large windows at the front of the brewery allow for an extraordinary view of the sparkling stars. Soft music resonates through the speaker system and lends to my somber mood. I tried to hide my thoughts through dinner, to enjoy Carla and Aiden, who made me laugh and forget reality for a little while. But now the party is over, the McKennas and a handful of Kellys are all that remain, and I'm stuck in what comes next. *Truth or dare: confess or wait for it to be found.*

I sense Colin coming for me and I find him reflected in the glass. Hands stuffed in his pockets, he stands a few yards behind me. He hesitates, but then moves closer until his chest warms my back.

"You're faraway," he whispers.

Tears pool in my eyes as Etta James begins to sing about lonely days that are over. This song, the lyrics, they're so close to the feelings I want to share with him but never will. Turning, I wrap my arms around his neck and sink my fingers into his silken hair. The world could watch us and I wouldn't care. For these few minutes I'll claim Colin as my own.

It's as if we've practiced this dance a hundred times before. I look him in the eye, his as dark as the midnight sky. He holds me close and we move, hip to hip, as I hum and sing about dreams come true. Yet no matter how hard I try, pretending is not enough. His gaze sticks to mine until I tuck myself into the crook of his neck and soothe my ravaged heart with his musk and the steady cadence of his pulse. The words are heavy in my heart and I wish life were different, that I was different and the past could stay buried. But it is what it is. As the song ends, I lean away and stretch to kiss him.

"Let's go home," he murmurs into my mouth.

I nod as we turn and start our thank-yous. His parent's, Aiden—whose hug is seconds too long—Blake, and then Carla is my last good-bye.

She looks at me as if she's a gypsy, reading my future like a map in her hand. "You'll figure it out, Charlie. Don't let your worries interfere with your heart; let the heart lead and you will dance to the moon."

I don't know how to respond to her impromptu tarot card reading and its chilling accuracy, so I hug her.

"He cares about you. Don't lose sight of that."

I know he does, but I'm not sure it's enough. Not with the secret burning a hole in my chest. From restaurant to limo, it's a silent ride home. Tension hums between us. Although I lean into his side, my body is stiff, unyielding, yet I want to melt into him and never leave. Colin endures my distance mile after mile and then on our way to our room. I can feel his anxiety pulse from him in waves in the elevator and down the hall. As soon as we're behind the closed door of the suite, he grips my waist with one hand and my chin is between his forefinger and thumb of the other. Forcing eye contact, he growls out his demand. "Tell me what's going on."

I don't know how to explain this, and I'm not sure I want to. My fucking past is going to ruin this, ruin me again—he won't want me if he knows the truth. Oh God, why did I agree to travel with him? I knew it was the wrong thing to do. I'm going to get hurt again; not by Colin, but because I love him and I'll have to leave. There is no other way.

One day at a time. The mantra begins in my head and plays on repeat. I love him today; I want him tonight. For what may be the last time, I throw myself at him, hands fisting in his hair as my lips crash against his. He groans when I slide my tongue in his mouth, forcing him to respond. Finding the zipper on my dress he tugs it down and in seconds I'm naked but for the scrap of black lace between my thighs and the garter clipped to my stockings. He breaks away, panting and hungry, as I step out of the leather pooled at my feet.

Barely bound control punches off him as he reaches for my breast, a rough clench of his fingers, a soft palm to soothe, and my clit throbs a heavy, aching beat. Under the weight of his stare it becomes more insistent, but it's not my pleasure I'm seeking—it's his. I need to possess him, make him mine, so I unleash the woman who can tame his beast and rip the magenta tie from around his neck, tugging at his shirt so hard buttons ping off the wall and to the floor.

Colin's eyes flare. "Charlie," he growls my name and it inflames me further.

I palm his erection, rough swipes of my hand up and down through fine cotton. His lip curls and he takes my hair, tugging me up to his mouth as I work to release him. I jerk from his grip and fall to the floor, knees spread, tugging him free until he stands before me bare, his hard length jutting out from his perfect body.

I take him in hand at the base and our eyes meet when I look up through my lashes.

"Don't hold back," I whisper down his shaft. "I want to taste all of you." Drawing my tongue from base to tip, I flick tiny sweeps of my tongue along his corded length and around the strained crown. I glance up to find storm clouds brewing in his eyes, pulling me into the raging depths of blue.

"Put your mouth on me," he grinds between his teeth, veins bulging in his neck. I kiss the tip, lapping at it with my tongue. "Now, Charlie," he says, fisting both hands in my hair, "in your mouth."

His command does nothing more than soak my panties; greed is my motivator. I want him with a fierceness that scares me because it's raw, and new, and more than casual.

Hard, silky, slick, I take him in and suck. He groans. Closing his eyes, he thrusts and we find a swift pace that has the hair of his navel tickling my nose with each pass. My mouth and fingers act in tandem to prolong his pleasure.

"Christ, you own me," he grinds out as I take him to the back of my throat and swallow. He throws his head back and groans, loud and long.

It's good; the silky slide of him on my tongue feels good, and I want more—more of him, more of the heady feelings that come along with taking him to a place where he can let go, where freedom and passion combine. The place where fucking is really love and I can love him with my mouth and my body—a place where nothing and no one will drive us apart.

I can tell he's close by the tug to my hair, and his quick thrusts, fast, faster. I'm filled with him, filled with love and fear that it could all be lost, and I'll have loved for nothing. Nothing more than the memories I'll walk away with.

"Charlie, I'm going to come."

I want him to. I want to taste him; I want him inside me, a permanent reminder of our time together. My teeth graze against his swelling cock. He tries to tug me away but I clench my fingers into his ass and then he pumps wildly into my mouth. Lost to the demands of his body, he takes me until he pushes down my throat and comes, one long jetted stream after the other, until he's empty and panting.

"Baby," he moans again, shuddering.

Reaching under my arms, he pulls me up. I'm desperate. Climbing his body, I wrap my legs around his waist and kiss him, deep, long, hungry lashes. He staggers back, fumbling toward the bedroom, and once there he falls on top of me. I won't let him loosen his hold, there's a manic level of desperation in my grip. I can feel it and I know he can too. Matching my need, Colin pulls my hair, opening my neck to his mouth, teeth and tongue trailing down to my breasts.

I arch into his hold, hovering in the place between pleasure and pain as he sucks my nipple so far into his mouth I feel it in my clitoris. A strong, pulsing ache demands his attention. One and then the other, he tugs and bites the sensitive peaks, and I writhe beneath him, searching for his touch in the place I need him the most.

As if reading my mind, he slides his hand below the scrap of lace, spreading me open to find my clit. Three fingers press flat, rubbing me into a bright burning light. His teeth and tongue tease my breasts as I loosen my legs to let him have me.

My heads rolls to the side as I grip the comforter. "Oh, God." I pant, rolling my hips to mimic his movement, and then they move down my slickness and inside.

"So ready," he murmurs against my skin.

"Please," I beg, "please, I want to feel you."

In a heartbeat, he's on his knees and ripping against the delicate lace to bare me to his gaze. Pushing my thighs apart, he grips the base of his renewed erection and taps it on my clit, rubbing it through my folds. His earlier release did nothing to tame the turbulence in his eyes.

"Feel me, Charlie," he commands, and watches his cock sink in, slow, stretching, deep, and filling.

I whimper at the exquisite pressure. My lids flutter closed.

"No," he growls. "Look at me. Watch me take you."

I can't deny him. Not Colin when his demand is clear, with his chest and abs flexing as he moves. Fingers dig into the pad of flesh above my ass to pull me onto his erection, driving in with controlled strokes, over and over, again and again. So slow. So full. *So fucking good.*

"Do you feel how perfect we are, Charlie? How perfect I fit inside you?" He glides in until he hits my core and we're flush, proving his point, pressing against me to swivel his goddamn perfect hips. I whimper. "Please." *Please take me, pound out my fears, make me forget the real possibility that I could lose you.* I want to scream it, but instead I whimper again.

Colin's eyes never leave mine. "Tell me, baby. I want to hear you say how perfect this is, how perfect we are."

I moan and let my body speak for me with a rush of pleasure, the slick wetness easing every stroke, each thrust deeper than the last as if by sheer force he can make us one.

"Colin." I grab his wrists, using him as leverage to grind my clit, to rub against him when he's buried so far inside me I can't feel the separation of his body and mine. "Oh, God," I cry as the tension stretches me thin.

"Now, Charlie. Give yourself to me."

Yes, I will and I do. Clenching around his cock, I arch from the bed as pressure hits a peak and I snap, bucking against him, coming so hard I use his body to take me past thinking and into blissful darkness.

His groan and the pressure of his fingers digging into my flesh wrench me back to awareness. He falls over me, arms taut, muscles rippling as sweat beads on his brow and he enters me with long, deep strokes. Eyes caught on mine, he pumps his hips again and again, seeking his own release and tempting me with another. "Charlie." He breathes my name and sinks onto my chest, wrapping me in his heat. Cradling me, he presses his lips against my neck as his movements become quick and sharp. *I'm giving myself to you,* I think he whispers, but it can't be true because his breath is ragged on my skin. Then I'm consumed by the roar of his release beneath my ear and into my heart, beating at the same frantic pace as the pulse between my legs. He surges into me, once, twice, jerking with each offering.

I lick his shoulder, relishing his sweet saltiness before whispering what he needs to hear. "Yes, Colin. We're perfect."

We lie entwined until our bodies cool. Tears burn against my lids. I struggle to hold them in as he kisses and sucks on my neck. Reality intrudes one second at a time and finally he lifts to his elbows, eyes narrowing as he watches me.

"Are you going to tell me what's going on?"

"No." I shake my head with too much vehemence. *I can't lose him.*

He winces and then shoves up to his knees and off the bed, leaving me cold and yearning for the connection our bodies bring. Sleek and beautifully naked, muscles flex in his ass as he steps to his bag for a pair of boxer briefs, like those will protect him from what comes next. He hasn't looked at me until now, a lingering gaze as he glances up and over my stockings, still clipped to my garter. His cock twitches beneath the cotton and I try on a short-lived smile. At least I'll always know he wanted me.

"Charlie, I can't help you if you keep everything bottled inside."

He moves to the edge of the bed, pulling the covers out from under me and then back up to hide my body.

I shiver under the sheet and then sit up, knees pulled into my chest. "You can't help me. No one can."

Colin sinks to the edge of the mattress and waits; forearms on thighs, he stares at the benign carpet. But I don't know how to have this conversation, so the silence stretches on and stirs up the anxiety in my stomach. I need to tell him my truth. It's now or never.

I swallow and spill my fear in a rush of words. "I'm afraid of how much you mean to me and that one day I'll have to leave."

He jerks up to look at me. "You don't have to go anywhere, I don't want that. Have I ever given you that impression?"

"You don't know me. If you did, this never would have happened." I gesture between us and my voice breaks. "I never had any intention of wanting more from you; if I truly thought myself capable of feeling this much, I wouldn't have agreed to the campaign tour. I want you to believe that; please promise me you'll always believe I'd never do anything to hurt you."

"Charlie, I do. What's going on? I don't understand what you're trying to say." His brow settles into three lines, drawn down as he turns to face me full-on. "What is it you think could hurt me?"

"I can't tell you." Tears burst from my eyes. The first heave hurts; the second is unbearable as the past barrels forward to slaughter a future I only pretended could come true.

"No, Charlie, please don't." He grabs my arms and hauls me from beneath the covers and into his waiting lap. But his caress and the murmured words meant to soothe make me cry harder, and then I let it come. The memories I closed off years ago fill the space in my head like an unwelcome enemy.

It's better to end this now to protect my heart from getting more involved and to save his reputation. Wiggling free, I kneel, as if the separation will lessen the sting when it comes. Of all the awful things I've endured, this will be the worst. I love him, I *love* Colin, but not with the pureness I do my family; this is greedy, needful, stuttering in strength, hot and lustful, sweet and crooning love. And he will leave me when he knows. *He will leave me.*

This mantra slices through my feigned calm and lashes against my heart in hurtful strokes.

I steady myself with cleansing breaths, one deep lungful after another as I work through the pain. There is no preparation for the vibrant memories that are more real than nightmare, and in an instant I'm pressed into a filthy mattress. Warm, stale breath pants against my cheek at the same pace of his vicious thrusts, ripping into me. It hurts—it hurts so fucking much, the jabs rip into my innocence, dry with disgust and fear. He makes me bleed, screaming against the hand over my mouth.

A sob erupts from my chest and I close my lips around it. *Oh God, please help me.* I think it now, just as I did every night when I was fourteen.

I cough out the lump and glance at Colin, his expressionless mask is in place and even his eyes are steady, unreadable. "My last year in foster care was with the Kerrs; they brought kids into their home like it was a job. Money motivated them to open their doors to more children than was reasonable, but the system was overloaded. It's where I met Ali; she came to the Kerr's after I did."

Years disappear and my pulse accelerates as the picture forms. "Before she came, it was me, three younger girls, and a fifteen-year-old boy—Shane Roberts. He was evil, you could see it in his eyes, and the Kerrs didn't care to rein him in.

"One night, he snuck into my room when I was sleeping, put a pillow on my face, and raped me. That was the first time." I can't bear to look at Colin, so I focus on my fingers, teasing the line of lace on my thighs. I'm naked, open and vulnerable but he has never made me feel dirty or damaged. "Shane came into my room night after night. I fought him, God, I tried so hard to get away." I pant through the memories as if they were the jabs I'd throw to his kidneys and groin. "But he was so strong."

"I stopped sleeping at night. I ran away, and they brought me back, and then Ali came. She knew just by looking at me and then she saw the bruises. We just clicked, something about us fit. From that moment, I wasn't alone. But she gave more than me; her part of the bargain included a knife from the kitchen and a threat to keep me safe."

I laugh, as crazy as Ali was the night she stood at the threshold to our room and told Shane if he wanted to keep his dick attached to his body he'd better never touch me again.

"The Carters were in the process of adopting Ali, and she begged them to take me too. She went so far as to refuse the adoption if they didn't. Ali was willing to give up everything for me." A tear slips out of my eye and I push it away; she would hate that I was crying over her. "She saved me and then the Carters did when they took me home too."

Fuck. I gasp as my chest tightens and I blurt out the truth that's burned a hole in my stomach since I met him. "I was pregnant." I pant, ratcheting up my pulse as the rest stumbles from my mouth. "I didn't know what to do. I literally had just met and moved in with the Carters. In hindsight, I know I was in shock and not capable of thinking, numb to everything, so Ali told them. She told them everything. Mrs. Carter, my mom, came to me and rocked me in her arms as if she wanted me. As if *I* mattered. I . . ." Tears well and fall over my lids, blurring the span of Colin's hotel room into patches of gray. "I hadn't felt love in so long. It was so good and safe and I believed her when she said she'd support whatever I wanted to do."

I find his wide eyes and prepare myself for the pain. It was my decision and I have to pay for it. Every day of my life I pay for it in some way. "I had an abortion," I whisper. "At fourteen, I thought it would kill me, that I'd be tormented my whole life by looking into the face of the man who slaughtered what hope remained in my heart. But then I knew it was too late. I was already ruined.

"I hated myself. I hated the emptiness, I hated the fear crawling around inside of me and that I had to sleep with the lights on. I hated that I locked the bathroom door and showered in my underwear until I was twenty. And I hated that I didn't feel anything when a boy and then a man would pay attention to me. I hate that he *broke* me."

Colin's jaw clenches so tight the muscles in his neck bulge under the strain. But I'm going to finish because he needs to know. "And then I met you. I don't know why it's you, Colin, but the moment we met it was different. My pulse raced and my stomach tumbled. I *felt* you in a way I hadn't experienced before. And I wanted it; I've wanted for so long to be a woman, to enjoy sex, to stop being the scared little girl that stayed locked away with her family because it was my safe place. I did all of that with you. All the things I thought were impossible all of a sudden became a possibility."

He doesn't move and the silence strikes a chord against my raw feelings. Colin told me, and the world, how he felt about abortion the day we met. He could never care about a woman who ended a life when his baby was so tragically taken from him.

I crawl to the opposite side of the mattress and slide my feel to the floor. My stiff legs buckle and I grab for a chair near the bed. It's a crutch as the truth sinks in. Arms taut, my head falls. Chin to chest, I accept the emotion clamoring for release. Tears, thick, wet sobs well up and spill out of me. I've lost him. *I've lost Colin.*

No counseling could prepare me for this level of grief.

FOURTEEN

"CAN I TOUCH YOU, Charlie?"

What? Colin's heat is potent as he steps behind me, close, but waiting for my response. I nod. Not a second later he reaches beneath my knees and sweeps me up, tucking me in so my nose is pressed to my favorite place. And for each sob, the gasp that follows is full of sandalwood and him. We settle on the couch, his whispered words lost in my hitching breath and the bouts of crying that come and go until there's nothing left.

Reaching to the side table, he hands me a tissue and because I think it'll be the last thing he'll ever do for me, I start all over again. I hate my weakness, but I love him more, so I struggle out of his tight hold and stare into his shining eyes. They're filled with so much compassion he blurs again under the waterworks that seem endless.

"Baby," he whispers so softly I barely hear him over the pounding of my heart. "Don't cry, please, my sweet Charlie."

I sniff and look at him through wet lashes. "You don't hate me?"

He flinches. "Of course not." I blink until my vision clears. "You have nothing to be ashamed of. What that boy did to you," his voice drops into a ragged edge of violence, "is unspeakable. I wish there was something within my control to ease your pain."

"Colin." I touch his cheek. He nudges into my palm as if he needs me as much as I do him. "I was so afraid when you found out, you'd be disgusted. This means more to me than you'll ever know."

"My sweet girl." He cups my nape, tipping my head with the fingers in my hair. I'm a mess, yet he looks at me with the same appreciation I saw at the fundraiser. "All I want to do is erase those memories. Can I kiss you?"

Oh, God. I reach for his neck and drag his mouth to mine. He sighs as my tongue strokes against his. But then he pushes against my shoulders when I try to straddle him. He shakes his head as if to clear it.

"Careful," he says. "I don't want to hurt you."

My heart sinks; he doesn't want me. I knew he wouldn't. How could I have been so foolish to hope he would?

Crushed, I hang my head and mumble, "I should go."

I move, but his arms tighten around my waist and his growl vibrates between us. "I'm not being clear. Let me explain." He licks his lips, the bottom one red and swollen from my kiss. "I have little control when it comes to you, Charlie. From the very beginning I couldn't resist you, couldn't say no, not where you're concerned. I want to give you the world and at the same time protect you from the hurt that comes from living in it. When I look at you . . ." His thumb and forefinger find my chin, and he tips my head to steady my roving gaze. "Baby, I always want you, but when you kiss me like that"—he shudders—"I don't want to be gentle."

He sighs and tucks a stray curl behind my ear. "You've been through so much already. I can't fathom how hard it was for you to tell me, but I'm glad you did. Your trust is a gift. I won't add to your pain by losing control, not after you had to relive that."

"You still want me?" I ask, confused. How could this man, perfect in every way, want to be with Damaged Goods Carter?

Colin's eyes darken with intensity. "Always, Charlie."

Always; he wants me always. I raise my hand to his jaw, now rough with his growing beard. My fingers stroke over his cheek and up to his brow; I smooth out the tense lines and then move into his waves, longer now than when we started this journey together. I fist his hair and as his nostrils flare, I tug his mouth to mine. I'm not chaste or sweet, I want to feel every part of him, let him take away the memories that still haunt me.

When he pushes against my shoulders again, I growl and stick with him as he seeks separation. He manages to pry away enough to murmur, "Are you sure you want to do this?"

"Please, I need you."

He gives in with a murmured, "Always," and then he kisses me. So gentle, even when I try to deepen it, he forces the pace and it's slow, tender. Taking me back to bed, he worships every inch of my body, with his mouth and tongue, hands and fingers, then finally his body. Hard, yet soft at the same time, he takes me with a soothing glide yet I scream his name as I crash around him. Tears streak down the sides of my face and into my hair. "Stay," I whisper when he tries to roll away. In time he falls asleep still inside of me, and I whisper the words lodged in my heart. "I love you." A lump sticks in my throat. "I love you so damn much."

I STARTLE AWAKE. MY pulse pounds in my head as I struggle to remember a dream that's already gone. I'm exhausted. A glance at the alarm on the night table confirms it's been an hour since I closed my eyes. Memories ruin my attempt to get more rest. Shane Roberts. The Carters. Ali. And the baby I could never love. How could Colin want to work through the enormous baggage that comes along with Charlie Carter? In the middle of the night it's easy to bring solace to a lover racked with guilt, but he has to be second guessing himself when clarity arrives with dawn.

Tears spring to my eyes. I cried a river last night, there can't be many more left, yet they squeeze through my clenched lids. Damn it. *Breathe in, breathe out*. I follow this mantra so I can't think about where he is. The bed is empty next to me. I know it before I open my eyes to the soft indent where his head should be. Grabbing his pillow, I bury my nose where his scent is the strongest and my body instantly revs, my pulse, my heart; he calls to me on a primitive level to mate and make babies. *Oh for the love of God, get a grip, Carter*.

As I hug the down pillow and try for more sleep, running water breaks through the silence. He's in the shower. The panther is heavy on my wrist and a loop of last night plays in my mind: his gift, the party, my confession. I thought I'd feel free but instead I have an additional weight added to the bench press of my life, and it's crushing my chest. The truth is too much to overcome.

My spirit dive-bombs into a self-pity party, and no one is invited.

I can't fathom how I'm going to salvage a good mood for Colin's parents and our final visit before they return to Boston.

Colin. Why would he want me? Mr. McPerfect and Damaged Goods Carter are not Mr. Darcy and Elizabeth Bennett; we're so far from peanut butter and jelly you could call me banana and ask who in the hell ever thought about that combination.

The water stops and I know he'll be out soon. I relax my tense shoulders and feign sleep with slow, shallow breaths. I'm not ready to face where we go from here.

The bath door swings open and his bare feet pad across the floor. He's naked, I know it, I picture it: the low-slung towel hanging from his hips, skin damp because he barely took time to dry off. I roll my eyes behind closed lids. I'm hopeless.

The bed dips next to me and he runs his fingers from the bare crease of my ass and up through my hair to my neck. A shiver claims me at the same time my clit pulses. He does it again, but this time he smacks a cheek and sighs while he rubs away the sting. I try to stifle a smile. Without warning, his touch changes from tantalizing to tactical, and he attacks my sides in a game that can only be called tickle torture.

"Are you kidding me," I scream, trying to escape incessant hands. Rolling to my back, I begin urgent protection techniques, flailing my arms and kicking my feet. As always, he's proficient at what he does and finds holes in my armor where his hands slip through.

"Colin! Stop, please, please." I laugh and shriek at the same time. Through the gaggle of limbs, I glimpse his huge grin. "W… why'd you do that?"

He rubs the tickle out of my sensitive skin, but I push his conciliatory hands away; he can't be trusted to refrain from a repeat attack.

"Because I don't want last night to linger." When my only response is to mimic his drawn brow, he sighs and tries again. "Charlie, I want to be with you. I didn't care about your past before, and I don't care about it now. We'll make it through."

Now the wrinkles are in my forehead; I'm confused. "What do you mean you didn't care before; before what?" I ask and sit up, tucking the sheet under my arms as the conversation changes direction.

His eyes widen by a fraction, but otherwise he stays statue still—unnaturally so. A minute goes by and my heart counts the seconds as I wait for his answer. Finally, he reaches for my hand. "Only this: last night didn't change anything, not for me. You are forthcoming about your family, your life when you became a Carter, but rarely talk about anything prior to that, alluding it's private. I knew you had something you weren't ready to share. I didn't care about what that was because I enjoy being with you." His fingers wrap through mine. "Now that you've told me, my feelings haven't changed. You're a strong young woman; I admire that about you."

Is he for real? "You realize this is hard for me to believe, right? Colin, you're running for president; did you forget that?"

His eyes narrow. "Yes, Charlie, my campaign is top of mind. I'm also here with you. You're a part of my life now, and I'll support you any way I can."

"Okay, let me play this out for you the way I see it." I poke at my chest for emphasis. "I'm damaged goods, Colin. I'm not Ivy League, debutante, angelic and pure Charlise Carter that can socialize with heads of state. I'm a lost girl, lost in the world of the 'system,' raped and driven to abortion when I was in a mental state not worthy of humanity.*¿Comprendes*?" My voice rises with each word. "You're a Republican candidate running to capture the White House, supportive of pro-life initiatives. My past will hurt you, not help you. I can't believe you're of sound mind when you tell me you don't care!" I end frantic and winded, staring at him like he's unstable.

"Are you quite finished?" His tone changes from smooth caramel to deep trouble, meaning I'm wading in it.

When I nod, he continues, "I don't ever want to hear you say you're damaged goods again, Charlise." He draws out my given name. "I assure you I'm of sound mind and *body*. I have lived my life in preparation for the presidency. I make decisions to ensure nothing will taint my reputation. I'm calculated and in control of my destiny and my future. None of that has changed. So, let's review your attributes, shall we?" His eyes are scorching.

"You are a beautiful, intelligent, well-educated, well-spoken young woman raised by loving parents. Period. I can't change what happened fifteen years ago, but I damn well can and will support you, help you any way I know how and with whatever I have. It's yours. So I'll say it one more time: I don't care about your fucking past." In time his blue eyes gentle. "However, I do care—very much—for you."

"Oh," is my genius response. He cares very much for me. But I shake my head to get that out of it; I can't let it muddle my thoughts. "Here's the thing. I just don't get it, Colin. Look at you." I wave my hands over his chiseled, god-like perfection, and then in front of my face. "How can you want to be with me?"

He shakes his head as if I'm testing his patience. "You surprise me, Charlie. If only you could see yourself the way the world does. Stunning is too tame. Beautiful is a paltry term in comparison. So, think in this context: Have you no idea of the number of men that want in your pants?"

"What?"

His right eyebrow rises. The right brow I love. The right brow that's sexy as hell.

"Shall I give you a list? Just last night the waiter who refilled your glass every five minutes, Bill Jensen, and Alex Miller."

"Are you jealous?" I ask, stupefied. That's nonsensical.

"It's not an emotion I'm familiar with, Charlie, and I don't pretend to like it."

"Colin," it's my turn at exasperation, "you are the last person in the world who should be jealous. Have you met me? Let's start again." I reach for his hand and pump it. "Hi, I'm Charlie Carter. I've never been with a man, except in a forcible situation that turned me off from engaging with anyone for fifteen years—that is, until I met Mr. McPerfect McKenna. Smoking-hot, sexy-as-hell, perfect-gentleman Colin McKenna, the man I can't keep my hands off, nor keep my pants on when he's around. The only man I have ever wanted. The only man I will ever want," I finish, sputtering and breathless.

We stare and tension tightens my chest because his eyes sink into dangerous thoughts.

"So we're clear," he says, reaching for my biceps. "I'm not going anywhere and neither are you."

He hauls me out of the covers and onto his lap, but I press my fingers to his mouth when he tries to kiss me. "Can you forgive me for what I did?"

"Oh, baby." He drops his forehead to mine. "It doesn't change a thing."

The weight crushing my chest evaporates—freedom from self-doubt and self-preservation. Colin McKenna really and truly wants me.

I throw my arms around him and he falls to his back, holding me through his chuckle. "So, now that we've got that worked out, what would you like to do?" He stares at my mouth.

My grin gets even bigger. "I can think of a few things."

He rolls over so quickly I have no idea how, and I end up on my back. "Do tell." He nips and kisses my neck.

"I would much rather show you," I say, pulling the towel from his hips.

I LOVE COLIN. STAMPING it on my forehead may be taking it too far, and is unnecessary. I'm giddy. My smile is permanent, there's a lightness in my step and everything is brighter and better because he knows everything. The pancakes I had for brunch were sweet and Colin's hand on my thigh was not. His parents didn't mention my heated cheeks and they ignored my attempts to keep his fingers from crossing the line of decency and too far up my skirt. Wicked, wicked, man. It's no wonder I had to take my jacket off as Colleen and I walked through the court, shopping. He makes me hot. Our last stop was to the boutique where I bought my outfit yesterday. She finds a stunning dress and I got something for Colin.

The sun is high in a cloudless sky, sparkling against the glass windows as we make our way back to the pub. Beers and baseball are keeping the McKenna men busy while we enjoy a lazy spring Sunday.

"Charlie, I'm sorry if I stepped past my boundaries last night. I shouldn't have spoken out about your relationship with Colin. I truly wasn't trying to interfere."

I wave away her concern. "Please, don't worry. I'm happy for the nudge into self-reflection." God, I'm so damn silly in love I could skip down the street. "Colin and I had a good talk; in fact, more than one."

"You're really very good for him."

"He's just as good for me," I say, absently touching the bracelet I have yet to take off. Colleen stares at my wrist and I hold it up for her to see. "It's a gift from Colin."

She smiles. "It's beautiful. Confirmation he cares for you very much, I'm sure."

That's what he said last night. I stare at the panther, light bouncing off the diamonds, and I'm comforted to know that maybe we're closer to the same feelings than I had thought yesterday.

It's with this hope and a smile to go along with it that we find them. Father and son are at a four-person high-top table, watching the Red Sox on large screens hanging from every conceivable place.

Relaxed today, Colin's blue T-shirt is stretched across his chest and hugging his biceps, loose except for an inch tucked in above his belt buckle. He's anything but the reserved presidential candidate the world sees. He's my Colin. I flush and curse his effect on my panties.

His gaze is pulled from the game and toward the entrance, and a grin splits his face when he sees me. He watches me step toward him with so much of his own hope, it makes me feel like we can do this. My heart gallops at the possibility and then because Colin grabs my hips, pulling me against his as he leans down for a kiss. Double damn. I must be crazy or in the twilight zone, because its midday, with his parents a foot away, and his tongue is sweeping against my bottom lip. "You're terrible," I murmur.

"I know. Come," he says, tugging me to the table where he holds my chair as I get settled. We're leg to leg when he sits down.

"Did you have a good time?" He asks and drops his hand to the no-go zone on my thigh. I do the same, except my pinkie presses against something stretching the boundaries of his jeans.

"Great time," I say and smile.

His lids sink into that look, the one that says he'd like to toss me on the bed. "What'd you buy?"

"I'll show you later," I whisper, and then look away from trouble.

Colleen and Michael aren't trying to hide their amusement as they watch us.

"What about you, Mom?" Colin drops a hand to rest on mine.

"A dress for your sister's wedding. I'm relieved to cross it off my list. Now I only have to worry about your father getting fitted for his tux."

Michael grumbles about the fitting while the waiter approaches for drink orders. "When is the wedding?" I ask after he leaves.

"July 23, in Ireland," Colleen says. "It's been Ryanne's dream to get married on the family farm."

"Have you ever been there, Charlie?" Michael asks.

I shake my head. "No, I haven't. My vacations are spent in northern Michigan at my parents' cottage." Saying it aloud, I'm reminded of the upcoming trip I've yet to talk with Colin about.

"It's a beautiful country," he says.

"I'm sure I'd love it. It's on my bucket list for a one-day visit; my biological grandparents were both born there."

"Do you have family living there now?" Colleen asks.

"I'm not sure. Other than a box of things that followed me through foster care, I don't have anything from that part of my life. I've never thought much about it; when I was adopted I immersed myself into the Carters, I didn't want them to feel as if I didn't love them, or that I didn't love being a part of their family, so I let my past go."

"Would you like to learn more about your birth parents or other family members that may live out of the country?" Colin asks, squeezing my fingers that are still in his lap.

I shrug. "Maybe."

"We'll talk about it before we go to Ireland. If you want to research your family before then I'll help you do it."

His comment plays on a loop: before we go—*we*.

"What?" He smiles and it's a bit devilish.

"Ireland?"

"Yes. You're going to need to get another dress. This wedding is black-tie. Wait until you meet Ryanne and then you'll know why."

Holy wow. How has all of this transpired in twenty-four hours? Colin knows everything and he still wants me; I'm a part of his future and we're holding hands in public. I close my eyes, welcoming the flush of warmth, and for the first time in my life, complete happiness—full, abounding happiness—creeps in to fill every fracture of my heart.

When I open to find Colin, he's watching me. "Ask me again if I'm happy," I whisper.

His grin fades. "Are you happy, Charlie?"

I entwine our fingers and pull them into my lap. "I have never been as happy as I am with you. I'm so completely, wonderfully happy, Colin."

Leaning in, he brushes his lips against mine, his mouth grazing over my cheek toward my ear. "So am I." He kisses my hair and leans his forehead into me for the briefest moment.

"WHERE HAVE YOU BEEN?" Ali scolds.

"What, not a hello, how are you, I love you?"

"Hello, how are you? I love you. Now, tell me why you haven't called me in, like, forever?"

I roll my eyes. "I've been busy."

"Busy gettin' it on with tall, dark, and handsome." She giggles into the phone like a teenager.

"Ha ha, you're funny." But I'm laughing too.

"Tell me how good it is, or are you going to hold out on your sister for the rest of your life?"

"God, Al. It's so perfect. I never thought it would be like this." I pause and look around the plane to make sure I'm alone. "I told him."

Silence. Ali is never silent. I give her a minute to process this news and finally she asks, "Are you okay?"

"I'm good, really. It's kind of hard to believe, but Colin cares about me. He said it doesn't matter." Last night felt like the end of my world, and today I've never been happier in all of my twenty-nine years.

"Oh, Charlie, I knew he would. You're beautiful, and funny, and loving."

My chest hurts and the tears in my eyes have nothing to do with the past. I miss my sister. "I can't wait to see you Thursday."

"Ditto."

"Did you finalize your flight?" I glance at Colin and Evan at a back table and then shift to look out the window at the late-day sun.

"I sent my itinerary by e-mail last night. I arrive midmorning. Did you book?"

"I'll get in to Traverse City around ten; Mom's going to pick us up at the airport."

"Save the details until then so I can see your blush." Ali giggles.

I roll my eyes and catch sight of Colin taking the last few steps to my side and then he sits next to me.

"I've got to go, Al. Love you."

"Love you too. See you Thursday."

Colin takes my hand after I toss my phone down. "You're leaving?"

"I'm sorry. I spoke to Evan about it when I first started and I meant to mention it to you weeks ago. I'm going home for my gram's birthday party on Saturday. My whole family is coming home to celebrate."

I hate his crumpled brow and the storm clouding his eyes. Pushing back the displaced wave of hair on his forehead, I lean in and kiss him. My mouth open and inviting his tongue, I devour him in deep hungry strokes. I cling to him, palms flat against his cheeks. Colin fists my curls, tugging me up and over his thighs; both hands fall to my ass, digging in and bringing me flush against his raging erection.

Our mirrored groans vibrate between us, and the heat dissipates to slow, sucking kisses as we catch our breath.

"You're delicious," I murmur against his lips.

"And you're trying to distract me. When are you leaving?"

"Thursday. I've booked a 6:00 a.m. flight into Traverse City."

"How long are you staying?"

"I'll meet you in Arkansas on Tuesday morning. I've already prearranged posts for all the sites, and I'll keep up on the tour while I'm gone."

He huffs. "I'm not thinking about the campaign." My heart goes haywire and I drop my forehead to his. The hum of the engines takes up the space where words should be.

"I'll miss you," he says, and the tension in his arms speaks to not wanting to let me go.

Tucking my head into the crook of his neck, I breathe in Colin and close my eyes against the emotion that wants to run down my face. I love him. I'd like to say it, but instead I mumble it into his skin as I nip and suck up his neck to his ear. "I'll miss you too."

More than you'll ever know.

FIFTEEN

"CHARLIE, WE'VE LANDED."

The fog is thick, too thick to break free. I can hear Colin yet I'm so tired I only want to sleep. I think I may beg for it and push him away, but the vibration of his laugh feels real.

"Come on, baby," he whispers in my ear while removing a seat belt I don't remember strapping on. A second later, I'm in his arms with my head pressed into his neck. Voices come and go, so do the sounds of traffic, and in the next minute Colin's hands brush against my stomach followed by a soft tug as he strips me bare.

"Sleep well." The warm slide of his mouth against my forehead is my final focus and I fall into darkness.

Sometime later a harsh expletive jars me from sleep; my heart pounds.

"This is none of your goddamn business." Colin. And by the sounds of it, he's pissed.

After a mumbled response that I can't make out, he says, "No, it doesn't matter. I've told you to let me worry about this, about her. I'm not having this conversation again, do you understand me? Let it go." A muffled voice and then he says, "It's late and time for you to go."

The welcome sound of silence does little to regulate my thrumming pulse. A minute later Colin slides into bed. I tuck myself into his waiting open arm, my cheek to his chest.

"Were you talking to someone?" I ask.

"It's nothing, baby, go back to sleep." His lips press into my hair just before I pull myself up to look into his face. I can barely see him in the dark room, yet I know he's looking at me. I lean in to kiss him, short and soft; we linger for a moment before I pull away and tuck myself into his shoulder.

I'M IN THE DESERT, hot, sweating, and so uncomfortable I drag myself into a new day just to escape it. Colin is everywhere, legs woven through mine, head on my chest, one of his hands palming my breast. I smile and try to relax, but he's a raging inferno.

I hate to wake him. Serious slumber like the deadweight I feel now doesn't come easy for him. If we're minutes from the alarm sounding, I'll endure the furnace, but if I've got time on my hands I'm squeezing out of here to order breakfast. I reach for his wristwatch he rarely removes. Today it's on the nightstand so I grab it. Every detail screams expensive and it's confirmed when I see *Cartier* inscribed just under the Roman numeral twelve.

The leather band is soft from so much wear. I flip it over and find an inscription.

C— Remember me always —A

A gift from Abby. My heart shudders in my chest. He carries a memory of her around with him every day—just as the inscription asked for him to do, *always*. A word he's used with me. Bile rises from my stomach and I can't swallow it down. I haven't thought about her in months. Colin hasn't mentioned her, nor have I. I had hoped our time together distanced him from the pain that followed him so closely when we met. But now I wonder if he'll ever be able to leave her behind. He doesn't wear his wedding ring; why does he wear a watch from his long-dead wife?

The only answer is he can't let her go, or maybe he doesn't want to. If that's true, he'll never be able to love me. *I have no heart to give*. I never believed him, especially after this past weekend. A shiver runs down my spine, even though I'm sweating. But this is chilling apprehension, a fear I'll lose him, or maybe more accurately that I've never had him.

I need time, and space, so I slip out from underneath him. For some reason I want to run—run from the chaos in my head, run from Abby and the complications of not only Colin's life, but the challenges knotted so indelibly into my own. I haven't run in years, not since Ali started medical school and moved away. She would drag me out with her in the mornings, but I never found the love for it like she did. Today is different. I need to feel the freedom it brings.

Quickly I change into the only sports bra I own, sweats and a tank, and an old pair of gym shoes I carry for rare downtime on the campaign trail. Leaving Colin a note on my pillow so he won't worry, I slip out of the suite. The sun hovers above the horizon, welcoming a new morning as I step onto the sidewalk.

Although the temperature will rise into the high seventies, the morning air is cold, urging me to jump right into a fast jog. Tall brown and gray buildings of varying heights line the streets. For blocks I run and free my mind, concentrating on the wind at my back, the tempo of my breath, and the pull of long-dormant muscles in my legs.

It's not long before the city becomes a blur and my thoughts stray to Colin, Abby, his campaign, and how I fit into the intricate web. Colin's life *is* complicated. I thought I could simplify it, but it's only going to get more challenging as he progresses toward the White House. Am I strong enough to endure the demands that grow as his career does? Will I forever be detached from him in public? How is it *we* can work? He's always said *we'll find a way*, but doubts to the validity of that statement are becoming hard to ignore. How is that possible when the disparity between us is so great? Yesterday my secrets were revealed, and the relief from that burden was brilliant. Today the questions surrounding *us* are overwhelming.

And then I laugh, a bubble bursting from my chest with such freedom I stop in my tracks. I'm so overreacting. Leaning against a stop sign at a cross-section, I smile through my panted breath. I love him, more than I ever thought I was capable of loving anything. Abby isn't going anywhere, and jealousy over their relationship won't strengthen ours, nor will asking him to forget her. It's selfish and inconsiderate. I'm hoping to sit at the same table, not usurp Abby from her place. As his trust grows, Colin will make room for me in his heart. I know it's possible.

Cutting across the street, I head in the direction of the hotel. Footsteps fall in line with mine; it must be Colin running to catch up with me. For the fun of it, I pick up my pace to make him work for it before he catches me. My breath spikes as I push myself faster, expecting for him to call out when I jump into a side street without stopping for the possibility of traffic. Silence. It's not Colin. Glancing behind me doesn't produce anything but the dingy brick of the building I just rounded. Footsteps echo in the narrow alley I use as a shortcut—first mine and then a second set.

Driving harder, I propel myself the final few blocks to the hotel. *Faster Charlie, run faster.* Closed shop doors blur as I streak by. Panic bursts in my already burning chest as I chance a look behind me. The shadow of a figure turns the corner. Lines are elongated into a grotesquely misshapen man by the rising sun. I dart into the road. A horn blares, the car it belongs to screeches to a stop inches from my frozen form. Shit. Waving a lame apology, I race into the hotel twenty feet away. Hands on my knees, I gulp in air.

Through the window, I find a quiet street; no one is walking or running in my wake. I didn't imagine it. The heavy tread of falling feet still echoes in my ears. With one last look out the door I turn to the elevators and Colin, my happy place.

IT'S NOT EXACTLY THE peaceful homecoming I was hoping for. Colin paces with his phone pressed to his ear.

"Phil, this better not happen again." His hard, almost frantic eyes find mine. "No excuses. I've been clear about my expectations, let me state them again—every minute, every day, no exceptions." His chest rises and falls as if he went for a jog, but that's not the case because he's in a very tight pair of boxer briefs. Something happened. "No, I haven't. Yes, I understand it may make things easier, but that's not what I'm paying you for. I'm sure you can tell by my tone this is of the utmost importance; I won't compromise and I expect the same from you." After a pause, Colin says, "I'm trusting you will."

His eyes never leave mine as he ends the call and tosses his cell on the couch. I grab a water from the fridge and drink it down while watching his gaze streak over my sweaty body.

"I went for a run." I admit the obvious.

"So I see."

"I thought maybe I'd be back before you woke."

"You should have woken me. I would have joined you *in the hotel gym*," he growls and steps toward me. He's angry and I can't tell if he's upset with me, or the *something* that happened.

"Are you mad at me?"

"Why would I be, Charlie?" His voice is calm, yet I know he's not. "You think I'm angry because you left *alone,"* he pauses for a shaking breath, "in a strange city, without telling anyone where you were going, or how long you would be…."

I am the *something* that happened to his morning. "That's not true, I left you a note."

"A note? A fucking note, Charlie?" His tone rises and his eyes flash a blue I've never seen before. His anger has never been directed at me, not like this. "I can't find you in a city with millions of people from a goddamn note that doesn't tell me what fucking direction you went in, how long ago you left, what path you were on! Did you even stop to contemplate the crime rate in this city, the number of—" He stops and shudders.

"No, I didn't," I say weakly, remembering the footsteps following behind me at the end of my run. "I'm sorry; I didn't think you would worry about me."

His brow digs into three lines, deep, angry lines. He moves so close I have to tilt my head back to hold eye contact. "Not worry?"

The words fall from his tongue as if they're poison. "Not worry?" he says again. "All I do is worry about you, Charlie. My God, do you not know how much I need you?"

Oh Lord. Comprehension barely sinks in before his mouth crushes mine. Melting into him, I dig my fingers into his hair and stay flush against his hard body. He holds my face with both hands so I can't step away from the frustration he takes out on me with lashes of his tongue. I match his need, the danger of my thoughtless morning run rolling off me in waves. He takes it, takes me until I can't breathe but he doesn't let me go, punishing my lips with his for the careless worry I caused.

He rips away, panting. "Goddamn it, Charlie—don't ever fucking do that again." His mouth finds mine, this time in a tempered but passionate kiss that frankly has me breathing harder than my morning run.

I cling to him, arms around his neck as he maneuvers us to the bathroom, turning the shower on hot before he strips me. My tank is first, up and over my head; my bra follows it to the floor. He drops to his knees, eyes on mine as he licks below my navel and removes my shoes one at a time. I'm on to his game as he pulls my pants to the floor, so slow my panties are soaked with my need. He kisses me there, runs his nose along the lace as he breathes me in. I grab his hair and moan when he suckles me through the fabric. Fuck. I spread my legs. Slowly, so damn slow, he peels them off and the warm air tickles my clit. I whimper when his breath fans over me. "Please."

He stands. *Wait, what?* I want to scream, "Back to your knees," but then his boxers are off and I sigh with relief because he steps into me. I hiss as the tight buds of my nipples meet his chest. My arms are around his neck and I lift to find his mouth, but he turns his head and navigates us into the streaming water.

Shampoo is first. Every tender stroke dissolves his anger and fear, and works me into a bigger ball of need. It's delicious, but so is his thick cock jutting into my stomach. I reach for it and he's quick to knock my hand away.

I groan and he smiles, tipping my head into the water to rinse and then repeat with conditioner. My body is next. He soaps up every available inch. Collarbone and arms; my breasts he takes on one at a time, tugging on the tips. I gasp and arch into him. But he moves to my back and butt, around to my stomach and then, achingly slowly, he moves between my legs. Parting my folds with his fingers, he rubs. I drop my forehead to his chest, rolling my hips with the rhythm of his hand. He flicks my clit and I almost come.

"Colin," I breathe into his neck. My nails sink into his shoulder as he does it again.

He stops and drops to his knees. *Yes, I love his mouth.* I fist his hair, but he washes my feet. *What? No!*

"Your morning run left us little time for anything but to dress and leave." He smiles—the bastard smiles.

"That's not fair." I jerk away from him as he stands and slip my hand between my thighs. If he won't do it, I'll make him watch as I do.

His nostrils flare and he's on me in a second. In the next my arms are above my head and I'm cold, pressed against the tile. "Don't you dare," he snarls. "You made a choice, suffer with it until I have time to work the pleasure out of you. It's mine."

"I didn't know it was dangerous," I hiss.

"And now you do."

He wants to be mad, fine. Rage simmers beneath my skin and out of my mouth one word at a time. "Let go of me."

Understanding flickers in his eyes. He pushed too far. As soon as his grip loosens, I fly from the shower and on my way out of the room I grab two towels. One I wrap around my aching and heavy breasts. Damn that man. I don't know how to do angry with Colin. Everything's new for me: him, a pseudo-relationship where I can't escape because we, for all intents and purposes, live together, or when I do, it lands me here, worked up and pissed off because he's furious over my need for space.

I take it out on my hair, scrubbing it with a towel until it's a halo of fury. When he appears in the doorway, naked as a jaybird, I turn away. My movements are staccato and when he sighs my name, I start the hair drier and hum "America the Beautiful" because it's stuck in my head from a rally last week. It infuriates me more.

Everything I do is out of spite. My hair in a high ponytail to bare my neck, the smallest thong I own slips into place. The tightest pencil skirt follows it and note to self: add extra sway to my ass at every possible moment. I screw professionalism and decide on a body-hugging silk halter that flares at the waist and holds all my parts up top in place sans bra.

I add makeup as my final fuck-you. *I look good.* Slipping into four-inch heels, I add that hip-sway and saunter into the suite. For a second I feel like a cheap replica of Brigitte Bardot in her prime, but I push through and pretend I'm all that and a bag of chips. He's on the phone by the window, a replay of when I came home this morning. I bypass his eyes, yet notice he's wearing the magenta tie I like to believe is for me. It may be his surrender flag, but too bad. Battle on. I do good mad and I'm ferocious.

It takes a minute to pack my camera, and everything I'll need for this morning's event. The flush of energy is my first clue he's behind me and then the heat radiating from his chest confirms it. His hand lands on my hip, as if to turn me toward him, but I stiffen and stand my ground.

"This is how it's going to be?" He asks.

Anger burns below my skin and I almost scream it out of me and at him. "This is how you decided it needed to be." I swallow and turn. His eyes show how he hurts, but he crossed a line with me this morning. He needs to know and understand the consequences that follow a stunt like his in the shower. "You're a smart man, Senator. I see it every day, so I need you to connect the dots here, because it's not something I like to talk about. Don't use sex to punish me. I've been there, done that, and I didn't get involved with you to retreat into a place that isn't good for me."

His eyes pop as he gets it. "God, Charlie."

"Don't Charlie me," I growl through the peak of my mad. I step away and tug my bag over my shoulder for an easy getaway. "I like sex with you, I like it a whole lot. Teasing me gets me going, and nothing is better than when you lose yourself in me; the rough grip and your strength is a turn-on. But there's a great difference between driving toward mutual pleasure and being spiteful. Don't ever take it that far again."

Finished, I bolt from his room and down the hall, jamming my finger trying to get the elevator to arrive before he follows. No such luck. Colin comes up behind me as I'm shaking the sting from my hand. He presses the button and the car arrives, damn him. We step in and stand shoulder to shoulder, floors dropping away as the silence tugs on my heart.

"I'm sorry," he whispers. "I was… worried. I fucked up, Charlie."

I close my eyes, warring with making it better and staying on the edge of my boiling point. I find his face in the silver doors. He's drowning in sorrow so I search for his hand, hanging limp by his side. He punches out a breath when I wind my fingers through his. "Apology accepted. And for the record, I expect you to make it up to me with your mouth."

COLIN DOESN'T LET GO of my hand until he's forced to. It's either release me or announce *us* to the world as the media captures his arrival. Helping me out of the SUV, he throws me a conciliatory look and then walks ahead with Evan and a local member of the McKenna campaign team. My mood verges on reckless. Although I know his worry-turned-frustration got the best of him and he's sorry for it, I want to make him pay. Not in a crazy-town way, but one that will move us past this morning's debacle.

Glancing away from his retreating ass, I focus on the schoolhouse where he's scheduled to speak in thirty minutes. Three stories of windows line the red-brick building that's more *Leave it to Beaver* than *The Jetsons*. The only modern upgrade is a new awning over the back entrance.

None of the women, and there are a bevy working today, pay attention as I walk the halls or when I enter the room staffers are using prior to the event. I get a few sideways glances as I listen on the outskirts of three different conversations, but never an invitation to join. My camera keeps me busy for a few minutes as I document conversations, including Colin's. Fifteen feet away, he reviews his speech with Evan and an advisor. Boredom turns into a brilliant idea when I spot the fruit on the buffet table.

Colin searches for me like clockwork every two minutes. It's a miracle the man can concentrate, but today I take advantage of his overprotectiveness. I'm ready with a heavily whippy-dipped strawberry when he looks up. I lick it, the tip of my tongue drawing through the cream. I'm on point when his eyes flare. Sucking on it has him riveted, his jaw clenches in time to his fist wrinkling the paper with his written speech. I bite into it. What's supposed to be sexy is hilarious as I jump back from the burst of juice spraying everywhere, including my chin and on Mable, the poor lady to my left, identified by a tag on her plaid button-up.

"I'm so sorry," I whisper and wipe at her sleeve with a napkin. This is authentic Charlie Carter, seduction turned sitcom.

I find Colin when the napkin sticks to my mouth, gross. He's a statue and at first I worry he's having a problem with brain synapses, but then I realize he's biting his bottom lip. Hilarious, I know. I'm a stitch and I laugh because it's just what we needed. Evan glances over too. I salute them and then search for the bathroom to clean myself up.

The click of my heels echoes through the empty halls. Lockers line both sides of the hallway, classroom doors break up the rectangular monotony, and posters advertising the upcoming *Alice in Wonderland* prom hint at a visit from the Mad Hatter.

The girl's room is down a darkened corridor. The door creaks as I slip in to find the sink and stalls behind a second door. I let the water run warm and then wash my face and hands, glad I could change both of our moods with fun fruit. I'll have to keep that in mind for future funks.

With a high-pitched and nerve-wracking sound, the door opens. My heart thumps. I freeze, my eyes darting back and forth in the mirror waiting for I don't know what; someone to walk in? That would make sense; it's a bathroom for God's sake. It's probably Mable come to chastise me and ask for dry-cleaning money.

Nothing happens. After a minute of silence I walk out and find the foyer-like space empty but for a single red rose on the floor. It wasn't there when I came in. I'm sure of it.

SIXTEEN

It's hot in the sun. Or maybe it's because Colin is picture perfect with his sleeves rolled to his elbows—from the boardroom to the bedroom in a second. He exudes sex appeal with just his cut forearms, ripped with muscles and veins. A delicious flush sparks my body past the point of easy need. He made sure of that this morning in the shower and I still intend to have him make up for his lapse in judgment—sooner rather than later.

Speech complete, he's shaking hands and kissing babies. I laugh when a young mother shoves an infant at him and gushes and coos as she takes a dozen pictures. I've taped the entire event and already coordinated with a reporter from Channel Ten for a copy of his feed. I'll pick them apart for the website later today.

I snap a few shots for myself as Colin approaches; his half-lidded eyes and saucy smile are meant for me. He glances at my hand and I think he may want to take it. I know I'd like him to; touching him would be a nice way to finish making up.

"Did you find something to eat, Ms. Carter? I saw you were having a rough time of it with the fruit tray this morning."

I smile. "I was hoping for heavier food, thick meat. Something I could really sink my teeth into, but it was apparently not on the menu."

His eyes water and finally he laughs, a hand-over-heart chuckle that's good for his soul. "I'll see what I can do for dinner."

"Please do," I say, grabbing my bag from the grass at my feet. "A girl nee—"

And just when things are getting good, Evan huffs to a stop next to him. "Colin, a moment please—*in private*." He glances at me. "I'm sorry, Charlie. I'll only be a minute."

"Sure, I understand." Colin's gaze swings from him to me, like he's in a tug of war: Charlie or Evan.

"Phil's men are in position and this is urgent," Evan says.

"Don't move." Colin pleads with his eyes. "Baby, please?"

"Yes, but I don't understand—"

Silencing me with his finger to my lips, he says, "I'll explain later." He squeezes my hand before turning to walk with Evan twenty feet away. As they stop, Colin turns and squares off, listening with arms crossed against his chest in a formidable stance. Evan talks so fast I can't make anything out, he points toward the school twice, flailing his arm the last time. Colin leans in as if bracing for a fight. Unleashing his hands, he gestures in a rapid-fire staccato beat before running them through his hair. *This is not good.*

Evan produces a large manila envelope, the contents immediately reviewed by Colin. He pales. He glances at me and then looks away, as if searching for someone in the retreating crowd.

I do the same, scanning the parking lot. I'm drawn to a man standing to the side with a long-range lens pointed at me. Hair on my arms springs up with goose bumps even though it's eighty degrees. Instinctively I grab my camera and take random shots as the same something-familiar feeling washes over me. But I don't recognize him. A baseball hat covers his hair, dark sunglasses and his lens hide most of his face, a huge sweatshirt conceals his frame. He turns, sprinting through the lot of people and cars.

Two guards, who most recently stood behind the stage during Colin's speech, race after him. Colin and Evan stalk toward me. I pack my camera, but fumble with my video equipment. "Here, let me." Colin takes over and I cringe when he rams everything in the bag. With the same impatience, he grabs my hand and hauls me across the lawn. I try to pull free but he clamps down harder and drags me to the SUV, pushing me inside by my ass. He slides in, Evan gets in front, and we lunge forward.

What the hell? Evan snatches my bag from the backseat. "Wait, Evan," I say, reaching for and catching the strap."

We play tug of war until he sighs, a small grin twitching at the side of his mouth. "I just need the memory card. I'll give it right back. Promise."

I pull the bag closer, bringing him with it and forcing him into a full body twist to look at me. "What's going on?"

His gaze flicks to Colin and back. He nods in his direction and says, "He'll explain. Give him time to wrap his head around it."

The strap slips through my fingers and I turn to the man with the answers. Finally his eyes find mine, calm, yet the veins in his neck throb in time to my racing heart.

Grabbing my chin, he scans over my face before closing his eyes and tugging me forward. "*Fuck,*" he breathes into my forehead before his lips meet my skin. He tucks me under his chin and I hold on, waiting for him to explain. It doesn't happen. Mile after mile flies by in silence.

And then his phone rings, just once before he snaps it up from lap to his ear. "Phil, what the fuck is going on? Twice in one day is unacceptable. My instructions were explicit, yet this arrived, unsolicited. Explain how that's possible if your team was in place as they should have been?" He listens for a heartbeat before vibrating with fury. "Let me be clear: I want security present at every location, at the hotels and with her every second." Looking at me out of the corner of his eye, he growls, "Get them there. Yes, every minute. I don't want her left alone. Figure it out." Colin hangs up and looks out the window, pulling his bottom lip until we reach the next stop.

Evan and the driver bail, and although the air is kicking in the car, it's hot in here.

Colin tugs my chin, forcing eye contact. "It's best if you head to the plane; you'll be safe there."

"What don't you want me to know?"

The expressionless mask is in place, but his eyes flash with… fear? Trepidation? "Charlie." He sighs, gripping my hand. "I don't want to get into it, not now; my schedule is tight. Do you trust me?"

"You know I do."

"Then let me take care of this. I promise, it's nothing I can't manage."

"I understand if you don't have time to talk now, but you will tell me. I don't like being kept in the dark."

He pauses to brush an escaped curl off my face. "Don't worry about anything. I'm handling it. You're fine."

It's almost as if he's convincing himself, and then he presses his mouth against mine. Barely parting his lips he breathes me in, touching the tip of his tongue along the length of my bottom lip. I sigh, lifting my hand to hold his cheek.

"Let me stay with you, please."

He groans and kisses me, really kisses me, deep and hungry, the pent-up passion he squelched earlier raging between us. I'm just as hot for him. Speech be damned, I pull up my skirt and straddle his thighs. "Fuck, Charlie," he murmurs into my mouth. "I can't. I need four hours."

The heavy weight of his hands run up and down my legs, closer with each pass to where I need him the most, but I know he'll never get there—not now.

"I've had a really weird day," I say and climb off him. Tugging everything in place, I'm shut down again, frustrated.

"Baby, I know. I'll make it right, I promise."

I nod and that's it. With a final squeeze to my hand, he's out the door. He stops for a second to direct the driver, who rushes to the vehicle and climbs in. By the time I look back, Colin is gone. I'm left alone to wonder what the hell is happening.

"Per the senator's instructions, I'll have you back on the plane in twenty minutes, ma'am. Sit back and relax."

I roll my eyes; this day keeps getting better and better. In the span of twenty-four hours I've gone from miss to ma'am: *fabulous*.

Traffic is heavy on the way to the airport; bumper to bumper, we barely move. I pull out my laptop and work for another twenty.

"Is there an accident?" I ask.

"Must be, but nothing has been reported."

"Maybe we should turn around and wait for Colin. He'll probably be done with his meeting before you can return for him."

"I have strict instructions, ma'am. I'm to take you to the senator's plane and nowhere else." He inches up to an intersection and I think we'll arrive tomorrow.

"Do me a favor and call me Charlie."

"Yes, ma'am."

Right. We move an amazing ten feet and then screech to a halt. My seat belt locks. I shift against the restraint and glance outside to find a ginormous black F-150 barreling down the street perpendicular to us.

It's not stopping.

We're in its path. *I'm in the path.*

I stutter out a warning and reach for the roll bar to brace for the collision.

The huge grill roars forward. I scream and tuck my head into my shoulders just as the SUV spurs forward, pulling us up and around the next car in line.

"Holy shit," I pant. "He didn't even try to stop."

But I'm talking to myself. The driver's already on the phone relaying information to someone, leaving me with more questions than when I left Colin.

What the hell is going on?

I CAN'T FORGET THE crazy morning. I work for hours; select pics for the blog and social media sites, post updates, write a four-page article for *Tomorrow Today* and submit it to the publisher. I gorge myself on vanilla lattes and Mrs. Brenner's double chocolate chunk brownies with fudge on top. And still the thunder of the F-150 won't escape my brain.

Evan pops in, smiles, and takes a seat in the furthest row. Colin arrives. Tall, broad, sun kissed from a day outside, but his expression is taut until he spots me on the couch. He relaxes next to me without a word, taking my hand and holding it in his lap. Thirty seconds later, he tilts his head back and closes his eyes, jaw grinding out more tension. I need to talk to him about yoga—his stress level is off the charts.

"Colin?" I whisper, scrambling to my knees to get closer.

His lids open and he looks at me, tender, just like the brush of his fingers over my cheek. And then they reach the back of my neck to hold me in place, firm and possessive. His gaze slips in intensity and my heart stumbles. There's something there, like a mirror of my own feelings. Love. Devotion. Need.

God, it deepens as his chest lurches. I groan and lunge forward at the same time he does. Our lips crash together. While Mrs. Brenner prepares the cabin for takeoff, he pins me to his chest and devours me, hard, hungry, controlling this kiss until he pulls a whimper from my lungs.

He breaks away and growls, "Breathe."

I gasp, sucking in air as he tucks me into the crook of his neck. "My sweet Charlie," he murmurs, rubbing my back as a shiver chases his fingers.

"We'll talk tonight, I promise." He sighs. "I just need some time to decompress."

I nod and stay wrapped up in him until Mrs. Brenner reminds me a seatbelt is mandatory and I reluctantly slip from his lap, starving for answers and Colin McKenna.

Engines roar, we take flight, and Colin and Evan retreat to the conference room as soon as clearance is given to walk the cabin. *Judge Judy* does little to occupy my roving mind, after episode one I flip to the movie channel. Ryan Gosling slams Rachel McAdams against a wall, all wet and sexy-like, reminding me of hot showers.

Damn and damn again. *Cosmo* it is. I flip to page thirty: "You on Top, the Fierce New Secret to Success."

I toss it down. It's not fair. It isn't, I say to myself and stand. I'm a woman, damn straight, and I had a shitty, strange day. Fighting with Colin is draining; mystery men and racing cars are nerve wracking—for him and me. One step takes me toward the man who can make it all better. The second and third allow time to form a half-cocked stress relief plan. He needs it and so do I. It's *Cosmo*'s fault. That magazine could give ideas to the devil on how to be sinful. Smoothing my palms along my skirt, I pause and then knock, not light, but loud—I-am-woman-hear-me-roar kind of loud.

I don't wait for a reply. As I step in, two heads snap up. I've got their attention, but I only want one. Colin.

Evan busts out a grin and grabs his papers from the table.

"Don't be too long, Charlie. I need him one more time before we land."

He winks on his way out, and I flip the deadbolt behind him. The heavy clench of the lock settles and the only thing I hear is the heavy thud of my pulse pounding in my brain.

I turn, loosening my hair from the band holding it in place as I do. I shake my head and it falls in waves down my back.

Colin swallows and watches every step I take, every inch I pull my skirt up. I stop in front of him, legs apart, the barest string of lace hidden just under my hem. He licks his lips.

"You owe me, Mr. McKenna, and I've come to collect."

He growls and reaches for me, but I swat his hands away. Finger to shoulder, I push him back in his chair. "You left me hungry and I didn't like it."

I fall to my knees. His belt is an easy off. A spark lights in his already smoldering eyes and then our combined efforts take over to free him from pants and boxer briefs, just enough so I can take him in my mouth. Musk and maleness fuel my need. He grows with every lick until silk and steel come to life in my hand and drive to the back of my throat.

"Jesus, fuck."

I vibrate my appreciation around his shaft and take what's mine. Reinforce that I'm committed to whatever we've got between us, that I want him, want to learn how to be in a relationship, good days and bad. But it's a give-and-take. I'm going to take everything he's willing to give and then I'm going to force him to give me all of him.

His cock swells on my tongue. "Baby." A string of expletives is lost to the roar in my ears as he comes. But it's not enough, not after I swallow and lick every last drop. I'm starving.

I shake as I stand. His fingers steady me and push my skirt past my hips as I climb on his lap, a knee on either side of his legs. Pulling my panties aside, I take his still throbbing dick and rub him against my swollen clit, up and down and through my folds. I can't stop watching his crown touch me, soft yet unyielding. "You feel so good."

He tips my chin with thumb and forefinger. "Don't ever stop telling me what you need. Always, Charlie," he whispers, and then he grabs my waist and sweeps me up and onto the edge of the table where he spreads my legs wide. "I need to taste you," and he does, licking my entire length. Our mimicked groans collide and I press into him, offering myself and at the same time, demanding more.

Wrapping his arms under and around me, he holds me open to do wicked things with his mouth. "Good God," I cry and let my head fall back against the table. We get lost—lost in his lapping tongue and the scrape of his teeth, and we find a little bit of wild in the stroke of his finger there and oh… my…. *Holy shit. Right fucking there.* I scream at the unexpected fullness and arch up, his hand finding mine and holding tight as I lose a little more of myself. Our fingers tangle together and press to my stomach as he demolishes his meal and makes me come harder than I ever have before.

"Colin…," I whisper, barely remembering who I am and where we are. His damn mouth is awe-inspiring. "Oh, my God."

He chuckles. Kissing my clitoris, once, twice, he murmurs indecent things into my most sensitive place as if it's a favorite of his. He looks up through his lashes and moves to lick and bite first one thigh and then the other, stopping to pull me up and onto his lap.

"So good," I murmur, just before I employ the same techniques, licking and biting into his mouth until we both can't breathe. After a few minutes I pull away, gasping as I duck my head into his neck, reveling in all things Colin. He rubs my back. A minute later he has my chin again and I'm forced into eye contact.

"Does this mean I'm a part of the mile-high club?" I ask before he can get anything out.

At first he smiles, and then a laugh vibrates in his chest. Pushing damp hair from my forehead, he says, "You're exactly what I need."

I smile. "I wanted to help you decompress, there's time to talk later, and we will, about lots of things. But it doesn't have to be difficult, so relax, okay? Life is a bunch of lessons—one after the other—and as long as we learn from them, we'll get it right next time."

He closes his eyes for a split second. "I'm sorry about this morning. I was thoughtless—"

I hold up a finger, forcing the next word into silence. "I don't want you to be sorry, I want you to understand. I love being with you." I glance at the table behind me as if it's proof of my orgasmic ability. "It's amazing in many ways. Other than the obvious, let's just say for years the arctic tundra was warmer than I was toward the male population. Outside of Ali and my family, my best friend growing up was my therapist, Sylvia. She was on speed dial and I saw her three times a week. I've taken baby steps since my last name changed from Hilton to Carter. Baby steps that got me to you."

His brow crumbles into three lines. I smooth them away. "And I love the pace we're at now. I'm better than great. I'm happy, Colin. I am. But I have limits, and this morning we almost crossed one that wouldn't be healthy for me."

"I'm going to be what you need, Charlie. I'll wake up each morning and ask myself what I can do to make you crazy about me."

I laugh. "I think we've already determined that's true. Your mouth can make me crazy daily." I smack a kiss on his lips and stand, smoothing all my garments in place while he watches like a hawk.

He reaches for my hips, holding me in front of him. A world of emotion plays out on his face: self-recrimination, doubt, need. "God-damn it, Charlie," he groans, crushing his head into my stomach.

"I've got you," I whisper, holding him right back. Sometimes he's such a contradiction: tough but sensitive, strong yet vulnerable. Colin McKenna has his own past that haunts him.

One day maybe he'll let it go and love me.

TWO HOURS LATER, WE'RE back at the hotel, in bed with beer and pizza. Colin removed his shirt and pants and is eating in boxer briefs. Very un-presidential, but very, very hot. I smile, sipping my beer to hide it. He takes a huge bite from a slice and looks up. "What?" he mumbles with his mouth full.

"Nothing, I'm enjoying the view." And I am. His chest, tight muscles dusted with dark hair, ripped abs, the long bulge barely contained in his shorts, thick thighs. Dear baby Jesus, he's pretty. I giggle as his eyes darken. "Don't get any ideas. I'm hungry for food this time."

"Okay, but let me know if you change your mind. I'm more than happy to comply." He winks and rips another bite from the slice.

Sparks in my nether region tell me I like his offer. "I'll be sure to let you know."

But for the next fifteen minutes we focus on baseball, the Red Sox working on a no-hitter, and finishing off the large pepperoni and cheese. The man can eat. When the box is empty, I clear it from the bed and test his mood. "I thought the Montgomerys were in Kansas City. Why didn't we see them?" I watch for lines between his eyes, tension in his jaw, but he stays smooth and relaxed, stretching out his legs and leaning up on his elbow.

"They were there, but kept to their own itinerary. Ella assisted with some door-to-door campaigns. John had a fundraiser."

"They stayed behind?"

He nods. "Captain Greene turned around after dropping us off. They'll be here in the morning."

"Are you keeping them away from me?" I ask.

"Yes," he answers and then takes a long drag from his bottle, watching me as he does.

I smile. "Why?"

"I promised to protect you, Charlie. I've done a shit job of it so far, but some things are in my control, and the Montgomerys are one of them. Ella and you are like sugar and vinegar: you're sweet and she's distasteful." He drains his beer and sets it on the side table. "Everyone in that family is difficult. I recognize my parents and friends—the people important to me"—he reaches for my hand and winds our fingers together—"find them off-putting at best, so I've chosen to keep them separate from us."

"Is that why they weren't invited to the Kellys' party?"

He nods. "For the most part. The Kellys and Montgomerys have vastly disparate beliefs. They couldn't be further apart in principles."

"What do you mean?"

Shrugging, he says, "The Kellys value family and loyalty above all else; they're a close group that support and love each other through the highs and lows in life."

"A lot like you."

A small half smile appears, but it doesn't reach his eyes. "Maybe. The Montgomerys are not as tight. John and his wife, Joan, barely speak to one another anymore. John's career always took precedence over his family and then when Abby and Sara died…." He glances at our fingers as he starts a mini thumb-war. "When they died the family fell apart."

I wait until he looks at me to ask, "What is it about John and Ella that binds you to them?"

"It's complicated." He sighs. "I was a part of their circle for a long time, friends with Ella before I began dating and then married Abby. That entire time I was ensconced in their world and had their unerring support of my career.

"When my family fell apart it didn't affect John's approval and advocacy of either of those things. He's a political machine, the connections he has, his knowledge, all of it."

Colin rolls over to lay his head on my thigh and my hand goes directly to his hair, stroking. He closes his eyes. "I don't want them to interfere with what we have. You're important to me, Charlie. I'll take whatever steps necessary to keep you safe and happy, I promise you my actions this morning—they won't happen again, and I won't subject you to the Montgomerys negativity. I decided after our visit to New York you shouldn't have to endure another encounter such as the one you did. I've tried very hard to establish boundaries with John and Ella when it comes to you."

My heart races. God, I love this man. I work my way down to lie with him face-to-face, and he holds my hip, clad only in a pair of panties and tank top that meets the lace. Heat follows the pads of his fingers as he traces a circular pattern on my skin, and the very near reality that I'm going to miss him for six days makes my chest ache.

Suddenly every minute we have is very important. "What time are you leaving tomorrow?"

"Eight. Why don't you come with me?" His casual tone belies the tense grip he now has on my outer thigh.

"I can't do that. Your meeting is behind closed doors; even Evan isn't attending."

"Scott's offices are near a shopping district and an art museum. You could spend the morning there. I'll be out by two; we could eat downtown."

"Tempting, but while you're in a business suit, I'll be in my bathing suit by the pool. It's ninety in Florida." I shake his shoulder and smile. "You're dealing with a girl from Michigan. We don't see this kind of weather until mid-July. Florida is the tropics to us."

Three lines appear between his eyes. "Charlie…." He's using that tone, the you-will-do-as-I-say tone and salute me after. My woman parts like this tone and I inch closer to feel up the sexy indent above his waistband, also known as an oblique, also known as the perfect handle to grab as he fucks me into tomorrow.

"Yes?"

"Come with me."

"No." He huffs and rolls to his back, and I climb on top of him, straddling his stomach. "I've asked you to tell me what's going on and you won't, so I'll make decisions based on what I want to do, and I want to play poolside."

His hands are hot on my thighs; up and down they stroke and I squeeze him beneath me. "It's nothing for you to worry about."

"Tell me," I growl.

He hesitates and looks a bit sick. "There's an overly zealous campaign fanatic out there who wants my attention, that's all."

"That's all?" I squeak. "What the hell, Colin? Are we talking about a stalker?"

"It hasn't reached that definition at this point, but there is someone following my campaign closely."

"That's what Evan pulled you aside to discuss."

"Yes."

"What was in the envelope?"

He sighs. "A note, similar to a few others in which they plot out my schedule, nothing serious."

"Do you think this will become dangerous? What about the truck?" Oh, God. My pulse is near explosive levels.

"Hey," he says, pulling me down and tucking my chin into his neck. ". Everything's fine. It was unrelated. The police spoke to the driver five minutes after the near collision. He was texting. Apparently he had no idea he almost hit you."

I nod and hold him tighter than before. "Stop shielding me, I want to know everything."

"I don't want you to worry. I'll protect you, Charlie. I promise I will."

"It's not me I'm worried about. I'm not the one with some crazy stalker who's trying to get my attention. What are you doing for protection? Doesn't the Secret Service get involved in issues like this?"

"I have everything taken care of. The Service is assigned once the candidate is confirmed. Until then, my own security detail will be with us from event to event. Everything is fine."

"Colin, I—"

"Please, Charlie. I've got it covered. If you prefer to stay at the hotel, I ask that you stay on campus. You'll have a member of the security team assigned to you anywhere you go; you will not be alone, ever. Your stunt this morning almost gave Phil and his team a collective coronary. They weren't expecting an early morning run so no one was with you. Can you do that for me?"

"I thought someone was following me," I admit and shiver. "At first I thought it was you running to catch up to me, but then on some level I knew it wasn't and I got scared."

His fingers dig into my ass. "Why didn't you tell me?"

"I didn't realize it was important at the time. I had no idea this was happening."

"Charlie, never again, do you understand me? Never again are you to leave without me or someone from the security team."

"Yes." I give my consent. "But you realize I wouldn't have gone out had I known. You need to tell me what's going on. I can handle it, Colin, I can." Crap. I hug him, tight, and breathe in sandalwood and my own fear. "I'm afraid you'll get hurt."

"Nothing is going to happen to me. It's probably a woman who thinks I'm hot. I get that a lot, you know."

"Not funny. Promise me you'll be careful."

"I promise. And you need to do the same. Listen to me when I ask you to do something, and no more early morning runs unless you plan them with me." He tilts my chin up so our eyes lock. "I worry about you too." His mouth curves into a small, almost sad smile.

My heart is off the charts and I almost blurt out *I love you.* Instead I say, "Please be careful. I don't know what I'd do without you."

"I will, baby. I'll take care of everything." And I believe him.

SEVENTEEN

"CHARLIE?"

"Hmm?"

Colin nuzzles my neck, kisses his way up my jaw until he finds my lips. He is minty fresh. As I open my eyes, my vision is filled with freshly shaven, beautiful blue-eyed Colin McKenna. "Morning." I run my hands up his arms, which are pressed on either side of my head, up to his shoulders to cup his cheeks. White shirt, black tie, and fully suited. Damn.

His smile is breathtaking, and so is the dimple. "Good morning yourself, baby."

"Come back to bed?"

Pressing his lips into my forehead, he says, "You're more than tempting." He kisses my nose and then mouth, sweeping his tongue against mine and teasing me long enough that my pulse beats between my thighs.

"Hmmm, you're not going to, are you?" I squirm because he's getting me worked up and he's going off to work. Damn again.

He grins against me. "I can't, the driver is downstairs waiting. Remember what you promised: stay at the hotel." He eyes me suspiciously, as if I may make a break for it.

"You promised too. Be careful."

"Always. Shall I look for you by the pool when I get back?"

That brightens my mood. "Yes. While I wait for you, I'll find someone to rub sunscreen on my back. Ivory skin and all that jazz—wouldn't want to get a burn."

That does it. His eyes storm over. Without a word, he grips my chin and very deliberately, slowly moves his lips against mine. Pressing me against the pillow he devours my mouth, tasting and demanding an exact response. My hands are in his hair, pulling him into me.

I grab his tie with every intention of stripping him; the driver can wait. And then my arms are flat against the mattress, pinned by Colin McKenna. I groan as he bites my bottom lip, the piercing sensation has a direct connection to my clit. *Oh, for the love of God.* I lose myself as he dives deeper into me, biting, licking, sucking and my body bursts, a flush dampening my panties.

He groans as I give just as good as I get. But then he breaks away. I try to follow but I'm a prisoner, held captive with his hands pinning mine.

"Don't bait me, Charlie," he says in that tone. "I'll see you by the pool later, and I better not learn another man has touched you." He releases me and leaves without another word.

Shit. I lie there, all alone and panting against the mattress, missing him already. I shouldn't have pushed him; for whatever reason he gets jealous.

I'm determined to enjoy our last two days before I leave Thursday. I roll onto his pillow and breathe out my sadness. It's irrational. I've lived without him for twenty-nine years, why does it all of a sudden feel like I'm leaving the most vital part of me behind? As I reach underneath the pillow I run into a piece of paper.

I'm lost in you.
Colin

I hold it to my chest, tearing up. I never imagined love felt like this—this beautiful and terrifying gift that unlocked my soul, demands I live and seek out more than what I had. At the same time, it awoke the possibility of feeling the same kind of devotion. And now that the chance exists, I'm going to fight for the dream to come true.

THE SUN IS HOT, my swimsuit hotter, in a '1950s bombshell kind of way. I can rock vintage glam and I can't wait for Colin to see my new strapless one-piece that accentuates all of my curves. But let's be real. I'm as pale as the whitecaps rolling onto the beach, so the ten coats of sunscreen are necessary—unless I'd like to go home more lobster than sun bunny.

As I finish my final lather to my thighs, a shadow blocks my light. I glance up, seeing legs first, thick with a fine dusting of blonde hair, thick, muscular calves and thighs, tight shorts, wide chest. He's nice looking but blocking my view of the ginormous pool. Water beads all over said parts and his hair is slicked back from a recent swim. Glasses cover his eyes, but the weight of his stare is heavy and hangs on for too long. *Maybe the pin-up look was a bad idea.*

I smile because I bought the suit for Colin, but that was the wrong move. Mr. Swimmer thinks it was for him and he sits on the lounger next to me. "Charlie, it's nice to see you."

Hair bristles at my nape. Weird. I take a peek behind me to the men roasting in black slacks ten feet away. Colin wasn't kidding when he said I'd have protection: two very large, hostile, come-near-her-and-I-will-draw-a-weapon kind of protection.

They haven't moved but for the sweat dripping down their temples, so I'm assuming all is well.

"Alex Miller," he says, reaching out in greeting. "Friend from Blake's fundraiser."

"Hey," I say and take his hand. When I'm ready for release he hangs on a beat longer. "What are you doing in Florida?"

"Business in Orlando. I came down on Sunday for a few days in the sun before I get into my presentation tomorrow." He waves over a waitress. "Can I buy you a drink? I just ordered one myself and then I noticed you here."

"Sure, I'd love a mimosa."

He orders and then sinks back onto the chair while we wait.

"What is it that you do?" I ask.

"Natural products for pools—less expensive than saltwater and better for you than chlorine. We're finally on to the rollout phase, pitching to Florida suppliers this week."

"Do you travel often?"

"This spring and into the summer I'll spend a lot of time on the road."

"Where's the next stop?" I ask at the same time fumbling to raise the lounger.

Alex pops up. "Here, let me help you. I'll be in and out of every state east of Mississippi and south of Kentucky over the next few weeks."

He brushes against my shoulder as he pulls away and an uncomfortable shiver sparks down my spine.

"There, that should do it." He retreats as our beverages arrive. "Cheers," he says, raising his glass to mine.

"So, you were telling me about your upcoming travel schedule." I pause to sip my drink. "That must be hard, to be away from home."

He shrugs and looks out to the gulf. "I don't have a family to miss me. It's easy for the single guy to go on the road. Anyway, where's home for you?"

"Michigan, born and raised. The only time I've been out of the state was a trip to Disney when I was eighteen and then to visit my sister at school. I guess that makes me a homebody." I really am sheltered. This job and Colin are blazing a new path of discovery for Charlie Carter.

I smile but Alex looks like his gin and tonic is sour. He stands and an electric pull settles in behind me.

"Colin, I just sat down with Charlie. For a drink. I didn't know she would be here."

"Alex."

Colin's fingers brush my shoulder and I lean in to him; this is the kind of shiver I like.

"Why are you here?"

I glance at Colin and narrow my eyes at his sharp tone. But then I get lost in him in a swimsuit. If I could whistle, I would do it. A two-inch navy line rims the waist of his sky-blue suit. It doesn't hit mid-thigh, more boxer brief than board short, and I'm not the only one appreciating the view. Every woman here is staring. I glare, and then claim him with a hand to the back of his leg, fingers reaching under the hem. Mine. I'd growl, but that might be taking things a bit too far.

Colin looks down and smiles.

"Excuse me," Alex interjects. I drive my gaze away from my sex god to his friend. "Nice to see you, Charlie. Enjoy the sun."

"Thanks for the cocktail." I wave as he walks away.

Colin stares after him until he exits the swimming area. His expressionless mask is in place until he looks at me. His eyes are ocean blue and churning like a tidal wave. *Oh my.* This man is hot and he's hot for me and my body too. He drags a lingering look from the tips of my toes, up my legs, over the apex of my thighs, stomach, breasts and then my mouth and hair.

"Like what you see, Senator?"

He leans down, planting a fist on either side of my hips, and his lips hover next to my ear. "I want to strip you bare, Charlie. I want my mouth on you until you're screaming my name and pulling my hair."

Shit. I squirm as he leans away. He can't say things like that unless he means it. "Okay."

A slow, wicked grin relaxes his face as he sits in front of my legs. "What are you drinking, baby?"

I love it when he calls me that; it makes my heart swell and my groin ache. I beam at him.

"Why are you smiling?"

"Because that one word from your mouth makes me wet."

He growls and I giggle.

The waitress appears, spending way too much time enjoying my view.

But Colin doesn't pay her more than a second's attention before turning back to me, his grin spreading into a dimple. "You're stunning."

"Thank you. I bought my suit this morning; I'm glad you like it."

His brow rises. "I'm quite certain every man here likes it. What else did you do while I was away?"

"Not much. I got a pedi." Pulling one of my feet in front of him I place it in his lap, wiggling my bright pink toes. Colin wraps his fingers around my foot to look at the polished nails and begins to massage it.

"Very nice."

"And I bought a magazine."

"What, by chance, were you reading about today?"

"Nothing much." A blush rushes up my chest and into my cheeks.

"Then why are you turning red?" His drink arrives and he sips, waiting with an arched brow for my response.

"If you must know, I will tell you." I sigh. "Colin, I have zero experience, other than with you. I feel slightly inadequate in the seduction and sex department, so true to form, I have decided to complete some research. With *Cosmo*."

"Charlie." He chuckles, shaking his head. "You're everything I've ever wanted. I have never been happier or more gratified with my sex life than during these last months with you."

I roll my eyes, incredulous.

"Look at me," he says in that tone. "I'm serious; you're amazing. I'm more than satisfied. I'm astounded by you."

"Okay, enough, you're making me blush again." I push away so I don't jump on him in broad daylight—that would be some headline: "Redhead Accosts Senator Poolside, Charges Pending."

"Anyway, I was reading until Alex found me."

His lip curls.

"You don't like him, do you?"

"No. He was Aiden's friend more than mine. Alex was a loner, so he brought him into the fold of our group."

"Your mom told me he's friends with Ella, too?"

Colin hesitates. "Yes, they met through me. He didn't bother you, did he?"

"We were just making small talk." His short answer is frustrating, but I don't poke for a broader answer because Evan walks up, very much in his element—the California surfer boy finally by some water. Hawaiian floral board shorts look as natural as his suit. He's leaner than Colin, but his entrance garners as much attention.

I laugh when he rubs his chest, and looks around as if he has his pick. "What?" he says, as he sits on the lounge chair Alex left open.

"You're so full of shit, Evan Daugherty."

"Not shit, Charlie. Just confidence."

"Ugh, you sound like my sister."

"You've said that before. I think I'd like to meet her. But until I do, I'm enjoying a much-needed afternoon away from politics. You really need to speak with your boyfriend about time off. His piss-poor benefit package needs fine-tuning."

My heart races into a pitter-patter: *boyfriend*? Colin's fingers don't miss a beat with my foot.

"You get into trouble with too much free time."

Watching a blonde walk past in the skimpiest two-piece bikini I have ever seen, Evan answers, "You may be right." We laugh as he hops up and heads to the bar at the far side of the pool.

Colin drags his fingers from my calf to thigh. "And you, my sweet Charlie, what would you like to do?"

I'd like to rush him upstairs and into bed, but instead of holing away in our room all day I decide on an outdoor sport and he agrees to swim with me. We're up and setting our drinks down when I remember my back.

I turn and lean down for my sunscreen and push my ass into his crotch. *Oops*. Colin groans so I linger and wiggle until he tugs my hair, almost playful, but not. I giggle and hand him the lotion over my shoulder.

"Do you think you can win at this game?" he asks in my ear.

"God, I hope not."

He mumbles some very choice words about how I'm going to pay for a sassy mouth with my mouth while he rubs and rubs and rubs. Damn him. He ends with a kiss to my neck and then he pounces. Hand on my shoulders, he turns me so fast I don't have time to scream before I'm over his shoulder.

"You wouldn't." I spank his ass.

"I might," he says, bending so I fall into a cradle next to his chest.

"But not now."

He smiles and then tosses me in.

After sitting in the sun for so long, the initial contact is a freezing shock to my system. I surface, sputtering. Colin grabs me, but before he pulls me in I slip beneath the water to slick back my hair, and then come up, hands sliding to his shoulders, legs around his waist. The bulge in his shorts presses into me just where I like it, so I grind down in retaliation.

"Don't move," he growls, steadying my hips as I pulse into naughty thoughts. I'd like to kiss him, but we're already pushing boundaries in public. I suppose that's why he scheduled our stay at the posh private resort, so we could play with few people paying attention. To get my body back in line with our location, I look to the rock wall on the far side and his gaze follows.

"I'll race you," he says, and then it's game on. Using him as a springboard, I jump off without warning. My parents believe kids should be busy, so our after-school routine consisted of volleyball, softball, soccer, and swimming. And I was good at the fifty-meter freestyle.

I almost beat him, but his last minute push and lengthy arm reach give him a slight advantage.

His smirk is too much. I fool him with a congratulatory kiss and then with hands on his shoulders, I use my entire body weight to sink him under water. He laughs when breaking the surface, but I know him and try like hell to get away. As I dive, he grabs my waist, and using the rock wall as leverage he throws me three feet. I beg for mercy when I pop free and he pulls me close. This time I play nice, leaving my legs to hang limp next to him. Laying my hands on his biceps, I work to catch my breath. Colin's eyes narrow as he scans my chest and then yanks me against him.

"What's wrong?"

"Cover yourself," he snaps.

I look down. Shit, my suit slipped. My already racing pulse skyrockets.

"I'm sorry," I whisper, tugging it up.

"It's not your fault." The words are conciliatory, but his tone is hard. "I can't stand that someone might see you." He looks around.

I scan the pool and surrounding area to gauge the reactions on the dozen or so faces. No one appears amused or is studying our antics, but I sink in the water and closer to Colin. My unplanned exposé would be embarrassing for me, but downright scandalous for him.

EIGHTEEN

COLIN HAS HIS HANDS on me. In fact, it's been hard for him to keep them to himself since we met poolside. He's different. It's not just the touching but his constant stare, as though if he doesn't hold me or see me, I may disappear. And I will in thirty-two hours.

Time is ticking toward my departing flight and every minute we spend together seems to find us inextricably closer. So from swimming to lounging to showering and dressing, we talk about everything and nothing. Elementary school best friends, Evan and Ali, my ungodly fear of crows because of Alfred Hitchcock's *The Birds*, pets in the past and his hopes for a chocolate lab in the future, my guitar and how it helped bring me out of my shell, little things, big things, and everything that all at once makes it seem like two puzzles fell into the same box and the pieces work together to form a beautiful picture.

But on the way to the restaurant for dinner his silence becomes deafening when I ask about girlfriends. He begrudgingly admits to high school love, Becca Johnson, and in college it was Liv Gordon, but then he clams up. I let him have a moment as we walk in and become two of the fifty or so other diners at the Seaside Escape. The entire dining area is open, exposed to white sand and the rising tide of the gulf as it rolls in. A soft breeze manages to tame the evening heat as the sun hovers over the horizon in the distance.

We're directed to a table with a great view and after drink orders are taken, he leans over to kiss me. Just a touch of his lips, but it makes me shiver just the same. Although the atmosphere here is casual, wood beams wound with string lights and thick rope, it's more than romantic with the natural beauty painted before us. We sit with his fingers playing with mine, and watch the sky cast blurred layers of orange and pink as daylight comes to a close. Soon the only thing that remains is the leftover painter's palette in the distance and seagulls flying over the water. Cocktails arrive and Colin orders dinner.

With romance top of mind, I ask, "How did your parents meet?"

His head tips as if in reflection and it's a minute before he answers. "My dad fell for Mom in the sixth grade, but she despised him." He smiles, lifting his bottle for a drink.

"When did she realize he was the one?" I ask.

"Not until high school. They were friends through middle school, after she learned to put up with his incessant pledges of love."

"That's sweet."

"Not to the president of the student council, who only had eyes for the captain of the football team. Dad was a mess until freshman year when Mom finally gave in and went on a date with him. They've been together ever since."

"When did they get married?"

"Just after college. I came a year later and Ryanne when I was five."

"Tell me about your sister."

"So curious today, Charlie," he says.

"I'm interested in everything about you." I tilt my head to look at him and the insanely snug T-shirt clinging to his chest and arms. Casual Colin is better than the sunset.

Squeezing our linked hands, he says, "I don't mind. She's a Nurse Practitioner at Massachusetts General. That's where she met her fiancé, Brett. He's an orthopedic surgeon."

"She works with him?"

He laughs. "No, he did my dad's knee replacement."

"Love at first joint." I giggle but his face falls. The levity we were enjoying is sucked out to sea with a gust of wind and a newfound tension stiffens his shoulders.

"I guess that's how it happened for them."

"How was it for you with Abby; did you know right away?"

"Charlie," he says with an ounce of warning.

I've pushed him in the corner, partly on purpose hoping he'd open up and release the sadness that's a constant companion in his eyes. Even when he laughs and smiles there are shadows there, but for us to have any sort of a future he needs to sort them out. "You never talk about her."

"I've told you I don't like to."

"I'm trying to understand." He looks out toward the water, our fingers rolling together.

"She was beautiful," he whispers. "I suppose I fell fast. I wanted to have someone with me."

"You wanted a family?"

His gaze remains disconnected. "Very much. I grew up with such a strong sense of family; I wanted to have the same for myself."

"So you had a baby?" I watch him carefully, looking for his reaction and it comes in crashing waves, much like the ocean when a storm makes it angry. It hits first and then shock when pain grips him.

He shifts away. Releasing my hand, he toys with the paper label around his bottle and then he takes a long drag, all the while looking at the simmering sky—looking anywhere but at me. Minutes pass in silence and my heart thumps, uncomfortable. Finally he says, "I won't discuss that topic. Don't ask me again."

"I didn't mean to upset you."

It's a relief when he continues, even though his anger is palpable. "I've told you before, Abby isn't an easy topic for me. The child is absolutely something I will not discuss. I can't make it clearer than this, Charlie."

He stares for moments, devoid of feeling, so much like the first night we were together. Colin has an emotional limit. I drive him against it, and when I do he pushes me away. My stomach churns. Maybe we're meant for each other, two fucked-up souls mucking through the waters together.

"I'm sorry." He sighs. "One day I'll tell you, but not now."

I nod. "I didn't realize how hurtful the topic is for you."

"It's something I try not to think about."

"Maybe you need to confront your demons." I grab for his hand. "I'll help you get past them."

The sad half smile does nothing for reassurance. "It's not that easy. In one moment, the future I thought belonged to me was destroyed. I've spent years trying to forget and you're asking me to remember."

"I am. It may be the only way to truly move beyond it; deal with the past so you can have a future free of pain." *So you can have a future with me.* "I had to do it. After I was raped, and the other... decision was made, I shut down. I could barely even speak to Ali."

Colin's jaw works back and forth in a tense clench. He doesn't like to hear me talk about Shane Roberts.

"When I came to the Carters and after...." I wave away toward the sand so I don't have to say it. "For a long time I ignored what happened. I'd push thoughts of it and Shane to a corner in my mind; I'd do anything to forget, but it didn't work." I lean in and take his chin the way he does mine. "All the fear and sorrow channeled into other outlets and it was usually self-deprecating—I never felt worthy of anything, certainly not affection. I couldn't love myself; how could I let anyone else love me? I pushed away everyone except Ali." Even now it's hard to remember the pain I saw on my parents' faces and their struggle to help me. Colin's expressionless mask is in place, but his eyes come alive, compassion sparking in the blue depths.

"That's when Mom found Sylvia and eventually I told her every sordid detail, including how I felt when it happened and at the time of the telling. It wasn't a cure, but it allowed me a new beginning with my family, the fresh start I prayed for every night while I was in foster care. I started to let Shane Roberts stay in my past so he didn't prevent me from having some sort of a future. That was another turning point for me, and I've had a few." I move my hand to caress his cheek. "There's something cathartic in talking about the pain. Let it out of your heart so it doesn't cripple you."

He waits a beat and then leans in to my palm. "Are you going to be my counselor, Charlie? Lay me down on a couch until I bare my soul?"

I know he's directing our conversation away from his hard truth and I let him. "There are lots of things I'd like to lay you down on, buck naked as the day you were born, but counseling you isn't what I had in mind."

And just as he smiles a platter of steaming food arrives, along with two plates, handy wipes, and a bib. Colin holds it out.

"Your dress is beautiful. You may want to take precautions to save it from sure death by barbeque sauce."

I roll my eyes, but snatch the apron-like thing from him just in case it becomes a necessary accessory.

"You'll love this, trust me. Chicken wings, shrimp, scallops, slow-cooked ribs, homemade coleslaw, corn on the cob, and warm bread."

"Holy moly." My eyes widen. "How in the world is it possible to eat all this?"

"We only need to try, baby." He smiles and sets a plate in front of me.

We work through the food slowly, his appetite bigger than mine. It's delicious. I'm licking the sauce from my fingers after finishing a wing, when we're interrupted by a cowboy, Wranglers and a hat to boot.

"Senator McKenna?" he asks. His grin explodes on a lined face when Colin offers his hand.

"Billy Adkins. It's an honor to have you here at my place. Everything has met your standards?" His eyes sweep to me, and they widen as he stares.

"It's excellent, one of my favorite locations when I'm in the Tampa area."

"Uhh, Senator." Billy blushes. I smile as he shuffles his foot. "I'd like to get a picture with you if you wouldn't mind. We keep a wall of photos over there by the entrance and I'd be real honored if I could get one of you."

Colin eases off his stool with the grace of someone who experiences this often. "Sure." But as he says it, he reaches for me to join them.

I mouth the word *no* but he tugs me to my feet. Billy lines us up with the sky at our back, a server waiting with a camera. Colin's steady hand on my lower back drops and he smacks my ass. My squeak is lost in his laugh and then I'm blinded by the pop flash as the picture is taken. I glare at him while he smiles, damn dimple and all.

"Dinner's on me, Senator. You have my vote and my wife's too. Wait till I tell her you were here." He shakes his head. "She'll have my ass, err…." Billy pulls his hat off and mumbles ma'am in my direction. "Well, thank you both again. Enjoy the rest of your night."

I ask Colin as we settle into our seats, "Does this happen a lot?" The sparkle in his eye dulls, as does his smile leftover from the tap to my butt.

"Sometimes," he says, frown growing.

"Comes along with saving the country."

"I suppose that's true."

"Tell me why you're upset."

He shrugs. "I wasn't sure how you would react to the interruption or the breach to your privacy." Flicking his gaze to mine, I wait for him to continue. But he looks stupefied when he does, bewildered by what he's about to say. "I wanted you in the picture with me, but I'm not sure how I feel about it."

My chest hurts. I rub over my collarbone and the back of my neck to ease the tension creeping in. I don't know if I should laugh at his dazed confession or cry because it hurts him to want me.

"I didn't consider it an intrusion. I'm proud of you. Your ability to elicit this kind of response from so many, all because of your integrity and pure genius, amazes me." Anxiety squeezes out the last few words with a faltering scratch. "But why is wanting me so difficult?"

He flinches. "Charlie, it doesn't have anything to do with you."

Anger flares up and out of my mouth. "Don't you dare tell me *it's not you, it's me.* I'm trying to understand, Colin, but you don't share anything about your past or why you're like this." By the sound of his sharp inhale, I'd say that got his attention. Our eyes lock and I watch him as I pant through my frustration. I don't want to keep begging him for information.

"I'm afraid."

What? "You're the strongest person I know; fear isn't in your repertoire."

He leans forward. "Give me your hand." The tone that draws out my obedience does little to ease my temper, but my body responds and I let him have the connection he seeks. "I'm afraid to trust myself. It's easy to be with you, baby." His smile soothes my ragged emotions and the rigidity in my fingers dissolves. "I want so badly to have faith in my reaction to you and you to me."

"You doubt how I feel about you?" Incredulity has me seeking separation again, but he holds tight.

"That's a part of it, yes."

I gape at him. Heat burns up my chest and paints my cheeks in a flush.

"Charlie, please—"

I hold up my free hand for silence. "I don't know what to say." I swallow my shock and it settles in my stomach with the acid eating away at me. Dinner isn't sitting well and neither is his confession. "I've bared my soul to you, shared something only three other people in my world know about me, but you can't trust me? What more can I do?"

He closes his eyes for a split second. *I know*, he mouths. "I'm grateful for your honesty and the trust you've shown to share your darkest pain. You're a million years ahead of me. The pain I experienced with Abby is fresh, still very real. But when we're together, you and me, when it's Charlie and Colin, I forget all of it and dive into a true relationship again, not just physical intimacy. We have that." He tugs me closer, but I won't be swayed. Desperation drags his brow down into three lines and he inches near me. "I get lost in you. Everything disappears and I want you by my side every day, all day. I want to be with you, really be with you. Tell the world we're together, and then reality weighs me down. I'm a lot to take on."

He hangs his head as if what comes next is his breaking point. "I can't get over the past and give you everything you deserve, but I won't give you up. I won't let you leave me."

My heart thumps hard beats. "What brought this on?"

He looks up and glances in Billy's direction. "Instinctively wanting you in the picture and forcing you to stand by my side when it was taken. The next six months are going to get more and more challenging: the press, the people.... My privacy, *our privacy* will become nonexistent." He takes a deep breath. "I thought we were safe here. I was wrong. It doesn't matter where we go, from here on out the spotlight will focus on us both—if I'm elected it will only get worse."

"Are you having second thoughts?" My voice quivers with the soft question. "Are you ashamed to be with me?"

"No, Charlie. God no." He's emphatic. "I'm asking so much from you. From this moment on, your world will change. At any time in the foreseeable future your picture could be on the cover of every magazine in the country, the world for that matter. But the only commitment I can give you is this. I can't let you go."

I close my eyes and close him out. He's so tempting. I can't let him sway my thoughts into something not right for me. Hiding in the shadows is my comfort zone. The spotlight is more for Ali than me, and Colin is the most public figure in America right now. The number-one photographed man in the world, with his good looks, the hunt for the presidency, the infatuation within the political arena, and fan girls everywhere demanding the press feed their insatiable desires for Colin McKenna.

But besides all that, I'm amazed for the first time he's really talking and it's about a future with me in it. From where I sit, we were never very casual. Commitment may not have come with our sexual relationship, but we've been monogamous and clearly connected.

From the first night in Albany we've shared a room, a bed, a shower, morning coffee. Our movements synced. We've grown together and his confession is taking us down another uncharted path. He wants me with him, everywhere as well as always. Adding public acknowledgement is as good as stating a new level of commitment.

I open to find him watching me, intensely concentrating on the range of emotions that must have flitted across my features. "I'll get used to the spotlight and camera flashes. I want to be wherever you are, Colin. I'm not afraid of that, whatever it brings."

His mouth parts. Breathing out a sigh, he stands and pulls me from my seat. He flicks a brief wave to Billy, and then tugs me behind him and out of the restaurant, down the few steps until we hit white sand. With the full moon lighting the way, we walk down the beach. When we're surrounded by a thick grove of mangrove trees on one side and the gulf on the other, he pivots to face me. "I don't want to hide anymore. Yesterday at the school I wanted you by me, all day, behind the scenes and on stage. I want the freedom to laugh when you suck on strawberries."

I push out my bottom lip, but it tugs up to a half smile. "It was supposed to be seductive."

He grins, and reaches to cup my cheek. "You don't need to seduce me. I'm yours." Leaning in, he kisses me. He's soft, a mix of sweet barbeque, beer, and Colin. Fingers finding and digging into my hips, he pulls me flush against him. I whimper, giving in to hard lines and heat. And now he's hungry, taunting my tongue to play a deep, wicked game that has my pulse soaring. Breaking away, he presses his forehead to mine. "I'm an honest man; I don't want to hide you, waiting for someone else to figure out we're together and try to paint it in an unfair light. Charlie, I want you to do it. Tell the world we're together, write an article for the magazine or put it on the blog. You have carte blanche to do whatever you believe is right."

Me? "Don't make a rash decision; think it through. I'm not exactly the type of woman America wants by your side."

He growls and wrenches me closer. "The world will fall for you just as I have. You're irresistible." He smiles his dazzling, all-American I-can-make-you-believe-anything-I-want-you-to-believe smile and I do. I believe him, because I want it so badly to be true.

"I'm sure, Charlie. Are you?"

His eyes spark and I think about a future with him in it. "Yes," I breathe without further consideration of the complications I could cause for him or what it will mean for me. He's more important than anything else.

A dimple pops on his cheek and then his brow falls. Wrenching me into an impossibly tight hold, he buries his head in my neck and murmurs, "God, I'm going to miss you, so damn much." And then he drags his mouth to mine with an intensity I haven't felt from him until this moment. His lips worship and his tongue strokes my body into a needy inferno.

Panting, I pull away and say, "Come with me."

NINETEEN

MY DEMAND QUICKENS OUR steps, and in minutes we hit the hotel grounds and another finds us entering our suite. When the door swings shut and the lock seals us in, I turn to whisper, "I have a surprise for you."

"If it involves you naked in bed—"

I press my finger to his mouth, containing his sinful smirk. I've formulated a dirty plan to wipe it clean. "It wouldn't be a surprise if you've seen it before." His lids sink and my stomach falls with them. *This is going to be fun.*

Fighting off his groping hands, I back into the bedroom giggling. Blocking another advance, I state my first command. "Take your shirt off and lie down."

His right brow rises, but I don't wait for commentary before grabbing my bag on the way to the bathroom.

I pray the newest edition of *Cosmo* is giving good advice. Laughing, I pull out the black-and-magenta teddy I bought the other day. I haven't tried it on and suddenly the barely there lace and little strings are causing second thoughts.

My boobs and hips may stretch it thin, but what's the worst-case scenario? We get a good laugh, and I can deal with humor if that's where we end up. Stripping out of my sundress, I complete a fresh check and then step into seduction at its best. Magenta ribbons weave under the see-through cups and tie into a bow between my breasts. Lace falls beneath them in a flyaway cut. My nipples pearl with the anticipation of his teeth, the suction of his mouth and I slip on the matching G-string.

Colin's magenta tie is the final accessory. As I hang it loosely around my neck, I glance to the mirror. I like what I see. My body has changed over the last few months, the curve of my hips still present with a clear hourglass indentation between them and my chest, yet I'm firm, lithe even. Turning, I wiggle my butt and enjoy the smooth roundness and the curve into the small of my back.

With a last fluff to my loose curls, I open the door. Lying on the bed, hands folded beneath his head, he's naked from the waist up. Tan, defined, and brushed with dark hair, my Colin is mouthwatering with the fly of his jeans unbuttoned.

A sharp inhale slices the silence as he props himself onto his elbows for a better view.

"Charlie," he whispers as he looks me over, taking in every detail and catching on the barely there panties. A flush of warmth readies my body and my racing pulse thrums in my neck, my clit, everywhere. Dark, mesmerizing lust rolls off him while his gaze hangs on my breasts until they're tender and heavy. Finally, our eyes meet; his are hot and tempting, and I'm tempted. I have been for a long time. Now the attraction is more than I bargained for. A future with Colin, but will we stand a chance if he doesn't trust my feelings? I can't say the words, and if I did he wouldn't believe them, so tonight he'll feel it in my actions.

I approach slowly, one foot in front of the other until the mattress hits my knees. Tie in hand, I slide it between my fingers. "Will you play with me?"

He swallows but remains silent so I speak for him. "I ache for you, always. When you're absent—I'm empty."

I climb up and then crawl over the length of his legs, pausing at his zipper. The blunt end of his crown strains past the band of his black briefs. As I lap at his tip, he jerks and growls, "Suck me."

Murmuring my appreciation, I lick away a bead of precum, salty, sweet, meant for me, and when I kiss him he groans. Looking up through my lashes, I watch color spread up his neck. "Only when you come in me am I truly full, finally satisfied. But then I need it again." I suck his throbbing head. "And again."

"Christ," he hisses and bucks beneath me.

I press words into his skin, my love, my need, my plans for tonight. Hair tickles my nose as I move through the darkest patch below his navel and then up to the rippled plane of his abdomen, chest, and finally his face. His nostrils flare as I pull up in front of him, our lips an inch apart.

"Lie down," I demand. His eyes narrow, but he does as he's told. I sit on his stomach and watch surprise flash through his features as I slide the magenta tie from around my neck. "Hands above your head."

I smile through the rumble in his chest and tie his wrists together, tight enough he can't break free. My breasts sweep against his face while I work; his nose skims my cleavage.

"There." I sit back to enjoy my sex god as he tugs against his bonds, jaw clenching. "Now you're mine to do with what I want, and I want you—" I lean in to brush my lips against his "—naked—" one more light kiss "—hard—" I graze my mouth and teeth along his cheek, down his neck "—in my mouth—" his breath comes out in a rush "—and deep inside me."

He shifts his hips, bucking me into position to rub against him. "Don't move," I warn, sitting on his cock, clenching him between my thighs. I grind into him more than once and he finds my rhythm. Our breath picks up speed. His thick length bumps my clit and I shudder from the zing of pleasure. If I don't stop now we'll both come before we really get started.

I stop and wait for his gaze to stray from my panties to my eyes. "You've given me so much, Colin. I've grown under your direction and strong hands, built my confidence to share with you everything about me. I'm safe with you and yet your trust is still out of reach."

His abdomen retracts as he tries to sit up. "Char—"

"Sshhh," I whisper, my finger over his lips. "No talking. This is for me to do and for you to believe." His twitching erection is a comforting response.

"Untie me." He wrenches against the restraints and I fear for the headboard. "I'll show you how much I fucking need you."

I shake my head. "You make me powerful. I love your skin, smooth and hot beneath me."

He closes his eyes as I slide back, taking his clothes with me. Hips up, he does what he can to help and in seconds he springs free, heavy cock bobbing against his stomach. I spread his legs to make room and when he finally looks up, he finds me bent over him, lips an inch away from his sac. I blow. He twitches.

"Charlie, for the love of God."

I pull his cock taut and suck; male, musky, gorgeous, he fills my senses just as he fills my mouth. His groan hits me in the heart; it pounds against my ribs as I flick the smooth skin underneath his testicles, skimming over his sensitivity and down. The low, guttural sounds of Colin McKenna falling apart beneath me spark my own need and liquid heat clings to my inner thighs.

He trembles. I move to let him fill me, feel him at the back of my throat, throbbing, perfect and smooth and thick. As I pull back, I wrap my hands around his shaft and pump him in and out of my mouth, fisting him in tandem.

"Oh, fuck. Charlie." He's close. If his gruff whisper didn't give him away, his swelling shaft does. I rip off him with a pop.

Our chests rise and fall together, heavy, loud breaths as I position myself above him once more.

"I feel so much when you touch me. I love the rough pad of your thumb as it skims my nipples—just—like—this." I touch myself, pinching the aching points through the lace. He's a captive audience, eyes bouncing between my face and fingers, mouth parted.

"The silk of your tongue soothes the burn you've tweaked when you suck me. Here." I pull one more time and my groan mirrors his as I slide down, down, down to the place I need him the most. "And here."

"Charlie, so help me—"

"Can you feel how wet I am for you?" I roll my hips against his bare cock and I know he can. I'm dripping. "This is how I always feel when I'm with you, constantly ready, always needy, always wanting."

"Baby, please." His tongue dips to run along his bottom lip as he looks at my hands, low on my navel. I slip one under the lace.

"You make me feel so good," I whisper and dip down, spreading my lips open. Teasing my clit, I slide further into my slickness and bring it up to ease the circling motion. Oh, God. I do it again, sinking into my opening an inch this time.

"I love your fingers on me and in me."

Colin bites his bottom lip as my strokes become faster, deeper, but as a whimper breaks free I pull out and away, tearing at the strings that bind my panties together and keep me away from him.

He says my name on repeat, a low base pounding in my ears as I lift into position over him.

"But my favorite place is when you're inside me, here," I say while rubbing him through my folds and to my opening.

"Goddamn it, you're in so much…."

His words are lost in a gasp when his cock spreads me open and sinks in an inch. "But more than anything, I love to feel you here." I rub between my breasts and my heart takes off. He grips the bedpost as I sink down, filling me until he hits my core and he's everywhere. In my breath, sandalwood and sex mix, on my skin as the weight of his stare lingers, and deep within me, my mind and body, everywhere. A deep need demands I move and I do, head back, fingers on my neck as if they were his. I lose myself in the rise and fall. The slick sounds of love and lust meld into music, our fumbled words and grunted cries keeping time.

Yes, please feel this. Feel what I can't say, what's buried inside, but spoken by touch. I love you. "Please," *please,* find yourself in me. "Colin," *please*. "I'm so close. Come with me." *Love me.*

We move faster, harder, until my thighs quiver and I shimmer like the fire of the sun.

"Baby." He drives into me and we spring off the cliff together. "Oh, Charlie." His groan is muffled against my neck as I fall forward. Gripping his shoulders, I take in the pulse of his release in a warmth I only want from him.

My Colin.

I gasp for breath, exhausted. But I reach to loosen the knot at his wrists and then snuggle into his chest. Immediately his arms clutch me. Time seems to stand still as our bodies tick together.

Minutes pass and finally Colin rolls until we're lying on our sides, my head on his arm. I blink back into reality and find his staggered expression. I smile and rub his cheek, rough with the new growth of beard. He leans in to kiss me, light but lingering. In a second he dives into me, forcing my mouth open with his tongue and taking me to task, stroking into my mouth with long licks. Deep, carnal, demanding, until I'm flat on my back.

He pulls away. Propped on his elbow, he strokes over my cleavage and then toys with the ribbon holding me together.

"I like this." Rolling the bow between his fingers, he pulls. It bursts apart, his hand taking the place of a cup on my breast, the other I reach up to hold. One nipple is between my fingers, the other in his. Colin's eyes glow, wicked. And just when it had found a steady rhythm, my heart takes off in a sprint.

"Charlie." His voice is soft, but hot. Very, very hot. "Have you ever heard that paybacks are hell?"

"Yes," I whisper.

"Baby, I'm going to pay you back, over and over again." He doesn't give me time to respond. Pushing me into the mattress, he slips between my thighs and kisses me until I can't breathe.

CONSCIOUS THOUGHT COMES IN the form of Colin's lips nuzzling on the delicate skin below my ear. Chest even with my back, our legs tangled together. I moan, not necessarily from his delicious mouth, although I like it, I really, really do.

"I just fell asleep—go back to bed." I try to bat him away and hit nothing but air. He chuckles.

"Come on, sleepyhead, I need to get up. We have a big day."

He adds tongue and I'm thoroughly distracted. Tilting my head, I open for him to entice me awake. I groan. A good kind of sore reminds me of the sweet blissful torture I endured, along with the number of times I came on his hand, his cock, and his face.

"Good God," I moan as he rolls me flat. "Don't you ever get tired?" I ask as he runs his nose along mine.

I feel his smile as he moves against my lips. "Not with you, baby."

He shows me just how energetic he is, but he's slow and thorough, sweet and wicked. I cry out my appreciation and grip his ass, and then his hair until I'm exhausted and panting beneath him. Colin breathes into my neck. I could stay like this all day long, snuggled against him, our naked bodies pressed together.

"Go back to sleep." He lifts away, but I wrap my legs around him before we're separated.

"One more, please."

I pucker up and then smile as he hovers over me, arms straight and ripped with muscle. Tilting his head, he brings his mouth within a half an inch of mine, and then he jerks away. I growl and lift up to capture him. He's too quick, pulling just out of reach before I touch him. His rumbling chuckle inflames me. I let my head fall back to the pillow in defeat, very slowly moving my hands from his shoulders into his hair, all the while looking into his bemused eyes. I stay stock still and wait for his next move. He's patient, too patient, and I can see the inner workings of his mind as he watches me calculate a strategic plan.

He leans down. I do nothing. The tip of his nose connects with mine, and he tilts his head so his lips hover in perfect position. I wait. One heartbeat, two—I pounce. Pulling his hair, I lift to find his mouth. Oh, the joy of success. I suck his tongue when it's offered, bite and lick into him until he's moaning and palming my breast.

I release him and fall to the bed. "When will you be back?" I ask, batting my lashes.

He shakes his head, panting. It takes a minute, but finally recognition sparks in his eyes. The lightbulb switched from Charlie Carter to campaign. "Around one. Be ready to go."

One last peck to my cheek comes and then he unwraps himself from my arms and legs. Standing naked next to the bed, his eyes darken as he gazes at me.

"You could stay and keep me company."

"I wish I could, baby."

"Would you like me to meet you at the conference center?" I offer to make his plans easier.

"No." His voice is firm, as are his eyes. "I don't want you traveling by yourself."

So we're back to this. "I —"

Bending to reach me, he puts a finger over my mouth. "Charlie, I have a lot to worry about right now. I don't want to add you to the list. Please, do as I ask."

He's playing on my weakness. Smart, intelligent ass.

"Fine." I cross my arms over my breasts, pouting.

"Fine," he says, mimicking my tone, but his eyes are bemused. "Go back to sleep." He throws the covers over my head as he leaves for the shower.

I drift off and when next I see him he's clean, has a smooth jaw, and is dressed in a three-piece navy suit, stunning and brilliant. Kneeling on the bed next to me, he leans down to whisper in my ear, "Check the closet later, I've left something for you." He nuzzles against my cheek.

"I'll miss you," I mumble, still half-asleep.

"And I you."

He slips away, and I fall into a restless sleep with strange dreams. The colors are bright; red, purple, yellow, and magenta meld together in a pinwheel. An abstract painting of Colin forms. He reaches for me. His face is dark, and he's animated in a conversation I can't hear. I'm just under the surface and struggle to wake. Something's wrong. I can feel it and my heart hurts. But I'm paralyzed in sleep, unable to move.

Drifting again, the dream changes to a meadow filled with flowers. The wind stirs them into movement and the rolling field morphs into my body. Colin covers me and as I wait for his kiss, a black void swallows me. Empty. A sharp pain rips through my chest. He's gone.

Bolting upright, I hear the echo of my fading scream reverberate against the walls. Where am I? My pulse is fast, thrumming in my ears. Pushing damp hair from my face, I stare at Colin's pillow. Just a dream.

Debate prep. I sigh as the early morning refocuses. It's the last one before he accepts the formal Republican nomination this summer. It's a big day.

The alarm clock on the nightstand glows eleven o'clock, two hours since he left. I throw the blanket back to reach for one of his T-shirts.

My stomach reminds me I should call for breakfast. Coffee and blueberry pancakes will ward off the sticky touches the nightmare left on my mood. A quick call to room service and a walk into the living area later, I spot my bags on the floor. Work will keep my mind absorbed in the campaign. After quick media updates, I pull out my camera and get stuck in the feeds from the Kansas City speech. I download them to my computer to manipulate the frames. In the first few shots the man's lens, hat, and sunglasses cover his face, making it impossible to detect features. He's nondescript. Medium height. A large sweatshirt covers his build. There's nothing to identify who he is.

A knock startles me breathless. *Leave the discovery to Nancy Drew*, my heart begs as it pounds in my chest. I peek out the door; no one but the guard left to watch me.

He turns away as I open and mumble a quick hello, tugging the cart in. My stomach somersaults and I hold my chest as love swells inside. Roses: a huge display of at least two dozen. *Colin.* A card is hidden deep in the stems.

My finger collides with a ginormous thorn. "Ouch, ouch, ouch," I whine and then suck on the stinging wound. A second try is injury free and successful. The note reads:

I always come for what is mine.

The harsh possession doesn't sit well with me. Up to now, the few notes from Colin have been more sensitive. But I send a quick text to let him know they arrived. *Flowers—they're beautiful and so are you. Thank you.*

Debate prep lends to unsurprising silence. For the next twenty minutes I stuff myself with coffee and pancakes and revisit the photos. Studying them does nothing to solve the mystery so when breakfast is over, I head to the shower.

Colin has a stalker. Someone interested in his campaign… but why is he taking pictures of me? It's possible he's discovered our affair. My heart stops. It stutters into a heavy thud under the weight of how that could affect Colin's campaign. What if this person is threatening to release information about us, specifically about my past and me? Is this why Colin suddenly wants to move our relationship into the public eye? Is someone threatening him? Instantly, I know he's holding back; he may have told me a portion of the truth, but it's not everything. I'm sure of it.

I'm quick to dry off and then head for the closet to find what was left for me. I open the door to a dress. Thoughts scramble through my head with exclamation points. My mother would be appalled by the string of profanity I can put together, a consequence of years with little supervision. I'm insulted Colin doesn't trust my judgment for my first public appearance as anyone other than a staffer. I growl at stiff and drab, but when I pull it into the light it's not so conservative after all. In fact, it's my perfect style. A demure boat-neck sheath, the front mirrored in the back only at the neckline. Two buttons hold it together up top and then it opens to a large diamond cutout. The peplum flare will acccntuate my waist and mimes my favored retro style. I smile and twirl with it in front of me, the same shade of Colin's eyes and the suit he left in this morning.

Blow drying takes time, but is worth the smooth affect. The end game produces a sweeping part and a low side ponytail. Adding liner and a heavy coat of mascara, I like what I see—especially when I slip into my new favorite dress. It fits like a glove. I love it; demure and sexy at the same time.

I add my panther to my wrist. Four-inch red heels add a pop of color and as I walk into the suite I find Colin, brooding by the flowers. Mystery man is large and in charge on my laptop screen just beside them. Legs parted to shoulder width, suit jacket pushed behind the hand in his pocket—he's stunning—if only his jaw wasn't clenched in anger.

In a few steps I fit myself to him and slide my fingers down to find his. He weaves them together but continues to stare ahead.

Minutes tick by; my heart counts each second. Finally he turns, whispering my name as he grabs and lifts me up into a desperate hug, his head dipping to the curve of my neck. I hold on, not sure why I'm soothing him, but I try to, clinging to his nape and murmuring reassurance. When he releases me, my hand lands in his hair, tugging.

"What's wrong?"

"The flowers are not from me." The words are ripped from his throat, raw.

"Who then?" A whirlwind of thoughts spin around before reality sinks in—mystery man. My stomach churns with understanding.

Colin doesn't have a stalker: I do.

TWENTY

"THIS IS NOT THE first time he's sent something to me, is it?" Colin has been holding out on me for far too long. It's time to hear his confession.

His jaw clenches and frustration bubbles up to a familiar rage. Breaking all contact, I push him away. Separated by ten feet I turn and cross my arms.

"Stop trying to protect me and tell me what the hell is going on. How long has this been happening? And don't tell me Kansas City. I know damn well that was just the first time I found out about it." I show him my best glare. "Enough with the overprotective *keep Charlie in the dark* bullshit. You have some explaining to do. Talk, McKenna."

The corner of his mouth lifts. "You're right, Kansas City was not the first time. It started in New York. In fact, I thought you may have known and that was the reason you thought of leaving."

My eyes close as I digest the information; he's right. That's when I received the Facebook message and Ella's smarmy commentary had me second guessing where I belonged.

"Go on," I prompt, without confirming the truth. "What did you get?"

"Pictures of you in the alley, post your charge out of the kitchen, and then the two of us in New York City." He takes a steadying breath.

"Just pictures, or was there something else?" He opens his mouth but stays silent. I growl, "Goddamn it, Colin, tell me. I need to know."

He blinks, squeezing into a tense brow as if the knowledge he's about to share hurts. "There was a note: *I'm watching you.*"

"How many times have you been contacted?"

"Several."

"How many?"

"There has been something in every city on the tour. We started planning ahead; a member of my security detail cased our hotels, intercepting what was sent in advance of our arrival. For a while that worked. Until Kansas City, when it was waiting at the location of my speech." He stares at me, sickened. "And today when the hotel made an assumption the flowers were from me based on the delivery details and the package I indicated would arrive—you're dress."

My head swirls, light passes into darkness for a second and then Colin is in front of me clenching the soft pads of my arms. I shouldn't be surprised by any of this; I am Charlie Carter, after all. Strange shit happens to me all the time; this is just another anomaly at the bottom of a long list.

"This is the last thing you need to deal with," I say with a tremble in my voice.

"No, Charlie. Look at me," he implores. Our eyes connect, green and wary to blue and determined. "I know what you're thinking, and the answer is no. You can't leave me. I need you. I'll figure this out and end it. I won't let it take you away from me."

I sink into his chest and take all the comfort he offers. "Who's doing this?"

"I don't know, baby. But I'll find out and keep you safe at the same time. Please try not to worry. Security has been stepped up; someone will cross-check every item meant for you. You'll never be alone. From the moment you return from Michigan, an agent will be your shadow."

I blanch, leaning back so I can see his reaction. "My family, do you think he knows I'm going home?"

"No, I honestly believe whoever is responsible for this is after me, not you. He's trying to get to me through you."

"That doesn't make sense. Why would someone be after you?"

"Many people don't want to see me succeed. They'll look for my weak spot, use it against me to bring me to heel. Hope I'll drop out of the campaign."

"And I'm your weak spot?"

"You're the only thing that could make me reevaluate the presidency."

"Colin," I gasp.

"Are you so surprised?" he asks and grips my chin. "I've been given a second chance with you. I'm not willing to give that up, to let you go. I won't sit back and do nothing while someone tries to take away everything I've worked to achieve. We'll figure this out and put a stop to it, I promise you." His eyes storm into dark clouds.

"Have you been threatened? Your campaign?" My worst fear is that I could hurt his White House goal.

"No, nothing."

I glance at the roses. "I need you to open up. Stop holding back; I want to know everything. Promise me."

"I will."

"Next week we're sitting down to discuss this. I want to see whatever you have."

"I wish you would let me deal with it, but you won't let it go, will you?" He waits, I think in hopes I'll acquiesce, and when I don't he says, "Fine. I'll show you everything."

"Good," I say, laying my head on his chest and holding him tight. "I'm sorry I've made you late."

"I always have time for you, baby. Always," he repeats. Closing my eyes, I let his words sink in. *Always*. There is so much potential in that one simple word.

"STOP FIDGETING, YOU'RE ABSOLUTELY gorgeous." Colin's voice is hot, his eyes hotter. Before I can comment, he takes my hands as we climb the steps of the conference center. He has not hidden his affection for me today. When we arrived, he introduced me to a young staff member as his girlfriend. I felt whiplash set in as I snapped my neck to gape in astonishment. His response was a slow, sexy-as-hell smile that squeezed in his dimple.

He wasn't kidding when he said security would be tight. I have a new shadow, and his name is Drake. He's tall, taller than Colin, with black slicked-back hair and sunglasses—they're on inside when there's only fluorescents. He's yet to speak and I fear he's more cyborg than human. If he opens his mouth and *I'll be back* comes out, I'm running. Anyway, if he scares the hell out of me, he'll freak the pants off anyone trying to get too close. I feel better already.

Evan and the Montgomerys are backstage in the anteroom designated to the McKenna campaign. Documents, laptops, and iPads are out on tables. Staffers rush to complete final prep for the debate, but their candidate is calm and collected. Colin's hold doesn't falter as Ella shoots me a death glare and John turns away.

"Charlie, you're stunning," Evan says as he approaches. He nods as he looks me up and down. "Nice dress."

"Apparently she's not even safe from my best friend," Colin deadpans.

"Just telling it like it is." Evan claps his back.

"Thanks, I love it." I shimmy my hips. "It makes me feel beautiful."

Colin brings my knuckles to his lips. "You're always beautiful, baby. Dress or no dress, you're gorgeous."

I ignore the heat in his eyes. "Who's responsible for it anyway? I'd like to thank whoever picked it out."

"The same boutique you took my mother to. I asked Rebecca to ship something in," Colin confesses.

"It's truly perfect. The only question I have is why?" I eye him speculatively.

Evan smiles and pats him on the back with a parting "Good luck with that" before stepping away.

"I knew you wouldn't have an opportunity to shop and I wanted you comfortable and confident. It's our first night out as a couple. The media may catch wind and it'll be hard enough for you; I didn't want self-confidence issues layered on top of your stress."

"Colin, we should have talked about this before…." I motion a crazed back-and-forth signal between us. "Before… this… us as in *us*!" I whisper shout.

"I thought we did?" His eyes narrow. "You're not going anywhere; neither am I. I'm not letting you go. You're my second chance, and we're about to announce it to the world. Which, by the way, we need to talk about: I'll prep John so he can be ready for a formal response. We'll prep you too, baby. When this gets out it's going to change life as you know it, and it will reach your family too." His right brow rises in that beyond-sexy way. "Are you ready for this?"

I can't help my eye roll. "Yes, I'm just surprised you are."

"I'm a simple man, Charlie."

I choke out a laugh and his brow hits new heights. There's nothing simple about Colin McKenna, but okay. Go ahead and think that. I pat his chest and let him continue.

"Soon your picture will appear everywhere, all the time, in any paper in the world. That's the truth. We're together and I'm not going to wait for someone else to figure it out only to sensationalize our relationship. I'm not hiding us anymore."

"Hence the matching color?" I ask, motioning again.

His smile is breathtaking. "A happy coincidence, but we do look very patriotic." He laughs. My sometimes stern, sometimes dominant, sometimes stubborn, a lot of times sweet Colin McKenna laughs at a happy coincidence.

I eye him skeptically. Cyborg or human? "Who are you and what have you done with my ultraconservative serious *boyfriend*?"

He leans in and smacks a kiss on my mouth, his grin returning immediately. "You have a unique ability to loosen me up, Charlie—or in most cases, an uncanny ability to keep me hard." His deep, caramel-smooth voice hits a new low and belies his calm façade. He wants me. He *always* wants me.

I swallow down my surprise. I'm his girlfriend. Senator Colin McKenna's *girlfriend.* A silly giggle bubbles up and I lift my hand to hide my smile as it turns into a laugh. It's crazy and I'm giddy with the sudden thrill of calling him mine.

Colin's brow creases in a wry wrinkle. I grab his face between my palms and force eye contact before I kiss him. Not quick, or light, but branding and bold, this kiss screams *mine* with sprinkles on top. Mine with a prancing pony and unicorn with purple hair, mine with everything a little girl dreams of at the best birthday party ever. And although my big day is months away, this is better than any present ever given. The cherry on top comes from his low growl, the grip he has on my lower back, and the sweet abandonment he pours into this kiss. *He's all in.*

He's my *boyfriend.*

I pull back with a gasp and beam at the world. Confetti should fall from the rafters with balloons and silly string. His grin mirrors mine. It's way prettier, and just as sincere.

"God, I love you," flies out of my mouth.

The world stops spinning. The party screeches to a halt as the needle is dragged along an old album. In the biggest vacuum known to man, air is sucked out of my lungs and I deflate.

Fuck. How could I be so stupid?

I drop my head in my hands and tear up. "Charlie." He sighs and wraps me in his embrace, his fingers tracing my bare skin.

We're at his debate, for God's sake, surrounded by key advisors, not to mention Ella and John and this is where I confess my love. *What in the ever loving hell, Charlie Carter.*

I force myself to peel away and look at the carnage, unsurprised I find his expressionless expression. But his eyes, God, they gut me. So sad, not the response a girl wants after baring her soul.

"I'm sorry," I whisper. "I shouldn't have said that. It just slipped out."

He shakes his head. "Don't."

A hard one-word rebuttal has me turn in fear the well will overflow my lids. His hand on my waist tugs my back to his chest. "Don't be sorry," he whispers in my ear. "I wish I could say the same to you."

The lump is hard and too big to swallow down. I can't cry here. Not now. "I want to take it back so it doesn't hurt you."

"Did you mean it?"

My heart pounds so loud I barely hear my own "Yes."

The pause lengthens and I don't want him to feel forced into something he doesn't mean. I turn. "Let's not do this. Our focus is the debate. Okay?"

He doesn't move. The wheels churn behind his eyes and then he nods and we move on like nothing happened.

FINAL PREP COMPLETE, COLIN is with the moderator and the other candidates before they take to the stage. I don't want to be any more of a distraction so I wander, but not too far. Behind the scenes allows for a view of the four podiums, the red-white-and-blue backdrop erected for tonight's event. An eagle stretches across the panels, symbolic and a stern reminder to uphold the republic our forefathers left as their legacy. Audience in place, their hum melds with the last-minute rush to get the details in place before the overhead lights shine and the cameras roll.

Ella and John arrive, and with them is Alex Miller. I round to the back of the room and watch the three of them together. They're chatty and for the first time Ella actually looks normal and not reptilian. John even cracks a smile. They're animated and clearly friends. Five minutes into my assessment, Ella searches out Colin.

She watches him with suppressed appreciation, features softening as she comes to his side. Pressing against his arm while he leans down, close, too close, she whispers in his ear. My blood boils. She wants him and although Colin is indifferent toward her, I sneer.

"Charlie?"

Shit. Trying on a smile I don't feel, I turn. "Alex, what a nice surprise."

"I didn't realize I was coming tonight or I would have mentioned it yesterday," he says. A dark brown suit looks good on him, and his glasses are more adorable than dorky. "Ella invited me last night."

"How thoughtful of her." My sarcasm isn't disguised well.

"Will you be in town tomorrow?" he asks.

"No, I'm leaving in the morning. What about you? Are you sticking around for a vacation?"

He nods, ignoring my question. "Where are you off to next?"

"Georgia. Colin is moving on directly, he'll campaign hard from here on out."

"Aren't you getting tired of the constant travel? I would think the never-ending upheaval would wear on you."

"I haven't found it difficult. Actually, it's interesting. For a girl who rarely got out of Michigan, I'm enjoying the other states." His interrogation is prickling at my skin. "Is this the first—"

"What about you? Is he making time for you? Are you okay, I mean." He licks his lips.

Electricity pulls me out of my stupor and then Colin's hand is on my lower back. Alex watches the fingers that are now kneading my hip.

"Yeah, okay," he says and pivots, walking away.

"That didn't make any sense."

"Come with me." Gripping my hand, Colin pulls me behind him. He barks out a request to a staffer for a private office and only stops after we're ushered inside a five-by-five gray cell with a desk pushed in the corner. "Five minutes, Senator McKenna, and you're on." With that I'm closed in with a brooding Colin. Silence stretches on for an eternity and I shift my feet, tug my skirt down, waiting for him to say something, anything.

When he finally speaks his voice is deliberately controlled, yet exasperated. "Why is it every time I turn around Alex Miller is next to you?"

I shake my head. "That's not true. He came by to say hello, a strange hello but whatever." I can't believe he's jealous. Did I not profess my love to him an hour ago?

"Stay away from him, Charlie. We have," he swallows and shakes his head a fraction, "a past and I don't like him. He's a weasel."

I bite back a smile. "Weasel?"

Colin tugs me flat against his chest. He clenches my butt to pull me up and into his groin. I gasp. Why am I complaining? His reaction works for me—in all the right places. I'm tempted to flirt every day if this is the response I get.

His mouth slams into mine and I enjoy the hard line of his lips and tongue. I hike my skirt up to my hips and then clutch his neck, pulling myself into a snug fit with my legs wrapped around his waist. When he groans, I know his plan is to withdraw, so I use all of my strength to cling to him, forcing him into one last daring foray. He chuckles. When he breaks contact I thread my fingers through the back of his hair and accept his forehead against mine.

"Say it again," he whispers.

Oh. I find his eyes this time and slide my hands to cradle his cheeks. "I love you."

He kisses me, breathless. When he breaks away, I add, "A lot."

"Charlie."

A knock forces my legs to meet the floor and he holds my hips, staring at the apex of my thighs. "Nice panties," he says, and then helps smooth my dress back in place.

"I wore them for you."

"So I see. I had no idea lace came in red, white, and blue."

I smile. "You'd be surprised what you can find on the Internet."

His brow crinkles, but then the door opens. "It's time, Senator."

As he buttons his suit coat, I touch his lips to ensure they're lipstick free.

"How do I look?" he asks, tugging down his sleeves and checking his cuff links.

I look up and down six feet and three inches of perfection. "Utterly and completely fuckable."

"Wicked woman," he growls and turns.

"Go get 'em, tiger." I smack his ass and add, "If you nail it tonight I'll show you my matching bra. It has tassels."

He laughs all the way to the stage.

TWENTY-ONE

Turbulence jolts me awake. My stomach is quick to fall as the plane does. It's been a rocky flight for many reasons. Weather is only one. Tears sting my eyes. *Six days*. Six days has suddenly changed from less than a week to a lifetime away. My lids clamp down and I jam the tease-of-a-pillow against the window, begging to find a comfortable spot. Six days.

Jesus, I'm a lovesick wuss. I'm stuck in last night, remembering Colin's sweet and dirty insatiable appetite. The man can do quick and long, against the wall, in the shower, on the bed, and bent over the couch like no one's business. We didn't get much sleep; by the time the sun searched for the horizon my legs were weak and my insides quivered like Jell-O.

This morning was emotional. We drove in silence to the airport; my hand in his the entire ride, and then we said our final good-byes outside the terminal door. I held his waist and every time I kissed him and then turned to leave, he would tug me back to mumble something in my ear. After this played on repeat three times I kissed him hard and deep, murmured *I love you* in his mouth, and ran through the doors.

Once inside, I turned for a last look and my heart broke a little more. He stood where I'd left him, hands slung into his pockets, dejected and lost. I waved and his jaw hardened before he folded himself into the limo and left me.

I grind my teeth and fight against our differences. For one day, I want him to not be famous and so dedicated he has no free time for grandmothers' birthdays, barbeques, and cottages in northern Michigan. I want to bring my first and only boyfriend home to meet my parents, hang by the fire, roast marshmallows and do the cheesy stuff that makes my family awesome. Larger-than-life Mr. McPerfect McKenna doesn't fit in small-town USA on a pontoon boat in the middle of Traverse Bay.

The rest of the flight ticks by as if I'm watching the clock. Work, a movie, my Kindle, nothing takes my mind off what Colin's doing. Where is he now, who is he with? It's a sick loop. When we land, antsy energy bubbles under my skin and I bounce my knees, annoying my neighbor if his wry glance is an indicator. Colin upgraded my seat to first class and I'm second out the door. My pace is more jog than walk as I race to find my sister in baggage claim. Traverse City boasts a new but small airport, so I'm there in minutes.

Ali's bright blonde hair is hard to miss amongst the milling travelers—not just because of the color, but because she's drop-dead gorgeous. She has an athlete's body, lithe with the right amount of curves to feminize her figure, and her face is soft, with a small nose and high cheekbones. Warm eyes, a flaming honey-brown with a rim of blue, draw you in and hold tight.

Running up behind her I wrap my arms around her waist, squeezing. She squeals. Turning, she dives into my hug and we jump up and down, drawing attention from those closest to us. She pushes away and scares young children with her whistle.

"Oh. My. God. You're a smoking-hot babe, Charlie Carter." She grins, eyes widening as she takes me in from head to toe. "I mean, listen, you know you're always stunning. But something has changed. What have you been doing with that man?"

I tense and then crumble under her scrutiny, tears welling. "I love him so much." Hiding my head in her shoulder, I cry out the emotion that's been begging for release since this morning.

"Oh, Char, I know you do. I could have told you that in February. Why are you so sad? Wait; don't answer that. Let's get my bag and we'll talk about this later when we're alone. Don't cry, honey, everything's going to be just fine." I cry harder. She said that to me when we were lost kids, trying to survive in a world that didn't have a place for us.

Sniffles and a few wipe-aways later, I've got my mess under control. We grab Ali's bag and find Mom just outside the doors. She hasn't changed; petite and slightly rounded in the hips, with short brown hair and blue eyes. My heart swells every time I see her.

Her hands fly to her mouth. We lunge and take her into a bear hug as she sobs and pets our hair.

"Don't cry," I whisper. "No matter how long we're gone, we'll always find our way back home."

She kisses my forehead. "It was hard enough when Ali left the state, but you too. Your father and I are fighting empty-nest syndrome."

Ali laughs and takes her keys to pop the trunk. "But Sammy and Ian are there, and they're never quiet."

Mom smiles and holds her cheek. "It doesn't matter how many children you have, when one leaves, Sunday dinner is lacking, with two gone the table feels quiet no matter how loud the boys are."

She gladly slides in the passenger seat as Ali takes the wheel. In the back, I listen to Mom describe the changes to the neighborhood since we were here last summer. Then Ali fills us in on the latest news from Georgetown and the end of her third year. It's time to pick a specialty. Mom beams. Pride is an understatement. She nudged Ali into medical school one encouragement at a time. Ali proved her tuition was worth it by graduating top of her class. She doesn't do anything half-assed and her chosen profession is no exception.

My update has to wait for later as we pull up to the cottage. The same childhood thrill wells in my belly as the gravel drive crunches beneath the tires. This place was in the family before Ali and I became members. But my sweet parents have always said it wasn't complete until they found us. And then it became my haven as I recovered; the peacefulness helped heal my broken heart, and now it's a comfortable embrace from a long-lost friend.

As is common with homes on a lake, the front faces the water. Honeyed, knotty pine peaks at the pitched roof and windows line the entire perimeter, allowing the outdoors in at every angle. The front levels into a long, flat green yard, with maple and pine trees cocooning it until the grass meets the beach and the turquoise waves lap the shore.

The Carter boys jog to the back when our car pulls in. The youngest, Sammy, was six when Ali and I came, and now he's twenty-one, tall and super cute, with almost black hair and blue eyes. Two years older, Ian is just as pretty and even taller. I love them and their smiles.

Sammy gets me first, grabbing and swinging me around like I used to do to him when he was young. Well over six feet tall, now he can do the same to me. Ian kisses my cheek and squeezes until I pinch his kidney, and then he passes me on to Dad.

"You look so happy," he says, holding me out at arm's length.

I haven't stopped smiling since we arrived, and now it grows. A professor of journalism, he studies things for a living and I'm no different. His gaze roves over my face and a glance at the changes to the rest of me. Shorter than his sons by a couple of inches, he's thin with dark hair and circular glasses, very much a scholar. He likes old books and a rare find. I'm pretty sure he believes Ali and I are the best discovery he's come across.

"Charlie-girl, when is the last time you ate a proper meal?"

I smile; he's always worried about me. "A muffin on the plane."

Mom comes by, circling her arm through mine as we walk down the short path and into the house. "You have lost weight, are you taking care of yourself?"

"I'm fine, really. Better than I've ever been." In the kitchen she stops and takes my shoulders to look for the truth in my eyes. She grabs my cheeks when she finds it and a grin soothes her frown away.

"I'll tell you about him later, but I don't want you to worry. Colin is the best thing that's happened to me besides you and Dad and our family." If not for them I wouldn't have survived childhood. I shudder at the thought of what I would have become without their love.

"I can't wait to meet the man who stole your heart," she says, turning to the fridge to get lunch ready.

Colin here? It doesn't seem possible. For a second my good mood crashes, but then I'm caught up in the family fold. The day races by, playing catch-up with stories and laughter and food, so much my belly hurts after dinner.

Ian and Sammy start a campfire, it crackles and spits sparks high in the darkening sky. I take out my guitar; songs are sung and marshmallows are roasted. We're not *Leave it to Beaver* wholesome, especially with Ali's penchant for a potty mouth and Ian's proclivity to running a numbers game while he was in high school, but we're my perfect family. The freedom I feel here is liberating and so is the growth I've discovered with Colin.

Speak of the devil; my phone rings from inside the house, where I left it on the dining table. Sprinting inside, I grab it on last ring. "Hi."

"Hi, yourself."

I smile. Other than a short text letting him know I'd arrived, we haven't spoken since I left him at the airport. "It's so good to hear your voice. I miss you already."

"I miss you too, baby. Georgia would be much more stimulating if you were here."

I groan as my girl parts start to spark brighter than the fire. "Colin… I really, really miss you."

He chuckles. "What are you doing?"

"Singing songs by the beach. I missed my guitar too, and we're having a happy reunion."

"Hmm, bring it with you when you come home to me. I'd like to hear you play."

Home to him, um, yup. I'm all in. "Now tell me what you're doing?" I love my family, I do. But I miss him like a piece of me is lost in the jungle.

"John will be here any minute to work on a speech for next week."

"I wish you were with me," I whisper.

He takes his time to respond and he sounds surprised when it comes. "I do too. We can talk about working some downtime into the schedule soon. We'll do something, just the two of us. Would you like that?"

My heart pangs, and then it pings like a sonar bleeping *here I am, come and find me*. "I would, a lot. Don't work too long tonight and don't say you won't because I know you will. Get some sleep."

I can picture his dimple as his smile spreads. "I'll try, but it's hard when a piece of me is a thousand miles away. Keep my heart safe."

"Are you trying to make me cry?" I laugh, but wipe a damn tear from my cheek at the same time.

"Baby." He sighs, and then the knock sounds loud enough it's as if it was the cottage door. John's voice is clear, as is Ella's.

My eyes dry up and I pace, pulling my bottom lip like Colin does. "You didn't tell me she was joining you in Georgia." Jealousy waves a friendly hand—*here I am*. Damn it.

"It was last minute. Charlie, I have to go. We can talk about this later, okay?"

"No, I'm sorry. I didn't mean for it to come out like that. I just miss you, that's all, and I hate she gets to see your pretty face and I don't."

"I'll send you a picture."

"I have plenty on my computer and if I need more, I'll search the Internet. Did you—"

"No," he growls. "I—Charlie, trust me, please. Everything is fine."

"I believe you," I say, my heart thumping a hard beat.

"You're okay?"

"Yes, go do your thing. I've got songs and s'mores waiting. I'll talk to you tomorrow. I love you."

The pause hurts. “I know,” he says, and waits on the line an extra moment. Then he’s gone.

Tears singe my eyes and I blink them back. I hate the weird feeling in my gut, but it’s there as the phone trembles in my hand.

MIDNIGHT HAS COME AND gone, yet Ali and I lie awake. A lamp between our beds sheds enough light I can see her wide eyes. “Charlie Anne Carter, you really do love him!” she squeaks.

“I do.” I fall sideways on my pillow and hug my knees to my chest. Fear simmers in my belly; reality is too much to ignore with the miles separating us.

“What’s wrong?”

I swallow back the lump in my throat. “Colin and I will never work long-term. We’re too different.”

“He’s a man; you’re a woman. You love each other. That’s not a hard equation to figure out.”

“It’s not that simple. He’ll never fall in love with me and I don’t know that I can live every day knowing I’ve given him my whole heart and I get leftover pieces of his.” I give her a quick Colin McKenna history lesson. “And that’s only half of it. The other part is this.” I sweep my hand from the top of my head to my toes. “I not meant for the White House crowd. I don’t know how to act, what to say, what to wear. He should be with someone like Ella Montgomery or Raquel Meyers. They make sense for him.” My stomach churns. “They were groomed to be with heads of state: flawless manners, well-coiffed hair.”

“Did you say coiffed? Who says coiffed?”

I throw a pillow at her head, but she deflects it with her quick hands. “I do, okay? And, yes, perfect, everything about them is fucking perfect. I bet they wake up and look ravishing every damn morning.”

"All right. First, stop talking like Gram. Ravishing is taking it too far. Second, stop right now with this bullshit. You're a fit for whatever and wherever life takes you. Why are you so down about this?"

"I don't know." I roll to my back and stare at the ceiling. "He's perfect, Ali. Colin McKenna is gorgeous and good, dedicated, honest—the list is endless. And I'm… well, I'm tainted. I'm so afraid my past will hurt him."

"But you told him, so why is it a problem?"

"He doesn't believe me."

Ali's eye's narrow and I fear for Colin's safety. She fights boys. I laugh remembering the ass-kicking she gave Dermott Kinley while we were at the Kerrs. He wouldn't stop teasing me about the knots in my hair and she beat the ever-living snot out of him. He didn't say a word to either of us the last five months we attended the same school.

"No, he *believes* me and he's horrified by it, he just thinks it's a non-issue. But it is. He's pro-life and obviously I have a different perspective. If it gets out he condones it, but has been so opposed to it in a million speeches, the public will call him out on the double standard and his campaign will tank."

She shakes her head. "I don't think it's as easy as that. I'm with Colin on this one, Charlie. Let it go. Put that part of your life behind you and don't let it hurt you anymore."

I asked Colin to do the same thing two nights ago. *Leave the past where it is so we can have a future together.* Maybe it's time.

SUN BURSTING THROUGH THIN curtains is my morning wake-up call. Peeking at the nightstand alarm clock tells me it's eleven. Damn, I haven't crashed like this since college. But all things considered, I haven't slept through the night since February.

Colin. I roll my eyes. Missing him this much is not normal. I need a head check—I mean a heart check. One day, five to go isn't a productive or pleasant use of my vacation. I'm with my peeps, I love them to the moon and back. But there's an added tier to my seven-layer cake and he's sifted to the top. I lift his stolen T-shirt to my nose and breathe in the leftover remnants of sandalwood and Colin.

Grabbing my laptop from the side table, I warm it up to send a quick e-mail.

To: Colin McKenna
From: Charlie Carter
Subject: Good Morning SHSM
Dear Colin, I slept through the whole night. That hasn't happened in a long while because I've been sleeping with a super-hot sex machine for a while now. Although I feel well rested, my muscles miss waking with the knowing ache of overuse. I'm thinking of you, CC

As I'm about the close the lid, my in-box pings and I smile.

To: Charlie Carter
From: Colin McKenna
Subject: Good Morning Beautiful
My dearest Charlie,

In my dreams last night I felt your kisses, your heat and your hungry body against mine. I woke this morning with a very simple and pure need for you; my body craved your touch, my ears missed your voice, and my mind longed for your insight. Tuesday is a year from now. I wonder if you want me, in the way I need you. Very simply, your love is a testament to the growing and burning need I feel when your name crosses my lips and my heart.

Colin

Holy Shit. I can't believe he wrote that. My in-box pings again.

To: Charlie Carter
From: Colin McKenna
Subject: Re: SHSM

P.S. I do hope the super-hot sex machine is at least making the sleepless nights a worthwhile event. I miss you, Colin

I rest my hand over my heart. My sweet Colin.

To: Colin McKenna
From: Charlie Carter
Subject: Every Single Minute
Dear Colin,
Every single second that fills each minute, growing into hours, days, and weeks, is more than I ever hoped to have. Tuesday is an eternity away. I love you so much, CC

To: Charlie Carter
From: Colin McKenna
Subject: Re: Every Single Minute
Baby, I feel the same way. I have to go. I will surely be distracted by thoughts of you and your aching overuse while I speak about the hazards of global warming. I long to be with you, CM

I reread the string of e-mails—more than once. Falling to the mattress, I pull a pillow on top of my face to muffle a groan. I want to drive to the airport and hop on a plane to meet him but I won't, no matter how much I need him. It's Gram's birthday and I'll celebrate with her. I can make it until Tuesday.

THE DAY PASSES IN a blur. Ali, Mom, and I shop for most of it. Ali insists I try on a bikini and I look down at my hips.

"Have you seen these lately, they haven't found a new home." I pat my rounded curves.

"Do it." She throws it on my stack and pushes me in the door.

When it's on, I have to admit I kind of like it. Ali's words of wisdom: "Buy it. Colin will throw you on the bed not in the pool when you put that thing on."

"Right. I will admit he's a much more effective workout than Pilates ever was."

"Is this a good time to tell you *I told you so*?" She smirks.

"Sure, get it out now." I smile. "You're right, Ali, but you know I wouldn't feel like this with any other man."

"I know. He's the perfect guy for you to spend forever with."

Forever. One day at time is much easier to consider and I concentrate on that when I slide into the next dress. Ali's face scrunches up.

For the first time in my life I second-guess my style. Life has taken a turn into a very conservative world and it's not a place I'm familiar with.

Retro-chic isn't daring, but it's not staid or Ella's traditional sleek either. I've always worn what makes me feel good. I pay little attention to fashion trends or what other people are wearing but that might have to change.

But this is frump-tastic and as horrible as Ali's crumpled nose. I put it back and pick the outfits that make me feel good and hope Colin likes them too.

Party-necessary items come next, groceries and decorations, and when we get home there's enough time for a late dinner and food prep. The only thing accomplished after we eat is food prep and cleaning, sliding into bed at quarter after eleven I send a good night message to my missing person.

To: Colin McKenna

From: Charlie Carter

Subject: Counting Down the Minutes

Dear Colin,

It's night again and you are on my mind, as you are so often throughout the day. My bed is empty when I so badly want you to fill it. I miss your strong arms around me and your lips on mine. I love you, CC

There isn't an immediate response as there was this morning, so I close my eyes with my laptop open and wait. It's early for him to be asleep, so where is he, who is he with? I hit my pillow and glance at Ali. She's out like a light, a skill she taught herself in med school. If you want every minute of rest possible you need to get comatose quick.

It doesn't work for me. Minutes pass, one after the other, and eventually I run out of scenarios. Colin's not available and I don't know why.

SATURDAY TURNS OUT TO be the perfect day for a party. I wake early after a restless night and snub my laptop, choosing a shower instead. Colin hasn't given me any reason for this burst of jealousy, yet it boils under my skin like the sizzling energy I feel when he's around. I ignore it through my blow dry and makeup application, I tough it out when I slide into a new set of lace lingerie Colin would drool over, I set it aside when I don my new magenta ankle jeans that verge on capri length and then a sparkling black tank.

I'm way more fun than any of those bitches and Colin digs me. That's my motto for the day. I have no worries. When I get back to the bed, I log in and find the message I should have read when I woke. It would have changed my surly attitude, but I'm glad I got there on my own.

To: Charlie Carter
From: Colin McKenna
Subject: Sleepless Nights
Dearest Charlie,

I've had a long day, solitary and reflective. I found solace in your words, your voice a whisper in my ear of memories that bring my blood to boil. The passion I have for you cannot be tamed. I need you. Colin.

The heart pang is back. I hate that he's lonely. I call, but it goes to voice mail and I leave a message about missing him.

Running down the hall I bump into Ian, who's bringing in last-minute groceries from the car outside. "Hey, Char, you look nice."

"Thanks. Do you need some help?"

"No, but Mom does. She's struggling with some recipe in the kitchen." We laugh; Mom always struggles with recipes in the kitchen.

When I round the corner she has her head stuck in a book.

"What can I do?"

"Oh, thank goodness you're here. Can you figure out what this means?"

"Sure. Why don't you let me make Gram's favorite cake and you can check something else off your list."

"You're a dear." She kisses my cheek and then heads out front to direct set-up. And that's how morning transitions to early afternoon. Stringing lights around the trees, ice in tubs with soda cans, glasses, silverware, plates and everything else needed for a party.

Finally everything is done. The yard is littered with white-and-red-checkered tablecloths, with daisies in low vases in the center of each. A makeshift bar in the corner is open and business is booming. Gram arrives and feigns surprise when fifty guests roar a greeting. In truth she's known for months. Gramps can't keep a secret to save his life and he confessed as soon as she asked what her birthday plans were. I accept her hug and kiss with an extra squeeze.

"My favorite girl," she whispers.

I smile. "You say that to all of us, we know."

"And it's the truth every time. All of you," she says. "And Charlie, don't think because this is a party you're not going to tell me about Mr. Hot Pants."

My eyes snap open and hers sparkle. "Oh, I knew it, Ali was right. That senator has gotten to our girl."

"Martha, leave poor Charlie alone. She'll talk to you when she's ready." Gramps winks at me, and then takes Grams arm to pull her along the line up of family and friends waiting with birthday wishes.

"I'll find you later," she calls.

I wave and smile, but get lost in thoughts of Colin. To manage the melancholy, I take a self-induced time out by walking down to make sure the fire pit is ready for s'mores. The lake is peaceful. It's too early in the season for the rush of speed boats, and there are only a few pontoons lazing around. The water rolls gently into the beach, coloring the white sand dark beige. It slows down the fast pace of the morning.

My Zen is interrupted, not by noise, but lack thereof. Voices that were loud with laughter have dulled to a low hum. Turning to find the reason for the change, I search the crowd. Mom's hand flies up to cover her mouth. Dad's eyes are as big as his glasses. Gram smiles, ear-to-ear awe that's mirrored on many of the faces surrounding her. Aunt Alice fans herself with a paper plate. I have seen that look before and I know who has caused it.

TWENTY-TWO

It's impossible for Colin to be here, yet my brain has jumped on the fantasy train. When heads turn in my direction, a nervous energy simmers beneath my skin. *What the hell?* I catch Ali staring, the corner of her mouth lifted in a knowing smirk.

And then I turn and time ticks by in slow motion as my heart thuds to a stop. I'm in the state between waking and sleep, where dreams seem vivid and real. A shy smile lifts the corner of Colin's mouth as he weaves through stupefied partygoers. Gram's mouth parts, speechless, which is not like her at all. And she's not the only one checking out his low-slung jeans, or how his shoulders fill a white linen button-up, sleeves rolled to the elbow. This is how I picture him in my mind: relaxed and smiling. The wind plays with his hair, messing it to runway-model perfection. He looks good, really, really good.

His eyes glow as he approaches, but when he stops in front of me his brow falls.

"Charlie?"

He reaches to touch my hand; the electric current that runs so strong between us is there, humming as if it's a real entity even before we connect.

When he finally makes contact, the current sends a shock to my heart and it beats once more. I gasp, the mannequin come to life. In one instant I move from standing stock-still, staring at a dream, to throwing myself into his chest, my arms around his head as he lifts me from the ground. I'd like to wrap my legs around his waist but a modicum of decorum outweighs the joy of having him between my thighs.

Tears rush to my eyes. He's been the only thing missing and to feel him against me, to drown in the wash of sandalwood, sparks a joy I've never felt before. He came here for me. *Mine*.

He holds me close and the heat of his body quickens my already racing pulse. I had forgotten about the party until this moment, and now I've decided I don't care. Lifting my head to look into the blue eyes I love so much, I ask, "You're really here?"

His smile is so shy, I melt. "I told you I need you. I couldn't wait an eternity."

Without caring who may bear witness, I crush my lips to his. He accepts my tongue, but he's playing a chaste game when I want to get dirty. A caress to my cheek has me slow down even as my body revs up. Pulling away before I'm ready for his withdrawal, he leans his forehead against mine.

"I missed you, baby."

I tuck myself into my favorite place and breathe him in for minutes, the waves lapping behind us while the party hums near the house.

"Are you going to introduce me to your family?"

"Oh, shit."

He laughs, a rumble in his chest that makes me smile along with him. After a chaste kiss to the lips, he lowers me to my feet. I wobble, but he keeps his arm around my waist to steady my gait.

"You really know how to surprise a girl, Mr. Sex Machine."

I love his chuckle, laughing is not something he does often, and I couldn't be happier to see him so relaxed and happy. Yes, he's happy, and I am too.

Pulling our connected hands closer, I hold them against my stomach as we walk toward my parents.

Everyone watches, but I don't care. He's here and I keep glancing at him to make sure of it.

In seconds we stop. "Mom, Dad, this is my boyfriend, Colin McKenna." The word is easier to say than I'd thought.

"Colin, my parents, Keith and Anna Carter."

"It's nice to meet you. I hope you'll forgive me for the intrusion."

His smile is really quite stunning and it takes Mom a moment to find her voice. "You're welcome anytime." Her face flushes as she says it.

"Thank you, Anna. That's very kind of you."

I can't help my silly grin. Leaning into his arm, my thoughts stray to perfection. Life has never felt so good. Having him here, with everyone that I love, is more than I've ever thought to ask for.

With Dad distracting him with some lake facts, Mom mouths to me *he's so cute* as she fans herself and my grin grows. Ali's next. This ought to be interesting—beautiful Ali and Mr. McPerfect.

"Ali," she says, ignoring my warning glare for good behavior.

Colin smiles. "So this is the sister—"

She isn't interested in a formal greeting, standing on her tiptoes to give him an Ali Carter special. His eyes widen when her arms wrap around his neck in a firm hug. I'm still holding on for dear life, so the best he can do is reciprocate with a one-handed loose pat on the back. While reaching up, Ali whispers in his ear. Colin doesn't say anything, only smiles and nods in response.

They don't have time to chat, as Sammy and Ian are close behind. I take Colin to meet my grandparents next; they're sitting at a table with my dad's brother, George, his wife, Mary, and their children. My cousins are speechless.

"Gram, Gramps, my boyfriend, Colin." I say it for the second time and it sounds right.

"Well, now, you're a handsome one, aren't you?" Gram says while staring unabashedly. "Charlie-girl, you sure picked a fine man—took you a while to find him, but he looks worth the wait."

Colin laughs, an amused smile spreads into a dimple. Taking her hand, he says, "Happy birthday, Mrs. Carter."

"Call me Gram, everyone does."

Introductions take an hour. Ali brings us refreshments so it doesn't feel so much like a campaign rally. Colin sips beer and chats, as easy with my family and Gram's friends as he is anywhere. At last

I steal him away to a wooden swing partially hidden from view by my mom's garden. It faces the lake, the sun glinting bright streaks of light off the water. I hope for a few minutes of privacy, but you never know, with kids playing hide-and-seek and the adults just plain peeking, how long the semi-seclusion will last. I haven't let go of his hand, and he hasn't asked for it back either.

He pushes us into a slow glide with his foot. Pulling my knee up onto the bench, I fold my ankle under me so we face each other.

"I can't stop smiling."

He reaches to rub his thumb down my cheek and I close my eyes. I'm surprised into a smile when he kisses me, but then it's wiped clean when he offers his tongue. Yes, please. We lose ourselves in the familiar brush of fingers over skin. I love getting lost with him. It's easy to do. So when I get hungrier and my mouth demands more and I toss away my beer so my hands can dig in his hair, he pulls away, chuckling. He remains close enough that his breath washes over me, and I groan.

"I want you," I say, remaining in the dark. I can't possibly look at him for fear I'll straddle his thighs.

The rumble of his chest reaches my ears, before the vibration of his mouth sweeps against mine. "Later, baby."

That reminds me. "You brought things to stay here, right?"

"I didn't want to presume, so I booked a room at a hotel."

I shake my head. "No way I'm here and you're in town."

"If you want me, I'll stay."

"I'll always want you." His eyes darken to midnight, a color my heart remembers wishing for and now, I've found my way. I'm strong enough to explore as I never have before. With his guidance, Charlie Carter isn't so much of a mystery anymore.

"I was wrong." I say it out loud, even though I meant to keep the thought to myself. "I had a hard time picturing you here at the cottage, with my family. I've thought about you so much; everywhere I went I wished you were with me. When I'd try to imagine you here it was hard to picture you in this simple place." I wave around the yard, filled with my family, layered with homemade and homegrown things. "You're so larger than life, Colin; when you're onstage or on TV, in front of hundreds of people, it reminds me of how important you are." His jaw tenses, so I rush on. "Now I see you here and I realize you fit. You fit with me. You're perfect here and with my family." I smooth the rest of his concern away with my fingers.

Colin dips his head an inch to bring our foreheads together, resting there for a minute before he rubs his nose over mine. "I belong wherever you are."

Damn, that's nice to hear. His mouth finds mine and this time he doesn't hold back. Taking long licks into my mouth, he pushes so I'm pressed into the swing. He devours me. I can only hold on by twisting my fingers in his shirt, pulling him closer even as I feel the need to push away for air. I whimper when his hand grazes my breast and then digs into my side.

Always responsible, he breaks away. "Shit, Charlie," he says on a panted breath.

I would laugh but it's not possible when my brain is sending signals to the lower half of my body to conquer and control.

"This is a beautiful spot," he says, adjusting his jeans.

"Really, we're going to talk about the lake?"

His eyebrow rises. "You have something else in mind?"

I swat at his arm. "May I remind you of paybacks? Keep pushing me and I will take it out on your body later."

A shiver rolls down my spine when his eyes drop to half-mast. "I was hoping you would say that."

"Fine, the lake it is. Yes, it's one of my favorite places in the whole world. You'll have to come back in the summer when the water is warm enough to swim and we have the boats in. I'll take you for a ride." I smile and bat my lashes.

He laughs and takes my hand. "I'd like that, baby."

Ali pops in. "Mind if I join you?"

Before either of us can answer, she snuggles next to Colin in a space not meant for another human. She bops him with her hip. He laughs and scoots over. His arm drapes over my shoulder, pulling me in to his side like he's done a hundred times before. Except he's here, in Michigan; he left the campaign trail for me. God, this is so surreal.

"Did Charlie tell you I'm in med school?" Ali asks. I give her my evil-eye warning.

He nods. "I understand you've finished your third year at Georgetown. Have you decided on a specialty?"

"Mmmm, not necessarily, but I enjoyed the rotation in the emergency room. The people, the injuries you learn about in that element are unbelievable. You'd be amazed at the things I've seen. Once, I had to stitch a poor boy back together after he was stabbed—stabbed by his girlfriend's sister because he broke her sister's heart."

"Ali Carter!" I scream.

Colin throws his head back and laughs. I'm glad he finds her funny. I glare at her. She looks like a cherub sent from the heavens, but she's a devil. I narrow my eyes and mouth *Stop!*

He pulls me closer, still smiling. "You don't have anything to worry, Ali. There won't be a need for you to wield your scalpels against me. I'll protect Charlie's heart with my own."

As if it knows Colin is referring to it, my heart flutters; how is it possible he can be this romantic on top of everything else?

Ali beams. "I just needed to make sure." She pats his thigh, a friendly tap to confirm her consent and her eyes grow wide. *Wow*, she mouths, keeping her hand on his hard muscle.

I nod and say, "You have no idea."

He looks at my sassy sister and then me, unsure of what passed between us, but we giggle so he lets it go.

Ali is the first of many interruptions. We move when Mom brings my guitar and the kids sit around me to sing songs. Colin lies on the grass, elbow propping him up, and the view doesn't get any better than him. He draws a large crowd. Everyone gets a pick and I go through "Old MacDonald" to a jumbled version of Katy Perry's "Firework." Ali pops in and I'm afraid. I close my eyes and shake my head when she suggests "At Last," the song I sang to Colin at Blake's.

No one will take no for an answer, including Mr. Sex God himself and so I start.

Of course I'm drawn to him and my voice dips an octave too low. I sing for him and everyone knows it—including Colin. I'm sure my face is the color of my pants when I'm done, but my reward is his hand on my lower back as he rushes me to the rear of the house. Now this is a kiss. This is more than a kiss. This is a 911 alert because I'm on fire. Holy sinful things I want to do to him. I tell him so too and he just smiles. Damn man.

When we reemerge, Ian and Sammy ask him to play horseshoes with Dad. The four of them chat it up like long-lost pals and somewhere in the middle of their game I take him a fresh beer. As I cross the lawn, he steps from the sandpit to take a call. I smile when he's quick to hang up and before I know his intentions, he holds his phone up and snaps my picture.

"Let me see it!" I demand.

"It's beautiful, Charlie. You're beautiful," he says as he leans down for a kiss. Just for fun, I taste his bottom lip with my tongue. A low rumble resonates from his chest before he pulls away.

I bounce with giddy joy. "I'm going to go help Mom with dinner."

"Don't be gone long, baby."

My heart somersaults. I can't believe how much a word or a look from him affects me. I'm glad to have a distraction in the form of corn on the cob. It's boiling in a turkey fryer off to the side of the house. Just as I put the last batch in a roaster for transport to the buffet table, Max, the huge Rottweiler from next door, tears into our yard and knocks into the boiling pan. Max rights himself, but the fryer tips.

I jump, but not fast enough. It slaps against the back of my leg, my exposed right ankle taking the brunt of the heat. I scream because damn, that hurts. Somehow, Colin is at my side, his breath bursting against my cheek as he picks me up.

We're in the house seconds later and he has me on the kitchen counter, foot in the sink. Cold water eases the sting.

"I need your pants off," he growls.

What? Why now? Later would be a much better time. "It will swell and I need to get them off you before it happens. I can cut them if you prefer."

"No way, they're my new favorite."

He glares at me. "I'm not worried about your fucking pants, Charlie. I'll buy you a thousand pairs just like them."

"Fine, I can see you're not in a reasonable mood." I lean back and pop the button at my waist; I don't want him getting near me with a sharp object. He's all too happy to assist, lifting my butt to push them down my thighs, leaving me in my tank and a pair of pink lace panties. I bought them with him in mind, but who knew he'd get his first look with my mother ten feet behind him. Oh, and Ali now, too. Nice.

"Hold on to me, baby."

I grab his neck. What had been soft cotton now feels like a bristle brush as it scrapes against delicate skin.

"Damn—" The imaginative string of filth I normally hold back comes out in an easy rush.

"Fuckity-fuck-pooh." His brow rises, as does the corner of his mouth. "I have honestly never heard that before."

I laugh and Ali pushes him with her hip. "I taught her everything she knows. Come here, sister."

Dr. Carter is making a house call. She bends to look at my ankle under the water. Washing her hands in the opposite side of the sink and rinsing with the spray nozzle, she presses a finger to the burn. It smarts but I've suffered through worse.

"Keep the water running on it for another ten minutes and I'll be back." She grabs my face with both of her hands. "Why do you always do this?"

I shrug. "Who knows why things happen to me? They just do; I've learned to live with it."

Colin groans and I lift my eyes in time to see his rolling. Ali laughs, patting him on the back. "Better get used to it. She has a natural lure to all things dangerous or that cause injury."

"I've had the unfortunate pleasure to learn that she does."

Ali's eyes snap to mine. "What have you not told me?"

I glare at both of them. "Nothing, you know everything. Factory falls and cut hand. I've been great for months. I guess I hit my safety limit and was due. Go." I shoo her away; Mom too. "Don't let this silly accident stop dinner. I'm fine."

Mom glances at Colin and says, "I can see that you are." She follows Ali out the door and we watch through the window as the two of them get everyone eating.

Colin rubs my back and now we're alone with the running water.

"If you're trying to distract me, it's working."

He smiles and glances out the picture window and to the guests that can see us as clearly as we can them.

"You have a beautiful voice, baby. I didn't realize you sing."

"This is it. At the cottage and most often by the fire, maybe sometimes in the shower, but I'm way to shy for karaoke."

He laughs. "Never once have I thought of you as shy, fiery maybe, but not shy."

"Why fiery?"

"Well there is the obvious." He picks up one of the many wayward curls. "Your hair. It's beautiful, like you. In the sun it's a flame, and in bed, with your head thrown back, it's a low burning candle meant to tempt me."

Tucking the strands behind my ear, he says, "Your intense passion, how fierce you give love, and then there's your temper." He whistles. "Most definitely your temper."

I laugh. "Okay, I admit I'm good at overacting."

Our easy mood falls with the sinking sun. His gaze darkens, prompting my heartbeat to sprint. He doesn't lean in to kiss me as I expect, but takes hold of my cheeks and swallows what appears to be a lump.

“Why did you come here?” I whisper.

Colin’s eyes close for a second and then he says, “There are so many things I would like to say, yet each time I try, words don’t seem enough. If I felt less, maybe this would easier, but Charlie, you should know the moment my life finally made sense was when I heard your voice. It’s my true north and I’m intent on staying the course.” His fingers slip into my hair and his mouth finds mine at the same time tears rush to my eyes. This kiss is as fierce as his hold, a possessive grip that screams *mine* louder than any statement.

He breaks away in a rush of breath and his lips find my ear. “It will always be you.”

Just when his mouth meets my neck, the back door bangs shut. He pulls away, but only so far as to tuck my head into my favorite place.

“All clear in there?” Ali calls and I wipe below my eyes. She glides into the kitchen with a smirk and a wink. “Let me see you,” she says, washing her hands again.

After a quick exam and a couple of pokes at my leg, she says, “Okay, let’s get you down so I can wrap you up.”

She holds her hands out to help me but before I can move Colin picks me up, taking me to the chair she’s pulled out from the table. Instead of setting me down, he places me on his lap, turning so my ankle is held up for her. I tuck my smile into his neck.

After wrapping what turns out to be a mix of first- and second-degree burns, Ali hands over a pair of cut-off jeans she had setting next to the first aid kit. Slipping from Colin’s lap, I catch him staring at my butt and laugh when he licks his lips.

“Hungry?”

He growls and reaches for me. “You know I am.”

“I meant for food. Come on, let’s eat,” I say, grabbing his hand and pulling him to his feet.

Dinner is full of good barbeque and laughs. We eat and eat some more. I escape dish duty and when everything is cleared, we sit around Gram to sing happy birthday. Every year, she’s surrounded by her grandchildren; this year, that includes Colin. He has me on his lap again; much to my consternation, given my entire family is present. Using the argument that it was easier to elevate my ankle, he won. Even with ibuprofen it stings.

So here I am, with Colin's breath on my neck, cousins and siblings around us. I couldn't be happier. Every couple of minutes, his lips brush against my hair. In time, my leg gets stiff and I have to shuffle on his lap to readjust.

"Careful," he warns in my ear.

I smile, knowing very well what he means. We're close to running off into the woods. I wiggle again to let him know I'd be okay with that.

"One of these days I'll take you up on your offer, Charlie. You just won't know when, but right now I really want a piece of Gram's chocolate cake." His eyes are dark, but filled with humor too.

I pretend to pout. "You want cake more than me?"

"Keep that lip away from me, or I'll take it and you right here. What would Gram think of me then?" His voice is laced with just enough truth that I decide I better mind my manners. Before I do though, I kiss him on the cheek.

Mom walks out with the chocolate concoction that has at least twenty-five candles ablaze on top. Gram holds her hands up, covering her mouth as she does every year in mock horror of the light show. In reality she loves every minute of it, enjoying the song and everyone singing it. Colin joins in. She gladly accepts help from around the table to blow out the inferno and works to ensure everyone has a piece.

We dive in and I hum against the delicious goodness as it melts on my tongue. Lifting his second forkful, Colin's brow rises. "You made this?" he asks, incredulous.

"Yes." I laugh. "You think it impossible I can make a cake?"

"No, I think it impossible you didn't burn the house down." He laughs, as does everyone at the table.

"Good one," Ian says. Sammy gives him a high five. My response is to glare, waiting for an apology that never comes.

"It's very good," he says in consolation. "I had no idea you could cook."

"Well, to be fair, we haven't been anywhere I can cook for you. Next time we have a break I'll make you dinner. You can decide then if I'm good at it."

"Deal." He smiles and takes another bite while watching me. There's more he hasn't said; his eyes convey a shadow of his feelings. Maybe one day he'll speak the words out loud.

TWENTY-THREE

I REREAD COLIN'S NOTE for the tenth time in as many minutes.

Dearest Charlie,

When I am with you and only with you I feel as if I can achieve greatness. With you there is the possibility of renewed life and a dream I never believed could be a reality. I will give you everything I am capable of giving; it is yours. Colin

He placed it on my pillow yesterday, before he left. When I came down for breakfast my mom knew I wasn't staying through to Tuesday, so she helped me rearrange my flight. Less than twenty-four hours after he departed Traverse City, I'll surprise him in Arkansas.

The plane engines rev and I tuck the note in my bag. But before I shove it under my seat, I send Colin a quick text: *Dear CM, the weather in Michigan is cold and rainy today. Wish you were here to warm me up ;) I miss you. CC*. An immediate reply pops up and I smile from ear to ear as I read it. *Dear CC, Please keep in mind tomorrow you will be thoroughly hot and I hope bothered. I miss you too. CM*

A stewardess gives my cell an evil eye and I rush my parting message. *Stop, you're making me blush. I have to run. I love you.*

Seconds after I hit Send, the phone is in my bag and then they're both stowed away. The next few hours are a blur of stale pretzels, uncomfortable napping, and maneuvering out of the airport. Flying carry-on only allows me to bypass baggage claim and then hail a waiting cab. As promised, I reach for my cell to call my mom with an arrival update but it takes seconds to learn the battery is drained. *Crap, I must not have turned it off during the flight*. I'll have to wait until I get to the hotel to connect with her.

It's closer than I thought and my heart rate speeds when we pull up to the entrance. Colin had left instructions with the front desk to issue me a key to his suite and the clerk doesn't seem to care it's a day early.

With card in hand, I rush to the elevators, nervous only because my impromptu appearance doesn't include Drake. But I spend the quick ride devising how to ensure Colin will forgive me. My mouth, his… *ding*.

The bell announces the tenth floor and I say "Excuse me" to a couple pushing in before I've had a chance to exit.

But I'm thrilled to be here and I smile while practically skipping to Colin's suite. I'm greeted by silence and décor that's unfamiliar, yet familiar at the same time. The soft velvet sectional looks tempting, especially because the overexertion has my ankle throbbing, but I need to send a message home. I set my bag next to the couch and search for his computer. It's on the desk in his room.

The picture window on the far wall frames the cityscape. Clouds build in the distance and dusk casts the room in shadows. I sink down in the chair and touch the mouse to awaken the laptop. After a second my gaze flicks to the screen and I blink through the bright light to focus on what stares back at me. My heart stumbles. Shaking my head does little to disrupt the sharp wail ringing in my ears.

A picture of me floats in the middle of the screen, with a smaller one of another woman imposed on top of it in the lower corner. The woman looks exactly like me: auburn hair, clear, creamy skin, cherry-stained lips, a small straight nose and high cheekbones. The biggest difference between us is our eyes: gray to green.

The similarities are striking.

My gaze drags from the stranger to my haphazard waves and my mouth spread in a ginormous smile. I was so happy. In that moment, I didn't want for anything but what I had. Colin came for me and I was surrounded by my family at the lake house. So who is the other woman and why are we side-by-side on his computer?

Revulsion rolls around in my stomach and gets worse when I notice an icon on the corner of my photo. A double click on the title *C. Carter* opens a content list.

The first link pulls up an article I wrote for a men's magazine last year. The topic: problems with big brother government. The document has a headshot I use for pieces like this one. The picture was professionally taken, my hair smooth, a serene smile playing on my lips, my eyes hinting at mischievousness. I always liked this shot.

Next comes a proposal I submitted for a freelance job, where I designed a website for a small business in Detroit. How in the world would he have a copy of this?

Link after link reveals articles I've written over the last two years. More disturbing is a folder full of pictures. One was taken on the Notre Dame campus as I rushed from the Inn and to my car. Two others are from last fall, the first when I sat on a bench in the park reading a book, the second while I was out with friends at a bar. At least fifty pictures chronicle weeks of my life and in every one I'm unaware of the photographer taking them. But in the last to pop up, I'm staring straight into the lens, brow drawn as if suspecting the intrusion.

The next link takes me first to my birth record and then to my biological parents' death certificates, and finally to my adoption decree. *What the hell?*

The last click causes the computer to think, as if stating a silent *proceed with caution.* I gasp. My hidden records are not so hidden. It's a scanned copy of a form, a social worker's account of my repeated rape and subsequent abortion, all so black-and-white and unfeeling. The wind is knocked out of my lungs as if I were punched in the stomach.

He knew.

The whole time he knew everything about me. *I didn't care about your past before and I don't care about it now.* He made me tell him.

He wrung out every sordid truth and he wasn't shocked because he knew… he knew everything.

Bile sticks in my throat from his deceit. *No, please. God, please no.* The room spins and I hold on to the desk for balance. Colin is calculated in everything he does. But who is the woman? The answer is a shiver clawing its way up my spine.

I log on to the Internet and type in *pictures of Abby McKenna.* Photos scatter across the screen and my worst nightmare is validated. In one of them Colin has his arm draped around her waist and Abby beams, posing with her hand tipped on her hip to elongate her petite frame. But it's the bracelet that has nausea churn my stomach. Without a doubt, it's the same one Colin gave me before the fundraiser in New Jersey. The weight of it pulls me down into a deep despair. In every photo, the similarities between the two of us are blaringly apparent.

I'm the spitting image of Colin's dead wife.

The knowing looks from his friends and family. The comments I didn't understand when they were said all make sense now. They were never fooled into believing I was along on the campaign as a member of the press; with my look-alike status they knew I was his mistress.

Colin must have seen my picture plastered on top of my articles. Intrigued, he researched my background, found out everything about me—*everything.* He manipulated me to be at his press conference and to accept this assignment.

Now I understand why he didn't want me to complete any online research about him and why I was asked late the night before to attend his campaign speech. I close my eyes and groan. I've been his puppet all along, he the masterful puppeteer moving me for his bidding, manipulating my actions and emotions with such skill I never suspected a thing. He finds broken things and makes them whole. I was the ultimate conquest, his biggest challenge. Take broken Charlie Carter and make her complete, fixed and mended into the long-gone wife he desperately wants back. A second chance at what once was.

I push back from the computer to bend over and shove my head between my knees. I'm on the verge of hyperventilating. While prostrate, the screen on the computer moves to snooze and the room goes dark. Blood pumps loud in my ears yet I hear the door to the suite open.

My shoulders tense. I don't want to see him. Not yet, not until I've planned my defense. But it's Ella's voice that rises to the forefront and my skin crawls. Her high pitch is annoying as she yells at Colin. His harsh retort shatters my trance. He's mad and loud, very loud. "This is none of your goddamned business! I've told you to leave her alone and stay out of my personal life." I sit up. He's talking about me?

"I have no choice," she snaps back. "You're thinking with your dick not your head. You've worked toward the presidency your entire life, and I'm sick of watching you throw it away for a whore."

"Watch your mouth," he growls. "You're walking a very fine line. My affairs are mine to manage. I know what I'm doing. I told you from the beginning, Charlise is the perfect person to report on my campaign. She's done exactly what we wanted her to do. She connected the campaign to women and young America. Our numbers in that age bracket have quadrupled since she began touring with us."

He's so calculating. *I leave very little to fate, Charlie*. His words play on repeat even as Ella continues.

"But then you started fucking her, and you're losing sight of what matters here. She's not part of the equation. While you're with *her*," she says, with venom dripping from her fangs, "your opponents are campaigning harder. They'll gain support. This has to stop. This sick obsession with Abby, trying to recreate her with someone else, isn't healthy. Can't you see what you're putting yourself through? You'll never get back what you had. Abby is gone."

Oh, God. I grab my chest to rub out the hurt in my heart.

"Get out," he says.

"I won't. I have always supported you, Colin, and for the life of me I can't figure out why at this moment you want to be with a woman who killed her baby. For God's sake, what the fuck is wrong with you? She's a murderer."

He told her. How could he betray me this way?

"That's enough. Don't you ever broach that topic again, or I swear to you, I will end our relationship altogether. You will no longer be a part of my life in any way. Do you understand?"

"No, I don't." Her tone softens. "You told me when this started she was just a distraction, something to keep you relaxed—*a good fuck* is an exact quote. You assured me she didn't mean anything to you, that you could walk away anytime. Now is the time. You've had your distraction; you've had your fun. Let's just hope you haven't caught an STD from the whore."

Blood drains from my face. A distraction? A good fuck? Walk away at any time?

I have to get out of here. Standing only confirms I'm trapped. I'll have to walk directly into the lion's den to flee. *God, I'm such a fool.*

Tears threaten my already blurred vision. A newfound silence pierces the ringing in my ears. The light snaps on and I turn away, eyes closed. Seconds pass before I blink them open to find Colin in the doorway, standing as still as a statue with an open mouth.

"Charlie," he breathes.

Surprise, you fucking bastard! I want to shout, but I'll try to leave with some dignity. Shame colors his cheeks and clouds his eyes. But there is more; shock, and something else. Fear?

"Charlie," he says again, "I wasn't expecting you today." He steps forward.

I lift my hands to block his approach. "Don't," is the only thing I say, but it holds so much vehemence he stops immediately. I'm so infuriated I'm afraid the tears will come, not from a broken heart—those will come later—but because I'm so incredibly mad, at him, at Ms. Bitchy, and at myself.

Ella pokes her head in. "If you'll excuse me," she says, the words dripping with joy. "Colin, do let me know if you need anything."

She curls her lip into a snarl before she turns and uses the door I so wish I had never entered and want to use now. This is the end. The end to what I had hoped was the beginning of my love story. But it's just another tragic chapter in the life of Charlie Carter. I wrap my arms around myself to hold in a tremor.

Without saying anything, I skirt around Colin and back out of the room. He watches me like I'm a caged animal; his eyes wide and wary, but they never leave mine. Steps away from the couch, I turn to go and notice my bag on the floor. That was his clue I was here; my black carry-on with the magenta bow tied to the handle.

"Charlie," he says. "Let me explain. Please." His voice is heartbreakingly low. I turn in response to his plea, not to offer solace, but to let him see me, the pain a stroke drawn perfectly in my lifeline. Freely letting the floodgates open, I think of the file I found on his computer. I think about the fact that I look like his dead wife, his betrayal, and his careless thoughts about me. I let him see the agony, my face contorted with pain. I want him to know for just one minute how his duplicity lacerated my heart.

He flinches and then lunges forward. "Don't—touch—me," I hiss and he stops a foot away. "How could you be so cruel?"

"I don't know what you heard—"

"Everything! I know it all."

"No, you don't. There's so much you need to hear from me. My feelings are private; I've never spoken to Ella about them. They're meant only for you. Please, let's sit down and talk. I'll explain. Please," he pleads again. Here he is, Mr. President, turning on the charm, the *believability factor*. I'm sure it's so I don't write a scathing article about his true character. I was right. All politicians are the same, lying sacks of shit.

Screw his plea. I want nothing to do with him. "Don't worry. I won't put any of this to pen and paper. I went into this with an open mind, with wonder and hope that you truly held the moral compass to effect positive change in this country. I thought you did. I won't ruin the hope of the American people who believe in you as I once did."

Colin's face crumbles under an ounce of the pain I feel. I stare at him one last time, his beauty unparalleled. I hope I never see him again.

Before I can leave he grabs my arms, shaking me gently. The intensity of our connection jolts through my body. "Look at me, Charlie."

My vision blurs on the button of his white oxford shirt and he shakes a little harder. "Look at me, *please*." Reluctantly, my eyes find his. Pain and fear paint a desperate picture.

"Please. Don't—leave—me. We need to talk, and I can explain everything. I—"

With strength I didn't know was within me I break away from his grip. "And listen to more of your lies?" He grabs his hair and pulls before his fist falls tight against his thigh. "I saw it all, everything in your sickening, pathetic file of my life!"

Shaking his head, he says, "No, you don't understand. Charlie—"

"Don't fucking say my name, you bastard," I scream. How many times has he said it, said my name passionately, or whispered it in my ear as we made love? It was never that to him. He used me. I'm the look-alike wife, a mirror into his past he can't move beyond. I groan and work to slow my frantic pulse.

"How could you do this to me? How could you hurt me so badly?" A tear escapes my eye before I can stop it. Pushing it away violently, I ensure he knows how deeply I'm scarred. It's the worst insult possible, but it's the truth. "I didn't believe it was possible to feel pain beyond what Shane Roberts did to me, but I was wrong, so very wrong."

Colin's shoulders slump.

There is one last thing to do. Glancing down at the weight on my wrist, I slip the bracelet free, my stomach clenching as I do. I've thought of it as a symbol of his feelings for me, but I'm wrong. As I have been on so many counts relating to Colin. His heart is owned by the woman he promised to remember *always*.

"This belongs to someone else." Holding it out, I wait for minutes. His frame is devoid of all emotion so I set it on the side table, next to the couch.

"It's my love, Charlie. The only way I know how to give it."

What? I can't think. I need to leave. With one last look at his ravaged face, I grab my bag and turn to pull the door open.

"Charlie, don't do this. I need you to breathe, to live." The horror fades behind me with the closing door, and my only thought is *I've lost my heart.*

The peace and utter completion I've always felt with Colin are gone. I'm an empty vessel moving dispassionately and all alone.

I call for the elevator over and over and when it doesn't come immediately I throw myself down the stairs, running as fast as I can down flight after flight. I don't know what I'm going to do; I'm in a strange city without any connections. I have no idea where I am, or what other hotels are around. Can I catch a flight? My cell is dead and I can't call anyone.

I walk quickly through the door and into an unknown tomorrow.

○

Also by Elizabeth Miller:

McKenna Chronicles
Midnight Sky
Midnight Sun
Only Tonight, a McKenna Chronicles companion novella featuring Kyle Sommerton

Recommended reading order:
Midnight
Midnight Sky
Only Tonight
Midnight Sun

AUTHOR ELIZABETH MILLER resides in Rochester, MI with her very sarcastic husband and two young boys. In 2013 she decided to flex her writing muscles and began her debut novel: *Midnight*. Published in 2014, she continues writing the McKenna Chronicles with the second installment released in early 2015 and the third due in 2016. Elizabeth loves to chat with readers.

Contact Elizabeth - emillerauthor@gmail.com

**Follow Elizabeth on Facebook at: Elizabeth Miller - Author

**Follow Elizabeth on Twitter: @emillermidnight

61869292R00149

Made in the USA
Charleston, SC
29 September 2016